Helen Townsend is the
books. *Balancing Act* is
also writes for film, tel
press. She was born in
three children and lives in

Balancing Act

HELEN TOWNSEND

HarperCollins*Publishers*

HarperCollins*Publishers*

First published in Australia in 1997 by HarperCollins*Publishers*
ACN 009 913 517
A member of the HarperCollins*Publishers* (Australia) Pty Limited Group

Copyright © Helen Townsend 1997

HarperCollins*Publishers*
25 Ryde Road, Pymble, Sydney NSW 2073, Australia
31 View Road, Glenfield, Auckland 10, New Zealand
77–85 Fulham Palace Road, London W6 8JB, United Kingdom
Hazelton Lanes, 55 Avenue Road, Suite 2900, Toronto, Ontario M5R 3L2
and 1995 Markham Road, Scarborough, Ontario M1B 5M8, Canada
10 East 53rd Street, New York NY 10032, USA

National Library of Australia Cataloguing-in-publication data:
Townsend, Helen.
  Balancing act.
  ISBN 0 7322 5761 1.
  I. Title.
A823.3

Cover photograph by Andreas Bommert
Printed in Australia by Griffin Press, Adelaide

6 5 4 3 2 1
99 98 97

Balancing Act

Chapter 1

Cassandra La Rosa. Her name. In gold lettering, on the bottom right-hand corner of the leather-bound briefcase. It looked vulgar and made her feel cross. The Human Resources Department had sent it to her while she had been interstate, a discreet birthday present for a top female executive. For male executives reaching midlife, DMC Dolan Engineering and Building had a tradition of ribbing jocularity and expensive booze-ups. Cassie was relieved that they had been scared off that course. When she opened the briefcase, she found a recent executive motivational book, *Beyond the Peak – the challenge of the hyper achiever*.

Cassie lay back, light from the venetian blinds striping across her body, a sense of relief at being out of work-mode. Small, lithe and blonde, in a yellow T-shirt and shorts, she looked childlike on the king-size double bed. *Discover new talents, double your salary, achieve inner power, pinpoint the meaning of work, life perspectives, beyond retirement* ... She looked up the chapter on true potential and found a quiz. She did it quickly and was not surprised to find that her potential was limitless. Flicking through the rest of the book, Cassie found she could work in another country, move into another business, retire at fifty-five. The only negative she was able to identify in her life was that she had never taken up golf.

The book was the only birthday present she had received. It was her own doing. She'd told her sister, Susan and Anthea, her best friend, that she would probably not be back till Monday. She had craved solitude after ten days solid work, but now, on Saturday morning, she felt a familiar pang of weekend loneliness. Looking at the present, she felt a longing for something more personal, even something akin to the male booze-up. But everyone knew that wasn't her. The world defined her in terms of work. Too often, she thought, she also defined herself in terms of work. Flowers would have been fine. Champagne and roses. Maybe she should suggest cutting the budget of the Human Resources Department.

She walked out to the kitchen and poured herself a glass of water, then picked up the wrapping and ribbon from the present and put it in the bin. Her apartment gave her enormous pleasure, the subtle interplay of light and colour, the expansive view of the harbour, the carefully chosen artworks she had collected over the years. But she often felt restless here. She noticed the light flashing on the answering machine and she clicked it on.

"Hi. It's Suzie. Imagine me having a forty-year-old sister. Happy birthday Cass! Have a good one. By the way, next weekend, we're having Nick's family over for Sunday lunch. It'd be great if you'd come too. The kids are dying to see their favourite auntie. Don't work too hard! Talk to you soon."

Susan's life was interwoven with births, christenings, weddings, funerals and family get togethers. Cassie loved Susan's young children, but her time, her energy and passion was directed to her working life. The exception was her mother who had Alzheimer's disease. Cassie thought of her two or three times a day, with a wearied, guilty despair. Her mother would not only have forgotten Cassie's birthday, but also at times forgot her name and perhaps her existence. Before the disease fully took hold, her mother had remonstrated with Cassie with bitter, paranoid suspicion for neglecting her. Now that her mother barely knew her, the visits seemed embarrassing and pointless, and her sense of childhood attachment to her mother more remote. Dutiful weekly visits had gradually shrunk to fortnightly or monthly visits. But she carried some nameless shame, as if she were betraying her mother.

Her mother still recognised Susan, maybe because Susan went to see her more often, maybe because Susan's life was essentially like her mother's had been, with a husband and babies. As a child, Cassie had been given more attention than Susan. In her mother's eye, Cassie had the potential of perfection. She was compliant, pretty and clever, although for her mother, no-one was beyond a sharp word of improvement. Her mother's pride in her had beguiled Cassie into feeling that they must be close. Only later had she felt a difficult, chilly gulf between them. Susan, the younger sister, often an unsatisfactory child, at least had more freedom to be herself.

She should see her mother this weekend. But she remembered all the things she had to do to prepare for the Monday morning meeting. Cassie stared out at the bright, cold blue windswept harbour.

Maybe next week.

On work mornings, Cassie always woke before the alarm. She liked to lie in bed, watching the transition from dark to light, as the early morning sun lit up the flat – the pale, polished walnut table, the tall sculpted giraffe coming to life with the dawn, the light hitting the Balinese bronze gong and enlivening the complex woven patterns in the sofa. Sometimes, she even had breakfast in bed, always using a deep yellow mug and plate for her coffee and fruit. It was her only period of idleness in the day.

She showered, enjoying the sliver of a blue harbour view through the window. It was a bright, shimmering morning and she could see a ferry, churning its way across her line of vision. Cassie got dressed in a dark red linen dress, and read the financial news. Wistfully, she flicked through the book on medieval art that she had bought herself on the weekend as a birthday treat. She took it into the bedroom and put it on the bookshelf. Almost all her books were either art books, business books or self-improvement manuals like the one the company had given her. Maybe, she thought, it was time to throw out the self-improvement books. Art was her real passion, but she only ever had time for snatches of it, rather than the immersion she craved. She picked up a small framed photo of an Italian peasant garden. It was her father's childhood home, which she had grown to love when she lived in Italy. The photo was slightly blurred, but it gave a sense of the dry summer heat, the dark cool under the vines, and the lush vegetable garden behind. She ran her finger over it, and then put it back in its place on the bookshelf.

Cassie's apartment and all her possessions were in her mind as a map. From the time she was a small child, life had presented itself to her schematically. As a four-year-old, she'd had a map of the family home in her head. Later, the plan had expanded to include the route to school, a plan of each classroom, the long unsurfaced road up the hill up to Brownies, the tortuous back street route to the hall where she learned ballet. Sometimes, walking along the track through the deserted bush up to their house, she'd had the sense of being a wild creature, a lioness stalking out her territory, knowing the safe havens, aware of the dark, the unseen, the unsafe around the edges of her map. But she liked to know that there was an edge, even in her mind, as if the maps had been on paper.

The known and the unknown, the light and the dark. Sometimes, as a child, it had seemed to her that she should explore the dark, map the unknown, but common sense and logic stopped her. The unknown was unknown. That was its essence. By definition it couldn't be mapped.

As she drove down William Street to work, Cassie thought about the personal geography of her life now, enclaves connected by ribbons of roads, the sanctuary of her flat, the active hub that was her office, yoked together by the capsule of her car, with strands out to her house in the Blue Mountains, the long, tense drive to her mother's genteel retirement home in the green suburbs. There was the jet strand to Japan, which she had so loved, but where she now sent her juniors. As she grew older, the map became less complex, less dangerous, more wholly her own territory. The edges were more defined. The sight of a prostitute looking blankly into the early morning stream of traffic, as if the night had passed her by, made Cassie think she preferred it that way.

The DMC Dolan Building was a large glass and steel city tower, grand and essentially anonymous. The interior was black marble, chrome and glass, but the foyer was painted in a pale blue, a receding sky, with wisps of cloud and the motto in silver . . . *There is no horizon, only the infinite*. Cassie had taken it to heart, believed in it, in both a personal and professional sense. Sometimes, though, it embarrassed her the way the words were emblazoned theatrically across the foyer.

"Hi, Denise," she said as she walked into her office. "Give me a few minutes, then we'll go over the day." She sat down at her desk and quickly flicked through the contents of the in-tray, then called up her personal diary and her e-mail. She made a few entries, then looked up at Denise who came in and sat waiting for her instructions.

"Nice weekend?"

"Great," said Denise.

Cassie smiled at her. "We've got to get this proposal to Onway Electronics this afternoon. There'll probably be a few changes made during the staff meeting, so I want you to check them with me at the end of the meeting. You'll need to make them straight away, no matter what else comes up. Get Alex to use the same format we used for the Century proposal, but with the new graphics and the bright blue. And see if you can book me a session at lunchtime with Frankie in the gym. Organise some irises to go to my mother, usual card, and ring round and check that the marketing people are still available this afternoon."

"Sure." Denise got up and looked at her hesitantly. "I was wondering if you got round to . . . you know?"

"Sorry," said Cassie, puzzled, "what is it, Denise?"

"My review." She reddened. "Remember I asked you? You said you'd do it when you were away."

"I couldn't," said Cassie. "I was flat out and, anyway, I need to look over what you've been doing." She felt a pang of guilt. "To do it properly," she added. Her staff reviews were badly behind, but there always seemed to be more pressing things. "Don't worry, I'm very pleased with your work. A review's not crucial unless you're thinking of changing jobs."

"I guess I'd just like to have it," Denise said, as she went out.

It had stopped raining, and as Cassie got out of the car she noticed how the fallen gum leaves shone wet and black against the grey sandstone of her sister's driveway. The damp soil, mixed with the pungency of the eucalypts, created a rich, fecund smell. It annoyed her that Susan never noticed such subtleties. When Susan got the money together to do up the house, she would obliterate this smell, creating a fashionable mishmash of her idea of a classic French garden – steam-cleaning the sandstone, folk-arting the furniture, and dispensing with the old, creaking charm of the place. Already, she'd installed a spa on the top balcony.

Cassie stood for a moment, looking into the dappled front garden, with its decaying bird-bath, aware of her ambivalent self-satisfaction at Susan's potential destruction of it. She felt superior towards her sister and this judgment made her uncomfortable. She wouldn't have married someone like Nick, pleasant and entertaining, but lacking any interests beyond the confines of his own life, as did Susan.

In adolescence, after a disastrous relationship, Susan became trapped for a time in bulimia and self-loathing. Cassie had told her often that she *would* find someone, that she would be happy. It pained Cassie that what she now recognised as condescending patronage had turned out to be true. It was as if her childhood perfection and Susan's imperfections still reverberated between them. Cassie had been so bright, so intelligent, so popular while Susan's weight alternately ballooned, then dissipated into skeletal thinness. Now, Susan's life was the traditional fairytale. Somehow, the emotional and disorganised Susan had achieved her dream.

Cassie pulled herself up, annoyed at her pettiness, wanting to be kinder. But she also felt oppressed by the obligation and tension of the family occasion before her, the hours of meaningless chat, the sense of her precious time being sucked away.

They were all there in the back garden, Susan and Nick, with baby Jack on his shoulders; Elin running down the lawn with arms outstretched; Kelly, the toddler, carefully peeing on a lavender bush; their distracted mother anxiously trying to make sense of who Cassie was and what was happening; Nick's parents, his sister Louisa, her child, her new boyfriend; the neighbours, whose names Cassie could never remember but who claimed her so voraciously as a friend that it would have been rude to ask; Nick's old school buddy; Nick's dental nurse Julie. A familiar, neighbourly tableau. Assembled in the autumn richness of the garden, beside the barbecue, they suddenly opened their mouths in unison to sing.

"Happy birthday to you, happy birthday to you."

Cassie burst into tears, not slowly or gracefully, nor in thanks, but like a primitive creature, whose life pain burst forth in a rush. She was surprised, powerless to suppress it, until Nick came forward and gently led her upstairs to the main bedroom, and told her to lie down.

"I'll get Susie," he said anxiously. At the door, he looked back at her. "I told her we shouldn't have made it a surprise. You're not good with surprises, are you?" He spoke it with such kindness that Cassie knew he had observed her and knew her far better than she had ever bothered to know him.

"I was really embarrassed," Cassie told Anthea over their regular Thursday night dinner.

"Crying like that. I don't even know what started me off. It's never happened before." They sat on the balcony, the only generous space in the small and inconvenient apartment which Anthea had bought to satisfy her longstanding desire for a water view.

"Crying's super trendy now," Anthea said. "We teachers can't do it at school because it would show the kids how weak and pathetic we really are, but I read it's the nineties trend in business. I thought *you'd* know that."

"I'm not worried about how fashionable it is," said Cassie sharply, missing Anthea's irony, as she often did. "It surprised me, I had no control."

"That's the essence of high fashion, though. The trick is to make it look spontaneous and uncontrolled." She saw Cassie was seriously annoyed. "Sorry. So it was more than the embarrassment?"

"I think it was a bit insensitive of Susan to surprise me with a party on my fortieth –"

"Aha! Avoiding forty," said Anthea, starting on her banana cake piled with icecream and cream. "That's why it happened. We're best friends and you didn't even tell me. Forty's a bitch."

"It's only a birthday."

"More than twice twenty, worse than sixty take away twenty. It's the hideous half of

12

eighty," chanted Anthea. "A sin, a crime, a misdemeanour." She stared out across the balcony at the flat, black expanse of water, and the containers stacked across the bay. The lights of a party ferry came into view, and they could just hear the faint tinkle of disco music. "Forty's like carrying round a big sign, saying, 'It's over, folks. And I blew it. Or never made it in the first place.'" She looked back at Cassie. "Only for women – part of the male conspiracy."

"I couldn't care less about turning forty."

"F-F-F-Forty. The F word. I heard a little cry of desperation in your voice."

"Well, how old are you?" asked Cassie aggressively, knowing full well that Anthea was forty-four.

"Forty-two," said Anthea. "And I've just finished two years of therapy helping me come to terms with my fortieth birthday. I am supposedly now a mature post-forty person." She struck a girly pose. "All I need to do now is lose two inches off my hips." Anthea was a tall woman, short blonde hair, with large blue eyes and a generous mouth. She always dressed to be noticed and she usually was.

"I never knew you went to a therapist."

"Don't use that tone of voice, Cass." Anthea took a large spoonful of icecream and cake. "Not only did I *go* to the therapist, but I fell in *love* with the therapist. Big mistake." Her face had a momentary flash of sadness. "He was good-looking, charming. I'm feeling fully forty, life's over. He's got one of those deep, smooth voices. He looks straight into your eyes. And he had the most fabulous brown eyes. You know what a sucker I am for the brown-eyed handsome man. He was post-gestalt, post-everything. So I slept with him." She was trying to smile, but her sigh came out more like a sob.

"With your *therapist*?" Cassie was genuinely shocked.

"You know, all these therapists say how it's vital to develop total trust, even if it is costing you eighty bucks a throw. How you can go anywhere, do anything, once you've learned to trust again. True self-realisation." Anthea flicked a spoonful of icecream over the balcony. Cassie didn't ask why. "Eighty bucks a fuck!"

Cassie finished her glass of wine. Drunk was okay, but she didn't want to be maudlin. "We should cheer up." She filled their glasses. "One disastrous fortieth birthday party is enough. No need to summon up the Horsemen of the Apocalypse to blow out the candles."

"Horsewomen only at this party." Anthea laughed, but in panic. Underneath it all she was forty-four. You could see her four years more than Cassie's, she knew that. "Look on the bright side, we're both gainfully employed, own our apartments. And we're both reasonably attractive." But past it, she thought grimly, whatever *it* was.

She glanced at the ferry. It was close enough now for them to make out the song, a disco version of "Norwegian Wood". The Beatles, redolent of wet kisses, dark, drunken, young, tender embraces. She looked back at Cassie, pretty little Cassie, sitting, clasping her drink, tears just contained in her eyes. Anthea watched with a mixture of resignation and sympathy. She leaned forward and patted her friend's hand.

"I haven't been out seriously with a man for two years," Cassie said suddenly.

Anthea hated the way Cassie used a prim euphemism like "going out seriously" for a sexual relationship. Especially because Cassie had the very best sort of sex appeal, a sort of sweet, wistful but extremely physical charm. She could still find a man, would always be able to find a man, whereas Anthea had not had a workable relationship for almost ten years. The dreams, the wanting, the carelessness with which she had discarded men in her twenties, felt like a painful memory of another woman's life. Now she seemed permanently reduced to distasteful or painful relationships, but ones too rare to forget.

"Sex," said Anthea lightly, "damned if you do, damned if you don't."

"I thought about having a relationship a lot last year," said Cassie. "Now that I've thought it through, it's hard to see how my life would be substantially enhanced by having one. There's not a whole lot to recommend it."

"Regular sex?" suggested Anthea. "The money you'd save on vibrator batteries?"

Cassie ignored the comment. "The only thing is when I want to eat out. I don't like going to restaurants alone. A few things like that. And sometimes, when I come home, I think it'd be nice to have someone to talk to about the day. And weekends. I'd like to go for a walk, but it's a little sad on your own."

"My God, I know. The walking along the beach shit with *him*," said Anthea. "Always strikes a chord."

"That's ridiculous," said Cassie, her voice brittle.

"You haven't really thought about it," said Anthea more gently. "We both live alone, which is not good for any human being. You've talked yourself out of wanting, but I still want. I want sex, and someone with a warm bum to sleep next to. I want someone to love me and admire me. I want to do all that back to him. And the tragedy is that the male is a threatened species.

For our age group, at least. All hunted down and taken captive, poor pets."

"If you feel that need, then you and I should go out and find a good man for you."

Anthea was amazed Cassie could talk like this, that she believed there were men to be had for the asking. Not, Anthea reminded herself, that she'd *ever* had anyone for the asking. In her twenties, she'd had the illusion of some prince, some knight on horseback somewhere. Then, he'd had an air of perfection. In her thirties, all she'd required was reasonable intelligence, good humour and the desire to stay with her. Mostly, she'd found the staying power lacking. They'd drifted away, married younger women. Now, she thought with desolation, there was no-one left. Maybe not even for Cassie. She and Cassie had often argued about the best way to live their lives. Anthea took life as it came, often shaken by its deep disappointments, but savouring erratic and unexpected pleasures. Cassie's methodical goal-setting seemed, to her, to shut out possibilities. But Cassie usually achieved her goals.

"We'll find out where you meet good men," Cassie said.

"Dream," said Anthea. "There's creepy Johnny Jamieson and his friends. That's it."

"Are you *still* seeing him?"

Anthea had given up trying to explain her relationship with Johnny Jamieson. She shrugged. "Now and then. He's not totally creepy all the time." Anthea raised her eyebrows. "You know, like when you're desperate." Cassie had met Johnny once and had suspected he was a bully under his suave flirtatiousness. But the women had known each other long enough to accept their different lives. Anthea got up and leaned out over the balcony railing, towards the ferry, its fairy lights, its music, the sound of laughter. "All that's left is friendship with the girls – going to the gallery, the theatre, learning Italian. Getting pissed. As good as it gets."

"Sounds fine," said Cassie, but her voice was small.

They looked at the harbour in silence. Cassie wondered if there was a void in their lives, a need which she had ignored. But she couldn't believe it was something as simple as a man. Being a perfectionist made many of her relationships unsatisfactory. In the last ten years there had been only one serious relationship – Phillip, with whom she almost lived happily. "Mr Perfect", Anthea had called him, but given Anthea's taste in men, Cassie didn't take the jibe seriously. And although he was almost the perfect partner for her, she always felt that there should have been something more profound and meaningful between them. Even their problems appeared trivial. In the end, after two uncertain years, Phillip seemed to be taking as much from her life as he was adding.

"I've been thinking of going to one of those agencies," said Anthea suddenly.

"An agency?" said Cassie. "To find a man?"

"Cass, it's hard enough anyway."

"Sorry," said Cassie. "It just seems vaguely tacky."

"Let me assure you, it's a whole lot less tacky than bars or blind dates organised by your friends, or sleeping with Johnny Jamieson."

Cassie was silent, not sure if Anthea was being flippant. "I suppose it's a nineties sort of thing."

Anthea looked at her crossly. "More a forty sort of thing."

Chapter 2

Cassie and Susan sat in Cassie's apartment, drinking coffee and finishing off lunch.

"It's bliss here," said Susan. "It's at least a month since I've been away from Jack." Cassie noticed Susan had put on weight.

"It's a month since I've seen them," said Cassie. She thought of Susan's children with regret. She loved them, unreservedly, and kept their photos in her wallet and on her fridge door. But in the last year, she'd seen little of them, because of the pressure of work. "My hours just get longer." She shrugged. "When I finish the bits and pieces on weekends, I've had it." She looked at Susan with concern. "Could you get someone to look after Jack sometimes? Give you a couple of hours off."

Susan sighed. Sometimes she felt her life was so separate from Cassie's they were beyond understanding each other. "Jack screams if I leave him. Sometimes Nick and I get a babysitter and go out at night, but only after Jack's asleep. If he's screaming when I leave, I know he won't stop. The woman at occasional care told me that he'd scream himself to sleep." Her eyes flashed angrily. "I don't know how people can do that."

"I guess he'd scream if you left him with me too," said Cassie. "But I'll take Elin up the mountains next time I go."

"She's needy," said Susan, "like Jack. It's harder because she's the oldest. Kelly's like Nick. Nothing fazes her. Stubborn as a mule, but tough as one too." Susan lay back on the couch. "Bliss being here with you, Cass. Absolute bliss."

"Maybe I should take *you* up to the mountains," suggested Cassie, not meaning it.

"It's like you and your job," Susan continued. "You probably need to get away, but it's so much a part of you that you never do. I feel as if I've got bits of the kids embedded in my brain." She put her mug on the arm of the sofa. Cassie quickly moved it onto the coffee table. "Sorry," said Susan.

Cassie looked around the apartment. "You don't have to see Mum so often, you know," she said tentatively. "It's not as if she remembers. The doctor told me that."

"She cries when I go. Maybe she doesn't remember everything afterwards, but that makes it worse. Perhaps she remembers a lot more than we think."

"It's the disease. Her mind is going. And you've got three kids." Cassie glanced at her sister's cheap, discount-store tracksuit, unaware of the expression of disapproval on her face. "You've got to look after yourself too."

"You sound like Nick," said Susan fiercely, "organising my life. After I've done the washing and before Kelly starts crawling into bed with us, I should do aerobics? Drop Mum and go to the beautician? I don't have that freedom. Don't worry about Jack crying? Go for a run while the dishes are piled sky high and we're having cheese sandwiches for tea again?"

"Sorry," said Cassie, remembering how defensive Susan could be.

"I owe Mum," Susan went on. "When Elin was a baby, I was nuts, on the phone to Mum every day. When Kelly was born, she'd come over and take them both out for a walk, so I'd get an hour's sleep. We weren't exactly buddy buddy mother and daughter. She had plenty of gratuitous advice too. But now, I'm supposed to forget that. Forget she's lonely, forget she brought us up – me *and* you."

"Okay," said Cassie, fighting to keep her voice under control. It had the older sister tone, the phoney parent ring. "We have different views." But it was more than different views. Black despair stabbed at her about their mother, anxiety, the fear of her death. At the same time, she almost hoped for an end to the horror of it. It was beyond Susan to understand her feelings. "I made a decision about Mum," she said evenly. "I haven't forgotten her. I help pay for her to be there, but I can't visit her as often as you do."

Cassie thought of the times she did go to see her mother – the long, empty silences, the uselessness of it all, how it unsettled her for days.

The atmosphere changed from cosy, sisterly companionship to a cold hostility. Finally, Susan stood up. "I may as well go."

"I'll walk you down to the carpark," said Cassie. Silently, they walked down the stairs and across the little courtyard. Cassie paused as Susan turned the key in the car door. "I don't know how to explain how I feel," Cassie said. "It's almost as if Mum's dead."

Susan twisted her hands together. Cassie had always disliked Susan's penchant for the dramatic. With her dark curling hair, her big eyes, she looked the part. Her theatricality went beyond her looks into the way she gestured and spoke. "My God!" said Susan. "How mum *is* and what you *feel* are two different things. You *feel* she's dead, but she's *not*. She's just lonely! It's no wonder she forgets things, stuck out in that place. You're bloody selfish!"

Cassie did not reply. Susan threw her bag in the back seat. They caught each other's eyes briefly, embarrassed, then kissed goodbye, almost formally.

"I'll ring you about taking Elin up the mountains," said Cassie.

"That'd be nice," said Susan stiffly, "whenever you've got time."

Shaken, Cassie walked back up the stairs into the apartment. It was the most open disagreement she and Susan had had for a long time. She put on a CD of eighteenth-century guitar music, which normally soothed her, then made herself a cup of coffee. Her usual choice was black coffee, which she associated with self-discipline and efficiency. Now, she was drawn by the comfort of warm frothy milk. She looked at a new marketing plan which someone had given her on Friday afternoon, then decided to work on it later. On the bed was a little dress she'd bought for Elin and had forgotten to give to Susan.

The disagreement with Susan wouldn't last, but there was no doubt that she and Susan had retreated from each other. In theory, their mother's illness should have brought them together. She thought back to the excitement of Elin's birth, the times she'd taken Elin and Kelly to the beach. But then Cassie became immersed in her job, Susan in another baby. They no longer had long phone calls where they talked about the children, nor did they talk about the new things Cassie was doing in her job. The illness of their mother had increased the distance between them. It had slowly widened, until now it felt impossible to bridge.

Cassie's life seemed to be getting harder. She loved her apartment, but it felt more difficult coming back there alone, every day, trying to relax or to motivate herself. The apartment felt not quite like home.

She sat back with her coffee, staring out at the harbour. Phillip came to mind, not as a name or even his face, but just a fleeting recollection of that look he used to give her – warm, sensuous. They had been right together in most ways. He'd wanted children, but neither of them had seen that as insurmountable. They had liked the same films, the same people. He was proud of her, she of him. But they had fought over things as petty as the colour of cups, the names of film directors, whether they would holiday in Bali, in Tuscany, or Provence.

Within a year of leaving her, he had married. She'd heard recently he now had a three-month-old baby. She had been so resistant about everything in the relationship, but when the end came, it was over in one weekend – the culmination of a long-standing fight over the fact that he had refused to shave on weekends. Anthea had said she was crazy, but for a long time it seemed to Cassie that it would have been just as easy for him to give in. Now, she hugged a cushion and thought maybe Anthea had been right.

Anthea pulled the sheet up over her breasts, as Johnny Jamieson smirked and kissed her passionately on the neck. She hated it when he started to hurt. He was adolescent enough to want to leave his mark on her.

When she'd met Johnny, she'd been attracted by his sharp aggression, his good looks and his intelligence. It was a combination, she remembered, too late, that was always fatal for her – invariably mixed with rampant ego and insensitivity. She'd fallen for him, with a familiar feeling of doom. He was the type of man who never fell in love. "Except with himself," she'd explained to Cassie. She'd continued with the relationship past the one-night stand it should have been. She told him things she should never have. Now, he had become proprietorial. Proprietorial and careless, in the worst possible way. Anthea rolled away from him, but he started fondling her bottom, kissing her spine.

She reached out, feeling in the bedside drawer, and handed him a condom. "Could you use this?"

"You know I hate those fucking things," he said. "And you're too old to get pregnant." She flinched and he leant down and kissed her breasts hard. Too hard.

She wasn't too old to get pregnant, but she'd never been able to, despite her longing to have a baby. Now, other aspects of Johnny's life were beginning to worry her.

"Not too old for AIDS," she retorted.

Her mind whirled, a growing horror of this loveless, sordid sex, which felt as if it had been endlessly and humiliatingly repeated. She was compromised, because she always asked him. But the edge to him, the meanness, made her increasingly reluctant to continue. There had never been any love, just a mutual need for uncommitted sex. She pushed him back playfully, kissing him lightly, trying to reduce the tension. Her hand found the condom package again.

"C'mon, wear it," she said lightly, "please."

He reddened, his forehead bulging. She held his gaze, trying to appear calm.

"Fuck you," he said. "I'm going."

She watched him dress, with a sort of calm despair. He didn't look at her again. As the front door clicked shut, she felt a combination of relief and defeat. She leaned back to the drawer and got out her vibrator. Better than crying, she thought.

"Just look at her! Isn't that the best smile?" Nick leaned forward across the breakfast bar.

"Can we have Sesame Street?" asked Kelly.

"We don't have TV at breakfast, sweetie," said Susan, as she detached Jack from her breast and put a crust in his hand. "We're watching this because it's one of Daddy's patients."

"The show's not that bad," said Nick. "I thought it would have been a lot more vacuous."

"How could they do that?" said Susan. "Make it *more* vacuous?"

Nick ignored the barb. He leaned back, swinging on his stool.

"Cosmetically, they're perfect," he said, satisfied. "Orthodontically, a little compromised. She refused to come back for the extra work. Still, she's out there, smiling, smiling, smiling. Prime-time television."

"Nick, get real. Breakfast television isn't prime time," said Susan sharply. "And she still hasn't paid the second half of the account."

"I made a deal with her – because of the publicity." He said it bravely, like a child fending off parental argument.

"I don't see a sticker on her teeth saying 'By Nick Scarcella'. That's almost ten grand."

"I fixed it with the bank," said Nick quickly. "I took Sutton out to lunch and told him about celebrity dentistry. He upped the overdraft, no questions."

Susan felt a sense of rising panic. "I'm supposed to sign that," she said, "as a director."

"You did sign it," said Nick, his bravado draining away, avoiding looking at her. "The other morning. The renewal."

"Was there an authorisation for extra?" asked Susan ominously.

"Second set of papers.

"You certainly picked your time," blazed Susan, "Kelly vomiting, Elin crying, sign here, no mention of the ten grand. No, 'Hey Suze, sign your life away.'" She strapped Jack into the high chair, went to the door and beckoned to Nick. "Kids, stay here. Daddy and I have something to discuss."

"Can we have Sesame Street?" asked Elin, sensing a window of opportunity.

Susan flicked the remote control to channel 2 and walked out into the hallway. Nick followed her. "You aren't a celebrity dentist," she said. "And hopefully you never will be. The way I look at it, we've just thrown away ten grand on your ego. Like maybe we could have had that holiday in Noumea. Or paid off the cards." She felt in her element with money. She knew she was good with it. It annoyed her that Nick treated her talent like an affront, as if she was questioning his ability to practise dentistry. She knew that the confines of dentistry frustrated him, but he would never sit down and work out how to overcome the frustrations.

Nick looked at her pleadingly, half apologetic, half peeved. "Every time I want to do anything in the practice, you stop me. Every expansion, every new piece of equipment." He looked at her angrily. "I'm moving beyond being a suburban dentist. Or trying."

"You used to be beyond it," said Susan. "Treating that poor kid with the horrendous overbite and organising the surgery for him. Paying the extra yourself. I never minded that. Or when you'd just graduated, working at that Aboriginal centre."

"That's before I married a woman who wants to holiday in Noumea every year." His remark hung between them, raising the stakes. Susan was furiously angry now, but aware of the children, screeching with laughter at Sesame Street and remembering her parents' terrifying arguments, the ineffectual shrillness of her mother.

"There's a balance, Nick! Creepy people who want big white shiny TV teeth deserve exactly what they get. But Jesus, make them pay!"

"I watched Donald Andrews reading the news last night. He's Debbie's boyfriend. There's probably enough in his mouth to get you your little winter sojourn in the sun." Nick picked up his bag and slammed out the front door.

Susan's first reaction was to ring Cassie for consolation, but since Cassie hadn't rung her, she wasn't going to call first. She always rang first, she thought. Instead, she got Elin into her school uniform, cut Kelly's lunch for kindergarten and changed Jack's nappy. He cried and twisted so ferociously that she wanted to slap him, although she didn't believe in smacking children. Sometimes, though, she changed her mind, and smacked him in private. Then she'd grow remorseful and wonder whether she'd done him some irrevocable psychological harm. Nick, although a generally indulgent and loving father, was in favour of smacking the children, but she'd taken a stand. Nick thought she spoiled them, especially Jack, whom he regarded as a wimp. Jack was very dependent, which was especially unfortunate for a boy, but as she explained to Nick, he couldn't help it. If he'd been born with a harelip or one leg shorter than the other, nobody would have thought of blaming her or Jack. But because he'd been born wimpy, everyone seemed to think it was up to her to change his personality, even though he was only fifteen months old.

She dropped Kelly off at kindergarten, then drove Elin to school. "Come in, Mummy. I ring the bell today," Elin pleaded.

"Darling, I'll listen from the car." Susan felt exhausted.

"You never have time for me." Watching American sitcoms had proved fertile ground for Elin, who had a natural ear for emotional blackmail.

"Elin, I came to craft last week. Jack's nearly asleep."

Elin slammed the car door. Guiltily, Susan watched her. It was amazing that a six-year-old had learned to imbue her walk with such pathos, defeat and neglect. Wearily, Susan unstrapped Jack and followed Elin into the schoolyard, but Elin had disappeared. When she came out to ring the bell, she looked cheerful, oblivious to Susan waving from the edge of the playground. Jack wriggled wildly in his mother's arms, struggling to undo her dress and get at her breast, and she sensed disapproval from the other mothers for feeding such a large and demanding baby. She ran for the car, where Jack roared wildly all the way home. She lay on the bed with him, crying, feeling he was sucking the life out of her, imagining Nick was having an affair with Julie, his nurse, or TV Debbie. She felt too tired to even try to remember Debbie's last name and wondered if that meant her marriage was in deeper trouble than she thought. But she was even too tired to think about that. Finally, Jack fell asleep, and she put pillows around him so he couldn't fall off the bed and went downstairs to clean up the kitchen. Almost all their appliances had been bought when she and Nick made up after quarrels – the four-cycle dishwasher, the two-door fridge with icemaker, the food-processing centre, the juicer, the waffle maker, the crepe maker, the natural bread machine, and the ultimate foolishness of an Alessi toaster. She wondered how many fights it would take before she and Nick ran out of appliances to give each other. Maybe that's when marriages went to the Family Court.

She stared at the list on the fridge door. *Buy nappies. Elin Yamaha 4 o'clock. Clean fridge. Don't eat leftovers.* She forgot that these last two were different instructions as she stood in front of the fridge, staring into it, miserably spooning last night's leftover chocolate pudding into her mouth.

Chapter 3

"I've demonstrated the need to be pro-active," said Cassie, "in all areas of our lives. Someone said to me recently that pro-active simply means you don't take life lying down." She paused. "Which was a criticism – a way of saying I should speak in colloquial terms and not use fancy, invented terms, what the media like to call Americanisms."

The audience laughed and Cassie sensed their support. "I came to the conclusion that all of us – in leading-edge companies worldwide – are using this language, because it means something that cannot be expressed in the language of the past. Pro-active is quieter, less aggressive, but infinitely more powerful." Her voice rose, and a murmur of approval ran through the lecture theatre. Cassie was suddenly very conscious of her own presence, the force that had the eyes of a hundred managers focused on her, as she stood at the rostrum in the conference room. She found herself moving beyond her prepared speech into a flow of rhetoric.

"At DMC Dolan, we have a commitment to quality, to integrity, to the best. We have a commitment, as is written in every one of our offices, to see beyond the horizon, to look to the infinite. Perhaps that sounds pompous, almost biblical in scope, but I believe we need that vision, that commitment, to survive in the markets of today and beyond.

"The key lies in authenticity – the absolute business of being yourself, of doing what is right for you. The most important thing you can know is that you are doing what you want to do – that you are on the path, at the place where you should be." Her voice rose, but remained contained. "The old maxim of sell, sell, sell, is dead. In its place is a far more powerful energy, of knowing that you are the right person, with the right product at the right time – the synergy of this company. And that time is now."

Cassie stood back from the dais and let the thunder of applause envelop her. Tim Bayliss, the head of New Product Development, leapt onto the stage to shake her hand, as the crowd began to shout and stamp their feet, whistling, hooting, cheering. "You got 'em exactly where I want them, babe," said Bayliss flatly as he pumped her hand, his faced wreathed with smiles for the audience. "They've forgotten what a shit of a year it's been."

Once the applause died down and the delegates began moving to the dining room, Cassie retreated to one of the hotel powder rooms. She was deflated by Tim Bayliss's cynical reaction and felt the need to steel herself for the dinner ahead. She thought of the book she had bought this morning, an indulgent, expensive book of Japanese prints. They were nineteenth-century agricultural scenes in which human busyness seemed antlike and inconsequential, no more important than the trees, rocks or rain in the landscape. She wanted to go back to her hotel suite, to study it and wonder what it would be like to be a figure in that landscape, rather than the feature she seemed to be in the landscape of this managers' conference. In the conference room, she had felt enlarged, powerful, almost mythical, but an undefined embarrassment niggled at her. When she had started attending conferences, it had been a challenge to deliver a speech in a way that would move the audience. She had risen to the challenge. But now, for the first time in her career, she felt doubts about the point of it all. It was uncomfortable, and she tried to put the feeling to the back of her mind.

She pulled at the heavy door of the ladies' room and winced under the bright lights as she saw herself in the mirror, somehow older, more worn than she felt. She was uncomfortably aware that her foundation was a little caked, the eye shadow settling in the fine lines that were beginning to form around her eyes. Her lipstick had smudged slightly into the tiny grooves above her lip. It was the lighting, she told herself, but that was no comfort. The lighting only showed up the lines, it hadn't created them. She wasn't vain, and she had never been coy about her age, but since her birthday, she felt something like fear about herself and her life. She opened her bag to retouch her lipstick and noticed a basket of shampoos, soaps and toiletries on the bench. Remembering how Elin loved these tiny bottles, Cassie picked up a couple. She was about to put them into her bag when the door opened and Jennifer Keen, National Promotions Manager, with whom she had worked closely in her early days in the company, stood, watching her, a slight smile on her face.

"So, Cass, how does pinching the shampoo fit in with all that honesty and integrity?" She said it with a laugh, but Cassie felt challenged.

"I take them for my niece," she answered coolly, but was betrayed by a rising blush.

"Yeah, kids do love them. I take 'em for the school fete," said Jennifer companionably, standing at the bench, wetting a finger and running it over her eyebrows. She got a lipstick out of her bag and ran it expertly round her mouth. Cassie noticed Jennifer had more lines than she did, then despised herself for noticing. She had always been a little uneasy around Jennifer. She was loud, sociable, aggressive, flirtatious. She used these qualities in her work. Cassie tried to see Jennifer as having a different style from her own, but she could never quite rid herself of her disapproval of this woman.

"How's the new campaign?" asked Cassie. "I hear you're travelling a lot."

"A whole lot," said Jennifer, washing her hands. "It's hard with the kid, but I try to make it up to her. And it's great to be away from the macho politicking and corporate bullshit. All this focus group crap, mission statements and visions. I want a job, not a bloody religion." She looked at Cassie, a dawning realisation that they were on different wavelengths. "You don't take it seriously, do you?"

"I think it's fundamentally very serious." She sounded schoolmarmish and wished she didn't.

"You're welcome to it. I'm skipping the dinner. I've done all my networking. There's a bottle of champagne and a cute young guy from

Adelaide up in my suite." She looked in the basket of toiletry products and picked out a sewing kit and a night mask. "My fete stall's very successful," she said, raising her eyebrows, "but I'm not sure it's due to authenticity."

She stopped at the door. "By the way, I've heard Bayliss has his eye on your Research Department. Bring it under his sheltering wing. Which would be hell on wheels for you."

"Julian has always insisted on Research being an independent department," said Cassie. "And he's always promoted a flat management structure."

"Tim Bayliss is talking efficiency. Which, by no mean coincidence, is also Julian's current baby," said Jennifer. "The board's running hot on it. I'd watch your back."

Cassie stiffened against what Jennifer was saying. It was the antithesis of everything the company stood for. "I know there's some discussion going on, but I have a very open relationship with Tim," she said, knowing it was not quite true.

Jennifer smiled at her. "So you know about the muscle that joins his brain to his balls?"

"I'm sure I can sort out any problems with Tim."

"Then ask him about the rumour he was touting that you were giving Julian head. Which, according to him, resulted in you getting to be head of Research. And while you're at it, maybe you could tell him I'm not a lesbian."

"This sort of gossip isn't the way I work." Cassie felt as if she'd been slapped.

"Me neither," said Jennifer. "I look at the reality of the situation and work from there. Watch out for yourself, Cass. You know what they say about executive level. Jump or be pushed. I'd be happy to help you on more constructive options. I know you've never been crazy about the female network, but it *is* there."

As the door swung shut, Cassie remembered how she and Jennifer used to be friends. They'd drifted apart. Jennifer had attitude. She worked differently from her. What Jennifer had said about Tim *was* true, but Cassie believed the only way to counter it was to work from principles and not give in to gossip. For a moment, she envied Jennifer. It seemed as if she had everything – the cute guy from Adelaide, her child, even her attitude. They weren't things Cassie sought, but they gave Jennifer freedom and confidence. Cassie quickly retouched her make-up and headed out towards the dinner. Tim Bayliss guided her to their table.

"That was a great speech you gave for those people," he said as they sat down. She smiled uneasily. Tim Bayliss was known for under-cutting reputations. He was also smart enough to make a convincing argument why his Product Development should take over her Research Department.

"Have accounts sent you that stuff on fringe benefits?"

"Insane, isn't it?" replied Cassie. "It's not worth doing all the paperwork."

Tim laughed. "I'm glad you feel like that. I thought it was me going mad in my old age. How's your Asia project going?"

"I'll be doing the preliminary presentation in a few weeks," she said. "We've got some fantastic material."

As the waiter poured them both a glass of red, Tim's eyes fixed intently on her face. "You know I'm right behind this push into Asia," he said.

Cassie took a sip of the wine and smiled. "I'm glad."

He looked round the conference room. "Funny business this," he said vaguely. "Sometimes I think about what else I could do." He laughed. "I mean, I'm fifty-four. Work all the fucking time. But what would I be without it?" He chuckled. "Angie would like me to get a sixty grand a year consultancy, four weeks holiday a year, no working weekends. I can see her point, but I couldn't do it." He picked up his wine and looked into Cassie's eyes again. "Could you?"

The Korean baths were white tiled, with a steaming aroma which was both spicily Asian and antiseptic. Cassie and Anthea sat naked on the scrubbed wooden benches of the steam room, sweating profusely as the steam rose. Anthea took water from the dipper near the door and poured it over herself. She could feel her skin shrivelling to goosebumps, as she poured another pitcher down her back.

"Oh, oh, it's so cold and hot. I love it!"

"I think you're supposed to pour it over the coals," said Cassie.

"I think you're allowed to do whatever you like." Anthea came here regularly, but it had taken months for her to convince Cassie to try it.

Cassie smiled. "It's relaxing, but I don't know that I'd want to do it every week."

Anthea laughed. "It would do you a lot of good to relax."

"Maybe. It's lucky I've got you around. I'd never do anything like this on my own."

"You never do anything on your own," said Anthea, "except go to work."

"I'm doing a course. On Japanese prints." She said it defensively. Almost every course she'd started in the last few years she'd had to curtail because of pressure of work.

"My God, I just don't get this thing about Japanese prints," Anthea said. "I think they're a bloody bore. Yet there's obviously a whole industry revolving round them – probably thousands of people crazy about them. How many Japanese print courses have you actually done already?"

"Five – which is hardly definitive. And most of those I've missed evenings here and there."

"Five's enough, even for someone as obsessive as you."

They sat, companionable in the steam, winding down on a Friday night, both retreating, almost retracting from their professional lives, into the safe, easy world of their friendship.

"Tell me about the dating agency."

"Social Scene?" Anthea chuckled. "My God, the first interview was totally demoralising. You fill in a questionnaire. Job, interests, financial status, that sort of thing. How do you describe yourself? Fat? Thin? Thank God I'm not fat because eighty-nine per cent of men specify they want someone thin. Eighty-nine per cent – I asked the interviewer if eighty-nine per cent also specify they don't want someone who's bad tempered or shitty in the morning. But none of them do. It's almost as bad with smokers. So I turned into a non-smoker quick smart, I tell you."

"But Anthea, you do smoke!"

"If I had the right man, I wouldn't."

"Anthea!"

"They ask you what *you* want. A wish list. Height – two inch gradations from five foot up. Intelligence – smart or super brain. Income in modules of tens of thousands. Looks to die for. Then they charge you five hundred dollars."

"So what happens?"

"Thirty bucks you can go to a party with every man and his dog. Fifty bucks, a dinner, hand-picked selection – the socio-economic tax bracket your heart desires. Being a cheapskate I went to the party, which was like the pub on a Friday night. Did my dough, seeing I know where to meet the creeps of the world for free." She thought of Johnny Jamieson, their last sordid exchange. It wasn't the sort of thing she told Cassie. Cassie tried hard not to judge her, but Anthea knew Cassie recoiled from certain aspects of Anthea's life. Anthea smiled. "I did meet a woman who told me to try the dinners, on the grounds that if a man was prepared to pay fifty dollars rather than thirty he must be a better person."

"So did you?" asked Cassie.

"Yeah. Four men, four women. Good restaurant. Classy. And comic."

"Comic?" said Cassie with a touch of disapproval in her voice.

"The first thing I notice is that the other women are tall, like me – over five eight. So we start laughing about it, kidding around that it must be a dinner for guys who like tall women. And then, in walks this guy – short – like literally, four feet; well, five feet, maybe. Pompous little lawyer prick. And then the other guys arrive – one's a journo, scrumptious. And two maybes. All the women are angling to sit next to the journo. And the little prick, telling us how he got his suntan in Tahiti and he'd parked the Beemer outside to take him back to Point Piper. Rich, baby! Rich and repulsive!"

"Was he *that* bad?" Anthea tended to exaggerate to improve her stories.

"Hideous. He told me the profile of his ideal woman – tall women who like short men, basically. So I check with the other women in the powder room. We'd all said at our interviews that height wasn't a big issue. But we decide there and then that four foot ten *is* an issue – a small issue but an issue nevertheless."

"The journalist?"

Anthea groaned. "Frustration! Both the other guys are chatting me up and one asks me for my phone number, which I gave him, hoping he might turn out to be a little less wet than he looks. But the journalist is super. So I asked him for a lift home because he lives in Balmain."

"My God, that looks so painful." They had walked out of the steam room. Cassie looked across to the massage area where two Korean women were pounding the back of another woman. "You don't get a massage here, do you?"

"Never! They're female karate champions who just do massage as a training."

"So the journalist?"

"Halfway home I realise there's only one possible reason for a dishy guy like that to be there – he's doing a story. I gave him a hard time about it. He denied it in a piss-weak way. Goodbye and good luck. The other one keeps ringing me, so we're going out next weekend. He's very herbal, though. So pleased I don't smoke."

"Shouldn't you be honest?"

"Maybe I should. Come into the spa," she said. "Then we'll get some Korean food. It's fantastic." Cassie noticed that Anthea's body was thickening, her hips fleshier, her breasts drooping slightly. Cassie worked out regularly, but the same was happening to her. Friends, getting older. Not a tragedy, she told herself, but somewhere she felt a pang. Lost youth. Not that her youth had been wonderful. She was better off now, but also more troubled than she cared to examine.

"I'm not crazy about Korean food."

"This is an adventure, Cass," replied Anthea firmly. "Life's an adventure." She slid into the spa, and almost disappeared under the bubbles.

On Monday morning, Cassie woke with a start, later than usual, conscious of the bright yellow light filling her room, the alarm clock hiccupping its way towards six. There was a picture in her head, left over from a dream, of her office at the top of its tall city tower. She could see the various floors, the floor plans in her head, sheathed in their glass and concrete shells. But instead of a sense of remote calm, the map showed tiny, grasping, hungry organisms, reaching out towards the light, feeding on each other, crippling each other in a bid to escape a nightmare of self-cannibalism.

Cassie sat up quickly. A sudden feeling of despair, then panic, came over her. Panic was familiar to her; she had experienced it since she was a small child, when she had withdrawn into a stubborn unreachable goodness. Then, only her father, with his abandon, his high moods, his habit of sweeping her off to work with him, had been able to unlock her. When she had been teaching Japanese, panic had made her rigid and unforgiving of her pupils. In the business world, she had found a way around it, identifying it, putting it in perspective, dealing with it. She read books about panic, so she could harness failure, crisis and despair; turning them into success, forward movement and creativity. She tried not to be mechanistic, and to soothe herself at a deeper level, but she still held the belief that panic was something to be dealt with, not expressed. Part of her irritation with Susan was the way she gave way to panic, allowing it to grow and feed upon itself. Yet Cassie had sensed an unnamed panic growing within her since her birthday, and those inexplicable tears. Maybe it was burnout. Nervous breakdown. Midlife crisis. Should she relax? Go with the flow, or get herself together?

Why had she striven so hard to get where she was? The challenge? To prove herself? To get a top job?

But why did she have this job? For the money? To belong?

What did she belong to? A company, with grandiose visions, healthy profits and a blue-chip share profile.

She liked the money, but that hadn't been her motivation to go this far. After all, she'd left teaching to do poorly paid data entry to support her through her MBA. She'd wanted the degree to take her places, to expand her horizons. Oddly, though, it was the data entry job that had led to her current job, plus Japanese, which, after leaving teaching, she had intended to pursue only as a hobby. But her fluency in Japanese, and her smattering of other languages, had landed her as head of Research, and now, to her shaping the marketing push into Asia. In her panic, it seemed a strange progression.

She took a large drawing pad from her bookcase and a thick texta pen and began writing. Mind maps had been the rage a few years ago and Cassie still liked to do them, although she had read that the technique was soothing rather than revealing.

STRESS.

FEAR.

LONELY. She circled this.

UNCERTAIN. Another circle.

With arrows from the two circles, she wrote the words LACK OF BALANCE. She examined the paper a little longer and wrote LACK OF INTIMACY. She circled this, joined it to LACK OF BALANCE and sent a quavering line to LONELY. She reached over and took the rest of the textas down from the bookcase and drew a red heart around LONELY. She added yellow slashes, which turned into trumpeting flowers, and then a jagged blue sky. It was like a child's Mother's Day card, reminding her of one she had made for her mother when she was Elin's age. She sat, cross-legged on the bed, staring at the page, feeling tears at the back of her throat – the beginning of what she had felt that day at Susan's when the tears had spewed forth. She put the drawing pad down, went into the kitchen and turned on the coffee machine, then walked into the shower.

As she turned on the water, tears did start, and Cassie found herself wondering if they were cathartic or self-indulgent. She hadn't even cried when Phillip left, and now she had cried, without real meaning, twice in the last two months. The tears kept flowing, as if there was an inexhaustible reservoir. Only when the hot water ran out did they stop. This coincidence made her wary of how genuine they were.

Anthea was lonely too, she thought, but Anthea had more friends and more interests. Anthea knew her neighbours, the local shopkeepers and even, amazing to Cassie, her postman. She felt little need to keep a distance between herself and other people. Cassie reminded herself that teaching was a less competitive career than hers and Anthea was a different sort of person.

Anthea saw the solution in finding a man. When Cassie was young, she had wanted to be married, but only because it was a goal everyone had, what her self-improvement books called an unexamined goal. She had been attracted to men, had fallen in love twice in her twenties, had nearly married once, but in the end had decided that relationships took more away than they had ever given her. Even falling in love had never been a deeply serious matter for her.

Cassie felt the need to deal with her emotions only when they interfered with other things, or to spur herself on. Moving out of teaching and into business was more exciting and fulfilling than she had ever imagined any relationship to be. She'd felt in charge of her life, that she was doing something of real significance.

There had been Phillip. Cassie had felt she was in love, but the feeling was continually eroded by the petty annoyances, by the sense of intrusion, by the energy and time she expended on the relationship, with its ill-defined rewards. What she felt for Phillip never went to the very core of her being. Sometimes she suspected a conspiracy, to elevate the importance of sexual relationships. At other times, she wondered if she was particularly unsuited to relationships.

As a small child, Cassie had longed for solitude. Susan had wanted to lie in bed with her, bring her dolls and swap stories, but Cassie had found reasons for privacy, for being alone. She wondered if she was too alone now and needed something to shake her mood. She remembered her promise to take Elin up the mountains. She must commit to this, she decided. Maybe "commit" was a word she should have had on her mind map. She glanced at the bedside photo of Susan's three children: Jack, still a tiny baby, held protectively by Elin, Kelly standing naked, except for her pair of new sneakers. Connection – another word. If she thought about it, it would be months off, hours trimmed and tagged, Elin just another event to be scheduled. She picked up the phone and dialled Susan's number.

"Hello?" Her sister's voice was muffled.

"Hi, Suzie."

"Cass. God, I thought you'd never speak to me again."

"Don't be silly." She tried to moderate her voice. "It was just a disagreement. Not serious."

"Sort of serious. I'm trying to be more positive. But actually, it made me think. I'm still seeing Mum as much as I can, but I am training Jack to stay with a babysitter."

"How do you do that?"

"Nick thinks it's crazy. I stay and she just plays with him. So it's sort of paying for nothing except sometimes I get to go to the loo by myself." There was a sense of desperation in her voice. "The good news is that Jack's finally crawling, which means I don't have to cart him absolutely everywhere."

"That's great! Backwards or forwards?"

"Forwards. Not like the girls. Proper neat little crawl."

"I can't wait to see him. Listen, can I take Elin up the mountains this weekend?"

"You sure can. Elin, do you hear that? Cass is taking you up the mountains. She says she loves you, Cass. Yes, she really wants to come. Friday night?"

Cassie hung up and looked at her Filofax. She was in a time frame again, with a marketing meeting, a presentation to the board and Elin. Her decorated chart now seemed frivolous. But maybe it had worked. The flat was filled with the smell of coffee brewing. She loved this place. She decided she'd do some work at home and go in late.

Outside, there was a high wind, and waves were sweeping across the harbour. The empty corner of the dining room caught her eye. She remembered that she had toyed with the idea of commissioning a piece of sculpture, of bringing some other presence into the apartment. An art dealer had shown her photos of work by an artist who sculpted in wood and bronze. She had fallen in love with what he did. She picked up the phone and called Denise.

"Hi, I'm going to tidy up some stuff here at home. I'll be in about ten." She smiled at Denise's surprise. "I'm just working on the Asia presentation. But I want you to do something else for me. Remember that sculpture I was thinking about for my flat? I gave you the artist's phone number to file. Could you chase it up? I need him to come here. Slot him in whenever. Thanks."

She looked up at the glazed white ceiling. She liked the idea of commissioning something. Smooth, sensual, maybe a yellow wood.

The phone rang.

"Suzie here. Listen, can Elin bring a friend? And why don't we all come up Saturday night? So I can see you too." Her voice sounded warm and full of affection, the best of Susan. "Okay, see you Friday."

Cassie put the phone down. She could feel the sense of panic again, although not its full impact. She always got more than she bargained for with Susan. It was never neat. But two children would be fine. Must be fine or Susan wouldn't have asked her. She'd invite Anthea to come up and stay on Saturday. That way, she wouldn't feel so overwhelmed by Susan and

Nick. Why, she asked herself, should she feel overwhelmed anyway? But she experienced a sudden desire for someone to take her away for the weekend, tuck her into bed, buy her treats, snuggle up with teddies, do her hair. She went into the kitchen and poured herself a coffee.

Chapter 4

Susan stood at the door of the surgery and watched as Nick handed the instruments to his nurse. "You'll need to make an appointment for next week," he said, smiling at his patient. "And no more drilling. We just fit the crown."

When they first married, Susan loved to watch him in these small, unguarded moments. He was so handsome, so professional. Now, she thought miserably, it made her feel suspicious and excluded. Suspicious of Julie and her quiet, intimate compliance with all Nick's wishes, which contrasted so markedly to the chaos and demands of his domestic life. And she was excluded from the business, which was half hers. All he wanted her to do was the bookkeeping. The split of ownership, he told her, was because she was his wife, not because she *needed* to be involved in the business. When she had ideas, he became prickly and defensive and told her she was a wonderful mother. He meant it as a compliment. She hated him for saying it.

She rocked the fretful Jack in the stroller as Nick took off his white coat and put on the soft bulky navy sweater she had knitted for him last winter.

"See you at two, Nick," said Julie, smiling at him. "Nice to see you, Mrs Scarcella. Baby looks great."

Julie said the same thing about Jack every week, Susan thought, as if he wasn't a real person. And Julie looked not only young, but happy and carefree. Julie wasn't bitter. That was it. It made Susan feel full of unfair fury. Julie was part of Nick's life in a way she wasn't. She used to be, choosing the furniture for the surgery, buying the fish tank, the big restful poster of a tree, the toys for the toddlers. Then, she had thought she would always be part of it. Her father had been the same. He had fussed over her, sung to her, but Cassie was always the one he took with him when he went out.

Nick turned to her and kissed her on the cheek, handed her the folder of accounts and picked Jack up out of the stroller.

"How's my bambino?" He kissed the baby's hands as Susan leaned over and fastened Jack's shoe.

"Busy morning?" she asked.

"Medium." He hardly ever talked to her about work now, the difficult patients, the interesting cases. She supposed it was her fault, nagging him, never calm. And he had Julie. Julie was very intelligent, he had said. It had stung her to the bone.

They went downstairs to the coffee lounge with its formica tabletops and suburban dreariness. Susan flicked through the accounts folder. She remembered when, newly married, they had leased the surgery. They had proudly brought his parents here to show them this clean, new suburb with their son's surgery. It was so different from their dark dingy shop where factory workers had trooped in, demanding pies and milkshakes. Nick had worked in the shop in school holidays and, when he was old enough, in the local smallgoods factory, where he'd been teased by a chorus of raucous women. No wonder the surgery had seemed like a bright new beginning.

"I've put in Debbie's latest account," Nick said sheepishly. "Her boyfriend never came."

"No celebrity dentistry?"

"It could have worked," he said, sullenly. "Shit, there's got to be a better way."

"If you let me run the business side . . ." she began. "If you look at the figures, taking a partner in makes some sense."

"I'm the professional," he said pompously. "I have to make those decisions."

"Shucks, I forgot," she said. She put the folder in her bag and took the squirming Jack back from him. "Why are we doing this?" she asked. "We could live in a cheaper house. Move to the country." This was a romantic dream which always came back to haunt her. "Live in the mountain house. Give up dentistry if you want."

"What I want has nothing to do with it. We've got three kids and we're mortgaged to the hilt. Wanting's irrelevant."

"But you're not happy," she persisted.

"Are you?" he asked savagely.

"Sometimes." Sometimes, the dreamy mornings when the two girls played quietly and Jack fed peacefully, against a background of the sun in the garden and housework that wasn't totally chaotic. Sometimes, when she sat in the sun with her mother. Then she could pretend her mother was how she used to be, but without the cutting criticisms she used to make. She could feel better and more virtuous than Cassie because she was the daughter doing the right thing, even if her mother wasn't quite aware of it As a child, she had loved her parents, but at times Cassie's perfection had cut her to the quick.

"You're lucky then," Nick snapped. She realised with a shock her "sometimes" hadn't included Nick.

"We should be happy," she said. "We've got three lovely kids, a great house. We must have more money than most people."

"More money worries. The practice needs capital."

"Get a partner then."

"And reduce the profits. We've got a house that needs a million things done." He sighed. "The kids, they're great, I agree. You're a wonderful mother." He patted Jack's bottom and Jack looked at him flirtatiously.

"Are you and me what's wrong?" Susan asked. They'd fallen out of love, out of excitement, out of even a pleasant sort of ease. He was a different person and she was too. She had known it was happening – her dislike of sex after the babies, his sharp remarks about her appearance, their disagreements over money. These things had an impact on their outer world, but she occupied a smaller, internal, private world, the only place where she could feel comfortable. It seemed terrible to her that her idealism about marriage had simply died.

She certainly didn't want Nick dead, but idly, without malice, she sometimes found herself running the role of his widow through her head.

It was tragic, bringing tears to her eyes, but also mawkishly agreeable. In reality he was greying at the temples, the image of the stern Italian patriarch gradually replacing the dark, boyish good looks he'd had for so long. A sense of pleasure had been replaced by bitterness that life wasn't serving up what he wanted.

"I never expected marriage to be one long honeymoon," he said. "You forget. My parents came here in the sixties with nothing."

"Yeah, well my father came here in the fifties with nothing," she retorted.

"Except an English wife. With money."

"Poms and dagoes," she answered dishonestly, knowing full well that her mother's English gentility and small private income had wormed its way past many a barrier where her father's Italian heritage would have barred them.

"Life is life," he said, "not some dream."

"Fuck it, Nick. You're so bloody tangled up in whatever it is, you're a pain in the arse."

He stood up. "Maybe I'm not the only one," he retorted. "I don't feel like lunch. I've got a two o'clock patient anyway."

As he walked out the door, she felt a stab of despair. "Hot chocolate," she told the waitress. "Cheesecake with cream and icecream." She brought a jar of pureed apples out of her bag for Jack. She opened them but he baulked at the first spoonful, and she sat unconsciously feeding herself as she waited for her order.

Later, when she walked into the schoolyard, she could feel the weight of the cheesecake adding to her despair. She sat out of the wind, in the shelter shed, watching the other mothers coming into the playground, the toddlers running wild.

Maria sat down beside her. "You look as if you've been crying."

"I had lunch with Nick," said Susan.

"So?"

"It's nothing major," said Susan. "I don't like him any more. We never talk. He bores me. And he feels the same way about me." It wasn't quite true and she realised she had stated it in Maria's black and white terms, not her own, which were less certain. She was like her mother, she thought, scared of people, not enough friends, retreating to home and family. If Nick would help her, would let her do things, she'd have more confidence.

"And you're stuck with three kids and a mortgage."

"I wouldn't mind being stuck," said Susan, "but it's the horrible emptiness."

Maria took Jack from her and put him over her shoulder. She walked up to the end of the shelter shed and back again, rocking him.

"You've got to give up this shit," she told Susan. "You and Nick are like ninety per cent of marriages. The other ten per cent are bloody lucky or bloody good actors. Look at my Gerry. Crashing bore. A bastard on the grog. We haven't got much in common, but he's another income, a father in an elementary way. I can get out. It'd be bloody hard and maybe I never will, but I could. And I've got other people in my life to have a good time with."

"Other men?" said Susan, shocked.

"Other women." Maria held up her hands. "Sex is far too complicated. Anyway, I can live with it, live without it."

"I know," said Susan feelingly. "I like the *idea* of sex, though. I miss the way we both used to feel when we did it. I wish I felt that now."

"Wish away," said Maria, as the bell rang. "But shit, Suzie, you've got to start getting a life. Nick isn't it. That's teenage dream stuff, kiddo."

"Do you sleep with Gerry?" Susan asked urgently. "Now that you don't like him?"

Maria looked at her puzzled. "Well, we're married."

"So you do?"

Maria shrugged. "It wouldn't work otherwise."

Susan looked out at the mothers in the playground, children running up to them, toddlers skittling away. She saw Elin looking for her, and called to her. She thought of her loveless lunch with Nick and wondered how it had come to this.

The driveway of the retirement home cut up through the green lawn, flanked by banks of azaleas that seemed to Cassie always to be in bloom. Whatever season she visited, the bushes were immaculately tended, but institutional, a little too neat, the edges too sharply defined. She pressed the buzzer at the big wrought-iron gates and was automatically let through. The lock was to keep the residents from wandering, not to keep visitors out. She walked along the path, past the neat brick villas, watching a white-haired man walking, head down, gesticulating. A woman was being wheeled by a nurse, while an old man lay back in a deck chair. The deck chairs were designed in such a way that the residents could get in or out of them without any sense of struggle. In the whole place, any sense of endeavour had gone. Easily, passively, comfortably, life meandered on, the calm exterior masking the loss of lives, the loss of memories, the loss of time and place with which all the patients were afflicted.

Besides their loss, they also had wealth in common – no urine-soaked beds, no tasteless pap for dinner, no harsh staff. "No loss of amenity," as the matron had explained to Cassie two years ago when she had first visited. It was as if the amenities and the luxuriousness of the surrounds made the loss of mind unmentionable. But it was the loss that haunted Cassie. From babyhood, her mother had imbued Cassie with a sense of the importance of good behaviour, of thoughtfulness, of strength of character, self-control. Cassie had responded, unlike Susan, with impeccable manners, high intelligence, high ideals. Now, the deterioration of her mother's character became more marked and more painful with each visit.

Cassie found her mother sitting on the verandah of her unit. She watched her for a moment, then walked towards her, steeling herself for the contact.

"Hello, Mum," she said. Kissing her seemed an intrusion on her mother's vacant stare. At her more desperate moments, Cassie fantasised that maybe her mother had a rich interior life. She could, at times, even understand Susan's insistence that their mother was "just forgetful".

"Cassie." She said her own name uncertainly as she sat down and tentatively touched her mother's hand. Her mother looked at it as if it had been dirtied.

"Cassie La Rosa," she went on desperately, "your daughter."

"Whose daughter?" asked her mother, suddenly sharp.

"Yours."

Her mother stared ahead. "He was very uninhabited," she said. "They say Italians are like that."

"Unin*hib*ited," corrected Cassie, without thinking, but recognising it was exactly the sort of correction her mother used to make.

"At me, all the time."

"At you?" echoed Cassie.

"Migrate – here, to this place. Strange place, don't you think, dear? He's never come yet." She sighed. "Pretty lonely, but I'm used to that." Her voice took on the tone of weary martyrdom that Cassie was so familiar with.

Her mother sat, prim and proper, not facing Cassie, but staring straight into the garden. She had never been a great one for direct eye contact, unlike their father, who insisted his children look him straight in the eye. Sometimes, like her mother, she had found him too bold, too confronting. She remembered the day before he died, she had sat with him, in the tiny stuffy bedroom in his mother's house. "Look at me, Cass," he had told her. "Tell me you love me." To her shame, terrified of death, she hadn't been able to do it. She had looked at him sideways, stroking his leg. "Papa, Papa," knowing he wanted more.

Everything about her mother was untouchable. It seemed that the disease hadn't stripped her personality, but had gathered it up and concentrated it, so she was here – angry, alone, polite. Her hair was perfectly done, although more simply than in the past, her collar turned neatly over the Pringle cardigan, her shoes precisely laced. Cassie had a painful sense of her mother's life, a life contained and unexplored, quite unlike her own. She had been a mother, with no ambitions or passions beyond that. Cassie had travelled, with the same passion and excitement as her father. She had fought, like him, to carve out a place in the world, to win. But recently, she'd a sense of herself, in the deepest part of her, as contained and constrained.

Cass noticed a cut on her mother's leg, red and bruised and angry. She couldn't look and she touched her mother's hand tentatively.

"I'll be going now." She had only been there a few minutes.

"You're La Rosa, are you?" Her mother said it quite impersonally, with no sign of recognition.

"I'll have a word to sister," Cassie said. She felt herself growing unreasonably angry and by the time she had walked to the office, she could barely control herself.

"I'm Cassandra La Rosa," she announced. "I'm upset to see that my mother's leg is ulcerated again."

The sister was young, but confident and competent. "Her circulation is terribly poor, and if she knocks herself, it ulcerates. Last week, she went down to the bushland park and scratched herself. She didn't want it dressed. Your sister came in and convinced her to let us do it. It got much worse. We had to get your sister to come in every day for a week, poor thing, so your mother would let us dress it. I know it looks awful, but it is healing." She took in Cassie's angry face. "I could ask Doctor to call you."

"No," said Cassie, ashamed. It must appear to them that she simply didn't care about her mother, that Susan was the responsible daughter. She wanted to justify herself, to explain, but instead, she apologised. "I didn't mean to snap at you. It upset me when I saw it like that. And that she's so . . . unresponsive." She shrugged her shoulders. "She doesn't even know me."

"She knows."

Cassie's anger flared again. "I'm some stranger. We don't even have a conversation."

"I'm sorry," said the nurse, "it is painful, but your mother really is different with you than she is with other people. I'm not sure it's recognition, but it's something."

"How is she different?" In a way, Cassie desperately wanted to know that her mother did recognise her. But more than anything, she longed for an end to the ambiguity so there would be no more reproach or guilt.

The nurse looked at her kindly. "I was watching you, through the window. If anyone else sits near her, like you were, she gets up and goes into the unit. Some of the other patients make friendships – go walking together, do things in the recreation room." She smiled. "Your mum's not a joiner. In fact, she won't stand for company, except you and your sister."

"My sister thinks she's lonely."

"There's nothing as lonely as this disease, is there? You see it in their faces."

Chapter 5

"Can we have McDonald's?" asked Elin from the darkness of the back seat. "If you've got enough money," she added politely.

"I think I've got just enough money for two things each," said Cassie, feeling the pleasure of being with Elin again.

"My mummy says McDonald's rots your heart," said Elin's friend Sarah.

"That makes *four* things for me," said Elin.

"I think I'd be allowed to have it as a special treat," Sarah said cautiously.

"That should be okay," said Cassie. "I'm sure your mum wouldn't mind."

"Or don't tell her," suggested Elin.

"I tell Mummy everything," said Sarah.

Cassie listened as the two children chatted, noting how the pure innocence of Elin's early childhood had given way to a somewhat soiled virtue. At every age, Elin, Kelly and Jack had enchanted her. Her feelings, when each of Susan's children were born, had surprised her in their simplicity and passion, in contrast to the relationship between her and Susan which was often so ambivalent and complex.

They pulled into a highway McDonald's, and Elin convinced Cassie that the two things didn't include drinks or dessert. Afterwards, in the car, the little girls snuggled down on the doona Cassie had piled into the back, and gradually drifted off to sleep. Cassie pondered on how she would get the house heated, the beds made and carry the sleeping girls from the car. But as they turned into the driveway of the old Blackheath house, Elin woke up, desperately excited. She shook Sarah awake and begged that they be allowed to sleep in the attic. Cassie opened the car door and was struck by the smell of pine needles in the cold night air. It brought back how she and Susan, despite the tensions in the house, used to revel in the garden and the bush.

She lifted the bags out of the boot and hurried the children into the kitchen. She clicked on the big gas heater, which she'd bought with her first pay cheque from DMC Dolan. It was the first of a series of luxuries she'd bought for her mother, until she realised that her mother much preferred the small, secreted luxuries that she had wormed out of the house over the years – the tiny circle of warmth round the fuel stove where she drank her afternoon tea, the lack of a toaster which forced her to toast crumpets in front of the fire in the lounge room, the window seat, with its worn tapestry cover, which caught a triangle of afternoon sun and the view over the valley, where she occasionally had a five o'clock sherry. It was with reluctance that her mother had even bought an old explosive chip bath heater, which gave them hot tap water after years of making do with boiling up the kettle.

Her father, by contrast, had indulged his more Italian and Italianate passions outside – great heaps of leaves which he burnt illegally, much to the fury of the local bushfire brigade chief, a huge woodheap, which came from scouring the local bush for suitable trees, the diversion of a small stream into a pond, where they could bathe in the dark, cold, slippery water, but which dried up if the summer was too dry or too long.

"Can we sleep upstairs?" demanded Elin.

"Yes, sweetheart, but pop up and turn the heater on. You remember how to do that? We want the house to warm up a bit before you go to bed. We'll have some cocoa down here."

"What's cocoa?" asked Sarah.

"She means Milo," explained Elin. "They didn't have Milo in the olden days." She skipped up the stairs, shrieking with delight. Cassie recalled how her mother's stories of England, her father's of Italy, their recollections of the war, seemed to be just as much the olden days as cocoa was to Elin.

Cassie began heating the milk. Standing by the stove, she recalled her parents' long-enduring struggle with one another, their hopeless rejected gestures towards each other. The chaste little gem scones her mother made to salve her father's hearty Italian appetite, the garden swing her father had made for her mother. He had eaten the gem scones without noticing. She had never used the swing, but had continued to take her old wicker chair out onto the verandah. The distance, the separation of their lives, the final humiliation of her father's death in Italy, had always seemed tragic. But now, standing huddled next to the gas heater, listening to the shrieks of the two children upstairs, made her wonder if her own life was almost as sad. She pulled herself up. Her mother's tragedy was that she had never had anything other than her family, a diminishing and unsatisfactory resource. She, Cassie, had a career, travel, a diversity of other interests. Already, she'd missed one of the lectures on

Japanese prints. A diversity of interests certainly, she thought wryly, that there was no time to pursue.

"We're bored," Elin announced at six the next morning, waking Cassie from a deep sleep.

"I'll come down and get breakfast for you in a moment," said Cassie.

"We had breakfast," said Elin. "We had the chips and the marshmallows out of that bag because Mummy told me not to wake you in the morning."

"And there's nothing on TV," added Sarah.

"No wonder I never had children," said Cassie, smiling at Elin. "Come here, you little rat. Come into bed, both of you. Your feet must be freezing." Elin snuggled into the doona with Cassie, Sarah perched shyly at the end of the bed, until Cassie threw the doona over her, embracing her into the circle. The three of them squirmed under the covers, writhing and chasing, catching hands and feet and faces with squeals of laughter.

"Mummy said you don't have children because you're too fussy," said Elin, emerging hot and breathless from under the covers. "Fuss, fuss, fuss."

"Too busy," said Cassie, feeling the sting of Susan's remark. She hugged Elin, feeling her tenderness for the child. "Bizz, bizz, bizz. Now you kids get out of here while I get dressed."

"What will we do?"

"Show Sarah the garden," Cassie told Elin.

"I hate outside," said Sarah stoically.

"Show her the pool."

"Daddy filled that in. It was all slimy and green and yucky like poo," said Elin.

"He filled it in?" said Cassie, a catch in her voice, "and the little waterfall?"

"He said it was filthy," said Elin, and ran out. "Come on, Sarah, let's tread on the frost. It's crunchy."

Cassie lay back, filled with anger. She had bought the house from her mother, paying more than market price, to allow her to go into a luxurious retirement village. She had taken out a mortgage, paid the rates, the upkeep, the repairs. In addition, she paid the gap between her mother's small income and her expenses at the retirement home. She allowed Susan and Nick to use the house whenever they wanted to. The change in the status of the house had never been discussed. It had been between her and her mother, her mother alternately agreeing to the move and then furiously accusing Cassie of treachery. She had done the older sister thing, taking care of it. But Susan's husband had removed the pool.

It's my house, Cassie thought, my pool.

The two children were finally reconciled to the outdoors, making a cubby house from a fallen pine branch, as Cassie pruned the roses. She remembered there was a particular smell to the process, not from the long-gone flowers, but from the sap of the rose. As a child, she had loved a game her father played, his hands over her eyes, making her guess the names of herbs and flowers from their smell. Now, although she could recall the smells, she could no longer remember whether it was the right time of year to prune roses. But she did recollect exactly how her mother pruned, above the buds, thinning the straggly crown of the bushes.

While her mother had taught her to grow flowers, her father had taught her to grow vegetables. Cassie had raised produce every season and sold it to the neighbours. Every Mother's Day she used to run a flower stall on the main road. She had felt such pride in her produce, a budding capitalist. But she had also loved the soil, the delicate green of the young plants, the tender act of creating and then caring for the garden. She hadn't had time to work the garden for years, instead paying a local man to maintain it. But by pruning the roses she was laying her claim to the garden, to the house and to the now defunct pool. This had been her territory as a child and she felt it passionately to be hers again.

She raged silently against Susan and Nick and sometimes against herself. She fought to be rational, to work out why the loss of the pool, which certainly wasn't particularly beautiful or functional, made her so angry. Was it the destruction of her father's work, the implicit siding with her mother, that tore her apart as it had done when she was a child? Or was it shunting the maiden aunt, a phrase with which she christened herself for this event, a phrase that sidelined and demeaned and demoted her, that was upsetting her? Or was it simply a question of the awful green painted concrete circle that Nick had replaced the pool with? Or Nick being married to Susan, three children, their simple happiness that was turning her into a harpie?

"I don't think you prune roses in winter, darling." Anthea's voice floated across the garden. "You've probably just cut off the spring buds."

"They're mountain roses," said Cassie haughtily.

"Like mountain bikes." Anthea laughed. "For inner-city wankers to have on their front verandahs for show."

"Something like that." Cassie relaxed and kissed her friend on the cheek. "I'm having a furious argument with my sister," she explained, "in my head. I need the roses to focus."

"Oh my God, is this going to be a *family* weekend?" Anthea sighed. "And I've brought a new beau."

"Is he bearable?" asked Cassie, thinking about Johnny Jamieson.

"He's the leftover from a Social Scene dinner," said Anthea. "A bit wet – not my usual bastard style, but I'm trying to be open-minded." She paused and looked up at a row of pines silhouetted against the bright blue of the winter sky. "Maybe he's slightly simple. No, not exactly simple. He's more naive, like a Rousseau painting. Here he comes . . . Peter," she called, "come and meet Cass."

Peter took Cassie's hand solemnly. Cassie noticed that he held on to it too long, as he looked earnestly up at the pine trees. "This is wonderful. Wonderful to be out of the city."

"Yes, it is," said Cassie. "I'll come in and make you a coffee, as soon as I've put these in the incinerator."

"I don't drink coffee," said Peter. He looked at her sharply. "Actually, you shouldn't burn those rosehips. They make the most wonderful tea."

79

"Turn your pee bright red, though," said Anthea. She shot a wry "I told you so" look at Cassie.

"You're welcome to the rosehips," said Cassie. "Anthea's trying to start a fight."

"You have to dry them before you can use them," he explained earnestly, "but I brought some herbal teas with me."

"Great," said Cassie. "I'll come inside in a moment."

"Why don't you get our stuff out of the car?" Anthea said to Peter. "I'll help Cass with these clippings."

They watched him as he walked to the car. "He's okay," said Anthea vaguely.

"Why do you bother?" asked Cassie. "If you don't really like him. I mean, it's not going to go anywhere."

"Lonely," said Anthea, not looking at her. "And randy. Arms round me in the night." She looked across the garden. "I suppose I should go and help him." She walked off. Compared to Anthea, Cassie felt clipped and contained like her roses. She noticed a thorn sticking into her hand. As she re-adjusted the bundle, a prick of bright blood appeared. She dumped the rose prunings into the incinerator. Was she a self-creation, spun out of nothing, a tissue of things she had grabbed from the world, things that had cocooned her safely within her own thinking? She'd always taken risks to get where she was, but now she felt squeezed into a small focus, a life entirely of her own making, with no surprises, no risks, no real passion, no real dreams. Or perhaps the dream of success had turned out to be less dreamlike than she had anticipated. She pushed the rose clippings in on top of the chopped-up poplar she had had the gardener remove. She'd light it this afternoon and watch the sparks arc up into the late afternoon sky, the flames leap at the top of incinerator, the coals glow at the bottom. She understood why her father so loved fire.

"I'm making us lunch," said Anthea. "Peter wants vegetarian lasagne." She put her arms round him as he sat at the kitchen table. "I sense incompatibility . . ." she crooned. "He likes herbal, I like synthetic, he likes spinach, I eat meat."

"We were planning a barbecue tonight," said Cassie. "For the kids," she added.

"We could go to McDonald's," suggested Elin.

"I want to go home," said Sarah, and burst into tears. "It's cold."

Cassie felt annoyed. Her sympathy for Susan's children seemed limitless, but she found it hard to extend this to children in general. She had an unreasonable lack of sympathy for this child who was clearly deserving of compassion. It was her mother's injunctions in her, her mother's observations of badly behaved children, of undisciplined children, of children not like her. Cassie had been restrained and disciplined, where Susan had been impetuous and self-willed.

"You're a bit homesick," she said lamely. Active listening might work in the boardroom, but hands-on empathy was needed here.

"I want to go home," the child repeated.

Anthea grabbed Sarah and stood her on a chair beside the stove. "Darlink," she said, mimicking a ridiculous foreign accent. "I need you to cry in my sauce, as I have run out of salt. When you have cried enough, we vill ring up your mummy. And then, she vill get on her fastest horse and come and rescue you from all the yukky people here. But we vill make her stay vhile we cook zee marshmallows on zee fire tonight. No?"

"Mummy doesn't like me to have sweets," said Sarah piously but less tearfully. "And she doesn't have a horse."

"She vill bring her car zen," said Anthea, "and we vill eat zee nuts and zee fruit, and put popping and exploding zings in zee fire." She lifted Sarah down and rummaged in her bag. "Sparklers! I brought sparklers, so we can all run round on the lawn and wave them around and pretend we're fairies in the dark." Sarah pressed against her and Anthea held her hand, helping her stir the sauce, stroking her hair.

Sarah pulled away and wiped her eyes on her sleeve. Cassie wished she had been able to do it.

Nick and Susan arrived as it was getting dark and the children raced around the lawn with the sparklers. Nick fired up the barbecue, and Cassie lit the incinerator, which sent out a shower of sparks into the night sky. A cosiness had emerged between Anthea and Peter, and Anthea sat beside him, as the others retreated inside to bathe the children.

"I really like you," he said, self-consciously.

"Thanks," said Anthea. "What do you want out of this?" she asked after a moment. "Sex?" She was suddenly aware of the harshness of her tone. "Love? Commitment?"

"I'm always in search of love," he answered, "which exists on many levels."

Anthea wondered why she had persisted. He took himself too seriously. It wasn't going to work. Even he, in all his cosmic togetherness, knew that. Arms around her in the night, but that was all. "Okay," she said, but with a sense of weariness. She took his hand. "We'll find our level, I guess."

Elin and Sarah and Kelly sat, angelic in their nightdresses, toasting marshmallows in front of the fire. Jack snoozed restlessly on a rug on the floor. Cassie decided on a direct line of fire.

"You filled in the old pool," she said, "without asking."

"It was stagnant," said Susan quickly. Too quickly, Cassie thought, for an easy conscience.

"It took me a whole weekend," said Nick proudly. "I saved you a bit on labour." He smiled at her, the bright, white, handsome Italian smile, so like her father's. A smile designed to charm women and put them in their place.

"It's so ugly," said Cassie. "And I liked the old pool. To tell you the truth, Nick, I was really upset you did it."

"You were in Japan," said Nick, not understanding. "It's always been a bugger of a thing, getting blocked and stagnant. Susan's always terrified one of the kids is going to fall in. Put a couple of big pots on it, it'll be fine."

"Dad made it. It had a lot of sentimental value," protested Cassie. "You've put up with it for years. You could have waited till I got back from Japan."

"I was only trying to help," Nick said crossly. "Save you time. Save you decisions."

"It's my house." It was the first time she'd said this.

"That's why he did it," said Susan decisively, picking up Jack. "We use it all the time and we thought we'd try to do something useful for a change. Of course, I forgot how sensitive you were about your stuff." She said it calmly, but it hit its mark.

"I'm very sensitive about my stuff," said Cassie fiercely. "And I don't see why I shouldn't be. It's done, but it can't stay like that. If I work out something else, Nick, maybe you could help with the labour then too." Nick looked at her in amazement. "And next time, ask!"

She felt a sudden ebb in her courage, from the way Nick was looking at her. She could see his mind ticking over, her character being slotted in – middle-aged, unmarried, neurotic. If she stayed here in the room, she would probably become hysterical and menopausal as well. "I'll go and check the oven." She hurried into the kitchen and turned the bread she had baking in the wood stove. It felt worse than when she'd lost the fight with the board last year, worse than when she'd lost the Cartland contract. There was something, in all these years, where simply by being single, she'd lost out on a grander scale. She lacked some essential credibility, which allowed Nick and Susan to ignore her. She was a woman with property, with money, with power, but a slightly ridiculous figure, because there was no man. It was wrong, but however much she fought against it, she couldn't shake it. She looked out and saw Anthea and Peter, arms around each other, silhouetted against the sky at the top of the hill.

Chapter 6

Anthea put a condom on the table beside the bed. She could hear him, in the bathroom, having a shower. She was annoyed he was keeping her waiting. But the weekend was her fault. She should never have accepted his gentle pressuring and insistent phone calls. Now she was here and, as Cassie said, what was the point? Embarrassment, single night of physical passion, no heart, arms around her?

She lit a candle and turned out the light. The shower seemed to go on forever. Finally, he slid into bed beside her. Earlier, walking up the hill, they had been warm, companionable. Now, her need felt urgent, but no longer warm. He seemed even more distant and removed.

They kissed, and felt each other's body, but Anthea was aware of a lack of tension, a lack of excitement on his part. They continued to kiss and stroke until, finally, he stretched and sat up.

"Great," he said, with a faked enthusiasm. "That was absolutely great."

She lay, mystified. "Did I miss something?" she asked. "Like sex?"

"Sex isn't everything," he said, "especially the first time."

"First time," she repeated. "Last time too, I think." She would have laughed if she hadn't been so cross. Even so, she knew it would be a great story.

Gently, Susan detached Jack from her breast, and rolled over and placed him in the cot beside her bed. Nick groaned, half asleep, and reached out to her, pulling her towards him. She resisted, not quite pulling away from him, but not acquiescing fully.

"Come on, Suzie, it's been ages."

In her bone-tired body she felt she had been so long full of other people, of babies, of birth, of complications, of people looking into her, the babies suckling out of her. Nick's need should come to her as something different, something for herself. But between them lay so many things – the money, the terrible thing he'd done concreting over Cassie's pool, his failure to help her, to see she needed help. But the worst was that he wanted her how she used to be, young and adoring. She wanted him to know who she was now.

"Hey," he whispered, and pinched her bottom. She ached with painful self-consciousness at this acknowledgment, however affectionate, of her flesh. Excess flesh, she thought. She cut off from him, but the stab of shame made her comply with his desires. She made love, mechanically and without resistance, aware that her body was motherly, matronly. She remembered when she'd met him, dropping out of uni, unsure of herself, working in a dead-end job. None of it mattered to him. He was enchanted. He'd described her, jokingly affectionate, as all tits and teeth, skin and bone. And she had been, alive, vibrant, with a physical energy that eluded her now. She had hopes – hopes for him, hopes for herself. Somewhere, deep inside, she still had hope, but it rested lightly, like a dissolving fantasy.

"Why don't we have another baby?" he whispered when they finished making love. She lay, as she had always done, in the crook of his arm, the wetness between her legs. She closed her eyes, resentful that he was more in love with motherhood than with her.

She sighed. "We'd have to get a new car."

"You can't not have a baby because of a car." His voice was insistent.

"We're in trouble, Nick."

"Shit!" He pounded his fist into the mattress. "Why do you always say that?"

"Because we are. We argue. I don't get enough support from you with the kids. It's not as if we ever sit down and talk about things."

"We're married, Suzie. We've got a business and three kids."

"That's a reason for not talking?"

"There are times in your life when you just get on with it."

"Before we got married, I told you about my father, how he and Mum never talked. And you said it was the same in your family –"

"Except my parents are happy."

"Maybe."

"What do you mean by that?"

"I don't know that your mum's happy."

"You don't know my mum," he said angrily.

"I talk to her more than you do."

"That's what women do – they get together and talk about how unhappy they are."

"I need to talk to *you*."

"You think that when I come home from a day staring down people's mouths, I want to hear how unhappy you are?"

"Do you care?"

"Oh fuck! Loaded question." He turned over. Susan turned over and patted Jack in the cot beside the bed. Her hip touched Nick's briefly, then she pulled away from him, separated herself. She imagined lying in the bed by herself, a small pleasure.

In the morning at breakfast, Nick lavished kisses on Susan which she accepted passively, a hint of resentment, displaced by Nick's determined good humour. Jack babbled cheerfully at his mother and laughed when Cassie poked her tongue out at him. The three older children replayed their night-time adventures with much shrieking and delight. Cassie watched Anthea as she sat next to the fire, contented like a cat, sipping her coffee. Cassie was aware of being separate and alone. She envisaged her relationships in map form, lines, coming from others, skimming against her like a spider web, but attached elsewhere. No-one knew her patterns of daily living, the small intimacies of her life, the larger desires. Maybe no-one ever would. She reminded herself wryly that the same was true of Anthea but Anthea threw out more lines, attached them more firmly and held them to her. There were more breakages, but a denser pattern. Not for the first time did she envy Anthea's courage, her ability to adventure.

"Where's Peter?" she asked.

"Gone," said Anthea. "Don't ask." She lit up a cigarette. "It's okay. Actually, it's good that he's gone. Great. *Magnifico*!" She laughed. "It's fag time!"

"Hey kids, I'll take you for a bushwalk," said Nick. "With any luck, the bunyip will just be getting up and washing his face. C'mon, get your boots on. Kell, I'll give you a hand."

He hugged Susan warmly, and picked Jack off her knee. "Did we bring the backpack?" he asked.

Susan looked at him doubtfully. "Can you manage the four of them?" She was brooding about the previous night. He'd had sex, and forgotten; busy now being a father. She hated his forgetfulness.

"The track's nice and dry. Elin and Sarah, you'll help Kell, won't you?"

Elin smiled at him and took Kelly's hand. "Baby," she whispered disparagingly and pulled her little sister towards the door.

"Go," Anthea told him. "We're going to sit round the fire gossiping."

Susan handed Nick the backpack and together they fitted Jack into it. The three girls were shrieking for him to come and show them the bunyip. He went to the door, and then turned round to Cassie, embarrassed. "I'm sorry about your pool," he said. "I thought about it last night. I know, I'm a real klutz at times. Suzie had told me not to." He walked out quickly.

"Nick's full of surprises," Cassie said admiringly to Susan.

Susan shot her a look. "Yeah, he is. As long as you explain things to him real slow."

"What happened to Peter?" Cassie asked Anthea.

"Doesn't like sex on the first date. Humiliating," she said. "Probably for him as well as me. So I asked him to leave."

"Impotent?" asked Susan.

"No," said Anthea. "We kissed and cuddled, and kissed and cuddled and then he leaned back and said how lovely it was. So I suggested he pick up his bat and his balls, metaphorically speaking, and get the hell out."

"I think that's okay, though," said Susan. "When you're young and single, you're under so much pressure to behave in a certain way. When you're married too."

"He should have told me first," said Anthea. "There are certain expectations, whatever your age and status." She smiled. "Sex being a paramount one when you go away for a weekend."

Cassie broke up a bar of chocolate, put it in a dish and handed it to Susan, who began to eat it. "But it is true that the expectations aren't as clearcut when you're older," Cassie said. "If I was searching for a relationship, I don't know where I'd start, what I'd want. I like my life now, I don't want someone intruding on it. There are all sorts of issues about money and lifestyle."

"And sex. You always forget the sex, Cass." Anthea smiled. "And the ex-wives. And whether the guy is gay or bi or for real. And AIDS. It's too much for one body."

"You need someone to screen people for you." Cassie turned to Susan. "You were only sixteen when Papa died. He wanted to do that for us. Find out all about any boy who came near us. To save us the trouble and the pain. Find out about their family, their tempers, their incomes, their expectations. It used to make me so mad. But it was probably sensible."

Anthea raised her eyebrows. "Oh my God! Let's hear it for being sensible and arranged marriages."

"Typical Italian father," said Susan. "Ten years and Nick'll be doing the same thing to Elin, I swear it. Trouble is, once you're married, that's it. You're supposed to have it right – the family, the income, the expectations. That's what you married and nothing changes. Set in concrete."

"What do you mean?" asked Cassie. She had seen hints of Susan's marital troubles in the past, but they seemed trivial to her. She wondered if that was because she was afraid of witnessing a repeat of the tensions in her parents' marriage. Or perhaps it was because she felt that her natural loyalties would be with Nick, as they had always been with her father. She had, for years, silently condemned her mother for her coldness to her father.

Susan sniffed and ran her finger round the almost empty bowl. "The Italian peasant heritage. Nick's line is that you get on with it," she said. "You don't worry about who's happy or unhappy, or why life is like it is, or whether you should be a dentist or a housewife or something else. You put your head down and get on with it."

"But Nick is such a darling," said Anthea.

"There is some merit in getting on with it," said Cassie, "if you do it intelligently."

"He's got tunnel vision," Susan went on, ignoring her.

Cassie started, surprised at Susan's perception, a map of her life in her head again, this time simplified – work, this house, her apartment – three circled areas, joined by lines. "I've got tunnel vision."

Susan stared at her, amazed. "You? Tunnel vision? You started off as a secretary, put yourself through uni, taught Japanese, then the MBA and before we know it, you're in the corporate world, headed for the top. I wouldn't call *that* tunnel vision."

"But from what you say, I'm the same as Nick." Susan wondered why Cassie always took Nick's side against her. Cassie went on. "And like Dad was, too. Wherever you are, whatever you're in, you put your head down and go for it. I look at my job, and I accept all the parameters. And now I'm thinking about it a little differently." Her tone was cautious. She was scared to tell Susan this, scared *not* to be as Susan saw her, scared to explore this narrowness in herself.

"I'm thinking about marriage differently," said Susan.

"And I'm thinking about why we didn't get laid last night," said Anthea taking Cassie's arm. "Beautiful women like us."

"Or why *did* I get laid last night?" said Susan miserably. "I think marriage is the worst tunnel vision because everyone's saying how great it is, and how wonderful your kids are. What do you say? Sorry, I hate being married."

"Do you?" asked Cassie softly after a moment's pause, almost hoping Susan wouldn't tell her.

"Maybe there's something wrong with me. I love my children, but some days, I don't want to look after them. I don't know about Nick. I look at our wedding photo, the same one as on the dresser there." She walked over to the dresser and picked up the photo. "Look at me, adoring him. You can see love oozing out of every pore. And look how he's looking at me. So proud, so protective . . ." She sighed, and glanced up at the doorway as the children tumbled in. Nick stood there, staring at her. She put the photo down. "How was the walk?" she asked coolly.

Anthea and Susan went out to find pastries for afternoon tea, while Cassie baked cookies with the children. Nick dozed in the sun. It was strange, thought Anthea, that both she and Susan knew quite a lot about each other, but all through Cass. The features of Susan that grated on Cass, Anthea didn't mind – her lack of sophistication, her mumsy talk, her naive, trusting hopefulness that there was a world of true love and pussycats and children with nice manners and affectionate natures. When something happened, as it obviously had now, it hit Susan with the force of a truck.

"Do you regret not being married?" Susan asked Anthea as they came out of the bakery.

Anthea laughed. "Do you regret not being single?"

"I wish I'd made more of being single," said Susan earnestly. "Like Cass. Had a career. Nick holds that over me. He's the professional with money and status. I've got kids."

"But Cass and me, we don't have your madonna status." Anthea stopped, and looked at Susan. "Every time I tell people I don't have children, I see the pity in their eyes. Incomplete as a woman. It's hard enough already, wanting a child like I do."

"It doesn't worry Cass," said Susan. "She's never wanted kids."

"True, but I think she still feels a need to explain it. Cass is always on display, always different. She's not only made it in a man's world, she's made it to the big time. I mean, she matters. All that money and power. She's amazing."

"What do you mean?"

"She lives in a different world from you and me, beyond our comprehension."

"Shit, I never saw her *quite* like that," said Susan. "I know she's well paid and it's a great job. Big office. Lots of glass," she added vaguely. "And she has the secretary instead of being the secretary." Anthea could see why Susan grated on Cassie.

They got into the car. The smell of the warm pastries embraced them. Susan took a small citron tart out of the bag and started eating it. She offered the bag to Anthea, who broke off a piece of warm bread. They sat, looking down the street of suburban shops, to the dark blue green haze of the bush.

"I want to leave Nick," said Susan, suddenly tearful. She didn't stop eating.

"Forever?" asked Anthea gently.

"I haven't thought about that," Susan said, "I only want to get over being unhappy every day. People don't leave for a little while, do they? I mean, leaving *is* about leaving for-ever."

"Not necessarily. What would you do?"

Susan sighed. "I'd like not to have to deal with Nick, not to have to worry about Nick and me being unhappy. Concentrate on the kids. They're enough for one person. And get over whatever it is I feel. Think about Nick after that."

"Why don't you?"

"I don't know." She felt fuzzy about the whole thing. Maybe, she thought, she should try to work it out. Make a list.

Leave Nick. Get petrol. Go to bank came to mind as an escape plan. Not good enough, she thought.

"You could live up here for a while," Anthea suggested. "The kids would love it. You'd love it. Cass wouldn't mind, would she?"

Chapter 7

When Cassie had first come to DMC Dolan, her university MBA supervisor had told her that it would be like joining a religious order. "A lifetime vow," he had said, "at least until they restructure. And a restructure has remarkable similarities to the purging, purifying process that the religious have been so good at throughout history." She remembered he had lectured in religious studies before making a midlife career change to business studies. "To either break you or catapult you to new heights."

Ever since her speech at the management conference, she'd sensed a change; that she was seen as being a legitimate target for others. Tim Bayliss had put the word around. Yet the Research Department, by its very nature, was quarantined. She didn't work on hunches, or imaginative leaps, belief, or desperate hope. Research produced facts and figures.

But Cassie's current project, researching the market for prefabricated construction materials in Asia, had come from her. It had also got away from her into being a catch cry, a cure-all for the fluctuating market in Australia. She had originally presented the idea with caution, but it had generated a chorus of over-enthusiasm which had somehow become associated with her, and carried the success of her past projects.

Six executives sat around the enormous polished black table. At the top was Julian Hammond, head of Marketing, who was above them, a new breed of marketer. He was small, solemn and neatly precise, and looked like the actuary he was. His only concern was results. In that sense, he and Cassie had always seen eye to eye. He had assumed the role of her particular patron and protector. But despite a fundamentally numeric nature, he was susceptible to gossip, to flattery and to intrigue. Under him was the gang of five, the senior marketing executives, currying for favour. There was Cassie, head of Research; Tim Bayliss, New Product Development and his offsider, John Anderson; Jennifer Keen, head of Promotion; and Simon Lewis, an Information Services specialist, new and untried, whose recent appointment created a wave of speculation, still waiting, metaphorically, to break. As Cassie sorted through her overheads, the others chatted.

"Fabulous product," said John Anderson. "It actually clicks together – whole sheets of the stuff. Having trouble getting a name though, aren't we Jen?"

"Chief of Engineering suggested we promote it with the name of Pre-fab sheeting five point two," said Jennifer. She laughed. "Wonderful, spontaneous creature he is."

Cassie clicked on the overhead. "Okay, let's start. What I am presenting today are the parameters of the Asia study," she began. "This is an interim presentation before we decide on the final models, and to get input on any factors which may have been neglected." Personally, she felt sure that there was no area of neglect. "In the next six months, I will go ahead with an in-depth analysis of growth and profit forecasts, modes of entry and target areas." She felt nervous, sensing hostility in the room. "As I said at the beginning of the project, Asia is not a single market, certainly not in the sense that Australia is. Asia is potentially a large number of markets."

"How many?" asked Tim Bayliss. It wasn't the done thing to interrupt a presentation. It happened to Cassie, and to Jennifer, because they were women. It was part of the territory, along with the occasional rumours, parading as jokes that they had balls, that they'd slept their way to the top, that they were lesbians. Jennifer gave as good as she got. Cassie tried to rise above the gossip.

"I'll answer any questions later," said Cassie evenly.

"Simple question," grumbled Tim.

Cassie put up her first overhead. "This shows the markets in terms of culture. Obviously here, we're dealing with the culture pertaining to building firms."

"Culture?" said Tim. "Oh shit, I forgot. Cassie and her Japanese prints."

He is gunning for me, thought Cassie. She paused. She could win battles too. She had the facts.

She slid in another overhead. "I've done some breakdowns of public expenditure and private income levels. Below this line, we can assume the income is too low for a market to exist. There are some surprises here. For instance, the general perception is of a large, unexploited market in China. Even in the strongest growth areas, it's pretty marginal."

"Cass, I reckon they still have to live in something, work somewhere." John Anderson's voice came from the end of the room. His antagonism was tempered by his familiarity, but there was more here at issue than the presentation. Another agenda. Perhaps as stupid as male versus female. Perhaps payback for her coup in the US market two years ago. Perhaps sheer boredom.

"In parts, it's barely a cash economy," she protested. The figures are in the report. We can toss them round later, but I think you'll find I'm right."

"Women always are." It was Tim Bayliss again. Jennifer rolled her eyes up and sighed loudly while the men chuckled dutifully.

Cassie went on as if she hadn't heard. "Now, if we overlay the income graph on the culture graph, we have markets with reasonable long-term return. But we have to take them one by one, which is what I'll be doing over the next few months."

"How long, oh Lord, how long?" intoned John Anderson.

"As well as culture and income, I've looked at ease of entry, political stability, potential rate of return and assessed each market on that basis."

"Not exactly new," grumbled John.

"If we can agree on the markets," said Cassie firmly, "we can look at the investment forecasts in depth." She could feel her confidence growing. She knew this stuff, back to front. She had a proven record in Australia and the US.

"While I don't believe we can predict profits with certainty, we can look to a return on these investments, plus growth potential."

Cassie switched off the overhead. Tim Bayliss leaned back in his chair. "So?" he said. "We don't even know if we're going to make a profit. I thought that's what the aim of this whole exercise has been. You're saying we can't find out till we get in there."

"Is that true?" Julian Hammond asked sharply.

"At the moment it is," said Cassie, instantly regretting the note of apology in her voice. "At this point, we need to research the most attractive options in more depth."

"China's not on that list." John Anderson stood up. "That worries me. The Chinese market is something in the region of billions. All the indicators say that. Cass puts her overlay up . . ." he ran his hand across his throat, ". . . and all of a sudden we're out of it."

"Is that a question?" Cassie asked.

"I guess it is." John Anderson had sat down again and was lounging back in his chair. "Yeah, it is."

"China is potentially billions," said Cassie, "but it isn't billions yet. It is an enormous market in terms of national income but it's only a viable market in very few areas. Let's face it, peasants aren't going to be flocking out of the paddy fields to buy condominiums. However, if further research shows Shanghai is feasible, we'd obtain more knowledge plus a base for expansion."

"Geez, it sounds more complicated than the AFL competition ladder."

"I should hope so," said Jennifer wryly. "I think we still make more money than them."

"We're in danger of missing out, being so cautious," said John Anderson.

"It could be a very costly exercise," Cassie said patiently, "as many Australian and American firms have found out. We tried that in Eastern Europe, but it's just too expensive."

There was a raucous laugh from Tim. "Beijing's an urban centre with a population of twelve million. I'd call that a market."

"I don't believe in going there to prove a point that's already been proved," Cassie said sharply. She caught a sympathetic glance from Jennifer. She was glad Jennifer wasn't antagonistic, but the idea that her support might be because they were both women made Cassie uncomfortable. She went on. "We have to decide whether we go ahead to develop a final plan."

"To tell you the truth, Cass," said Tim Bayliss, "I'm a little disappointed. I'd like to have the sense that we are actually committed to Asia."

"It's flawed thinking, Tim," said Cassie, firmly. "That whole notion of commitment to Asia, as a monolithic concept. I've examined that, on page 44."

Simon Lewis got up, having sat silently, almost languorously throughout the meeting. There was a sense of suspicion surrounding Simon, largely, Cass believed, due to the fact that he was new and wore retro suits and a diamond stud in one ear. He'd been nicknamed the Blues Brother. He picked up Cassie's document. "This is well structured," he said. "What it needs is more precise analysis, particularly in terms of projections. We need to give these cultural factors an actual weighting. I've got some ideas." He stood, un-self-conscious, relaxed, a contrast to the table-thumping manner of the other men.

But Cassie couldn't read the moment, unsure whether she was being supported or shafted. She looked at Julian. "What do you think?" she asked.

"I think what Cassie has done is well structured," he said to no-one in particular, but Cassie noticed that he echoed Simon's words.

"I agree," said Tim Bayliss, with total sincerity, "absolutely."

"But perhaps fast-track it," said John Anderson. "We don't want to miss opportunities."

"Absolutely," agreed Tim. "It would have been nice to be up and running sooner rather than later."

"Great to see you guys suddenly so positive," said Jennifer sardonically.

Julian snapped his folder shut and cracked his knuckles. "Simon could bring a lot to the next stage. He's coming up with some pretty revolutionary stuff in process re-engineering."

Cassie extended her hand to Simon. "Look forward to working with you," she said. She wasn't at all sure what to make of Simon. The best strategy was to be open and retain control. She needed to keep an eye out for shifts in the balance of power, that much was clear. She glanced across at Tim Bayliss and smiled.

Anthea had bought a pizza and she and Cassie sat at Cassie's dining table, eating the meal with a bottle of red wine, looking out at the sunset reflected on the harbour.

"Hideous day," said Anthea. "In-service on formulating a discipline code. Total brawl. If we could get the staff sorted out, the kids would be a piece of cake."

"I know what you mean," said Cassie. "I did my presentation today and I'm still shaking."

"Except *you* look great," said Anthea. Cassie never looked better than when she was in crisis.

"Jennifer had warned me," Cassie said. "And Tim was almost telling me he was gunning for me back at that management conference. Which I did for him *as a favour*. My God!"

"You look very sexy," said Anthea, glancing at her and then staring out across the black expanse of the harbour.

"My whole future is at stake," Cassie went on. "Bayliss and Anderson. I need a strategy."

"Erotic."

"Anthea!" said Cassie in annoyance. "Would you stop!"

Anthea got up, restless. Cassie didn't allow her to smoke in the apartment. "I won't stop. You've told me it's a crisis, and I understand the fundamentals, but you're the one who's going to solve it. Or not. But as your friend, I've observed this phenomenon."

"What?" said Cassie.

"That whenever you have a crisis, you look more aroused, more sexual, more passionate than at any other time in your life."

"That is idiotic," said Cassie shortly.

"But true. Or have you met someone?"

"I haven't met someone," said Cassie. She got up from the table, calmer. She gathered up the papers she'd been working on before Anthea came. She looked at the top page, her latest mind map, a web of relationships and options. She had circled Simon Lewis's name. "I don't want a man. Not now at least." She smiled at Anthea.

Next morning, Jennifer was in Cassie's office. She had a shoe box on the floor and was wearing a pair of very high-heeled red shoes.

"What do you think?" she asked Cassie.

"Great colour. Are they comfortable?"

"You're like my daughter. She tells me it's politically incorrect to wear high heels." She put the shoes back in their box and sat down. "We need to talk."

"You were right about Tim gunning for me," said Cassie, sitting down at her desk, "but he didn't get me. And the reason was that the research spoke for itself."

"Sure it did," said Jennifer. "And Tim's flying to Melbourne with Brian Brewer this morning. You can imagine the conversation up in business class. *Yeah, Cassie gave that presentation on Asia yesterday. It was good, but very academic. I mean, all this stuff about culture. You know she speaks Japanese? Where's the bottom line in all that?* And Tim knows, of course, that Brian and Julian play tennis every Friday night, their wives are best friends. And Brian's a bottom-line kinda guy. Etcetera."

It was always personal with Jennifer, Cassie thought, too personal. Jennifer always knew the gossip and was prepared to use it. Cassie had used it too, but she preferred to do it alone, without the air of conspiracy. Maybe Simon was her natural ally – he was new, he had liked her presentation, he had Julian's ear.

"Okay, Tim can be a snake in the grass," said Cassie. "So I simply do my job."

Jennifer sighed. "Cassie, let me remind you that you have played this particular game Tim is now playing. Bullshit baffles brains."

Cassie sat, tight-lipped. She'd handle this herself. It would be madness to get drawn into Jennifer's agenda. Jennifer was too explicit, but not serious enough, not truly committed to the company.

"Let's look a step up the ladder," said Jennifer patiently. "King Curran, on the board, has got the bit between his teeth to implement this flatter management structure. Which puts the pressure on Julian to rationalise. Basically, you and I know that this leads not to warm and fuzzy teamwork but to knifings in the back, and dirty deals. It's a cover for downsizing. Never mind we're making healthy profits and we've already downsized. Curran thinks more of the same will give us a competitive edge."

"I agree with a lot of what he says."

Jennifer smiled. "Me too, except when it comes to *me* being downsized. Anyway, Tim

Bayliss is ahead of the rest of us, basically because he knows he's in the firing line. He's made some dumb moves, so now his strategy is to make himself indispensable by incorporating your department and parts of mine."

"Julian wouldn't hear of it."

"Except he is under pressure. So Julian has to hear of a different plan – from you and me. We should join forces and develop a proposal for a joint department that would give us some efficiencies and a salary rise each rather than a salary cut. We could downsize Tim in the process. Which would be fun."

Cassie considered the proposal. She and Jennifer would be a formidable team. But Jennifer's style was different. In the end, she would rather be a lone player. She could work with Simon, with her advantage of experience and seniority.

"Whatever you're proposing, count me out. Julian has always insisted that Research should be separate. I hardly think that's going to change now."

Jennifer got up. "Are you okay, Cass? I mean apart from all this? Are you really okay? In yourself?"

"Of course I am." Cassie tried to smile. "Look, I don't mean to sound rude. Thanks for thinking of me. I know you mean well."

"I do," said Jennifer, walking to the door. "But I was really thinking of me."

Susan sat in the darkened car, watching the light in the surgery window. She had left the children at home with Nick's mother, so she could come and pick him up from work. She could see Julie and Nick as they moved about the room. It looked to her like a companionable, cosy, self-contained existence. 'Nothing but a Heartbreak' by Bonnie Tyler was playing on the car radio and she felt heartbroken herself, let down by Nick, jealous of Nick and his freedom, hating Julie, not only for her closeness to Nick, but for her youth, her carefree life. She beeped on the horn. Nick came to the window and waved.

She waited for the surgery light to go out. It then seemed an improbably long time till the door opened and Julie and Nick came out into the street, Nick talking animatedly to her. Susan beeped again. Nick came over and got in the front seat.

"What the hell do you think you were doing? I was embarrassed – you beeping when I was talking to Julie."

"So sorry to interrupt," she said. "Your parents are with the kids. They might want to go home." She pulled out onto the road.

"They're staying to dinner," he said. "We organised that this morning."

"Well, I was sick of waiting."

"I was just talking to Julie. It was rude."

"Why were you so long?" She said it accusingly.

"I was making money," he said sarcastically. "To pay the mortgage. So I could spend time in our lovely house with you."

"Yeah, Nick. Sure. You'd rather be spending time with Julie."

"Which is supposed to mean?"

She drew up into the driveway of the house. "You just think about it."

"There's nothing going on with Julie. She's a nice kid with a string of boyfriends."

"String of boyfriends?" said Susan sarcastically, at the same time hating herself for saying it.

"I'm not interested in Julie," he said.

"If you say you're not, you're not," she said loftily. "I certainly don't want a scene now, in front of the kids and with your parents here."

"Christ!" He slammed the door and walked up to the house. She shut the door and followed him. At times like this, she felt so desperate, so scared, so out of control. "Shut your mouth," she told herself. She went into the house. Mechanically, she got through dinner, put the children to bed, farewelled Nick's parents and then sat down at the kitchen table and howled. Nick walked in. He didn't have it in him to put his arm around her.

"What's wrong with you, Suze?"

"Nothing!" she said. She felt a daze of emotions – anger, despair, hopelessness, self-pity, wanting him, hating him, hating herself, hating Julie. It was beyond her to explain to him. She put her head in her hands and when she lifted it again, he had gone upstairs.

She looked at the fridge despairingly, knowing she would start to eat, to treat herself, to relieve the misery, to keep the confusion of feelings safely bottled up. For a moment, she wished for the bulimia back, to get rid of this weight she was carrying. But she'd moved beyond that. She didn't dare think where.

"I've been considering my life," said Cassie, as they sat, perched on bar stools, each with a martini. Cassie looked out of place here, thought Anthea. It was a place for assignations. Maybe, thought Anthea, she was trying out a new life.

"This turning forty is big stuff," said Anthea. "I told you. You'll be like the rest of us. Male hungry. Baby starved."

"I didn't know you were baby starved," said Cassie. "I mean, that you *still* were. When you didn't mention it, I assumed you were over it."

"I look at them," said Anthea fiercely. "In prams. Over people's shoulders, in the supermarket queue. Once, with that horrible man before Johnny, I put holes in the condom, then spent weeks worrying that I'd have a ghastly baby whose forehead bulged when it was angry. So I was pretty happy when nothing eventuated. But I've tried at other times. I even went for the frozen stuff, but that was the end of my baby dream, because I found out my eggs are low quality. I didn't tell anyone when I was doing it because it was so painful and humiliating." She put her glass down. "Sorry, enough bloody eggs and squiggles."

"You should have told me," said Cassie. She was aware she sometimes failed Anthea as a friend. "Tell me next time something like that's going on. You know, friendship and all."

"What have you been thinking about your life?" Anthea asked.

"It sounds pretentious, but I've been looking at the confines of my life. When you're a high achiever, the confines are supposed to be behind you. You look ahead, to what's on the horizon."

"So what happens when you look around?"

"I see a lot of things, which I don't really have time to dwell on."

"Tell me."

"I see the girl who stands on the corner in William Street in fishnet stockings. Some mornings they're torn, others they're not."

"Cass! How corny! Prostitute fantasy. You're such a late developer. Most of us are over prostitute fantasies by the age of sixteen."

"It's not a fantasy," said Cassie impatiently. "It's a question – her life, my life –"

"Her life really," said Anthea. "Unless you're going to go and do counselling at the Wayside Chapel."

"I'm not thinking of that," said Cassie. "She's a bad example of what I mean. It's more that things seem to be striking me. The Information Services guy. He's just a tiny bit unconventional. In a way I never could be. I'm such a rules person. He wears an earring, which is highly radical in DMC Dolan. He wore a black T-shirt the other day . . ." She grimaced and Anthea laughed.

"I know the type, " said Anthea. "Only way you can tell they're rich is that their sunglasses cost three hundred dollars. Otherwise, they live like pigs."

"See!" said Cassie. "I don't know that." She thought of Simon, compared to Phillip. He was attractive, but he was far too young, far too different.

"I don't know it either, really," said Anthea. "It's an observation based on a sweet and incredibly short case study of one such creature."

Cassie leaned forward and touched Anthea's hand. "And I've had this crazy idea, ever since we went up the mountains, to go and live there. Keep my place, but live there weekends – Friday to Monday. I felt such a buzz that weekend, working on the garden. And I can imagine a different way of life. Maybe get to know the neighbours. Invite people up." She felt a sudden loss of confidence as she said it. Confiding the dream to Anthea made it seem real, but at the same time she was wondering who she could invite.

"Will you?" asked Anthea.

"It's not will I, won't I. It's just alternatives, things I've never even considered before."

Anthea lit up a cigarette. "Cass. This is it. This is life. It intrudes on you. It's uncomfortable, difficult. You've been living it as if you ran it. It was bound to catch up. It runs you."

"But you make choices. You've made this decision about finding a man."

"Because I was forced into it. By the sort of person I am. Needy and greedy. No place to run, no place to hide." Anthea drew deeply on the cigarette. "No, that's not true. Of course, I do make decisions, but life is anarchic. We're at the mercy of circumstances, of our wants, our desires, things we feel and don't even know we feel. You've put off looking at your life, because you sense it's going to toss you around a bit." She finished her drink. "Are you going to sleep with the man/boy love item with the earring?"

Cassie pushed her drink away from her. "Hardly," she said archly. She and Anthea had such different styles. For Anthea, men materialised into possibilities before she knew them. For Cassie, Simon was a vague curiosity, a minor interest. She felt far more passionate about the mountain garden than she could about Simon.

Chapter 8

Cassie woke at five the next morning, too early, with a slight headache. She had never had a hangover, but she supposed that this was the beginning of one. She had never got properly drunk, always pulling herself back, away from excess. Last night, she had been tempted to drown herself in drink, to lose herself. She was struggling with a feeling of uncertainty when the fight against Bayliss should have been igniting her passion and harnessing her energy. Even the process of recruiting Simon was going slowly. She tried to dispel her uneasiness. Maybe Jennifer had exaggerated the whole thing anyway.

She decided to use the extra time to get rid of her old newspapers. Over the past month, she'd let them accumulate, although, as always, she kept them in neat piles, tied with a running bowline and a slipped half hitch. This meant the knot was strong and secure, but could be easily undone. Cassie's father had taught her the bowline and four other commonly used knots when she was ten. She recalled fondly that this had been his idea of an essential life skill. Perhaps hers too, because it was one she had never forgotten. He had also taught her to whistle through her fingers, a talent that had often surprised her male colleagues when she hailed a cab, but which had become less useful as she moved into a limousine lifestyle.

She put on an old pair of jeans and a sweatshirt and took down the first pile of newspapers.

By the last trip, she was sick of it, her hands and her sweatshirt streaked black from the newsprint. In the apartment, carrying them to the door, they shed tiny fragments, making an obvious pathway. Two ibis perched on the bin, their long beaks probing intimidatingly into the discarded paper. It was silly to be frightened of ibis, but she was.

Cassie got back into the lift. The idea of being seen blackened, dishevelled, distressed her. At least it was early enough to escape notice. But at the ground floor, the lift stopped. The man who got in was a stranger. From his clothes, navy drill pants and an old paint-spattered jumper, he looked like a workman, but he was carrying a portfolio under his arm.

"What floor?" she asked.

"Seven, please."

It was Cassie's floor and they stood in silence as the lift went up. When it reached the seventh floor, he stepped out with her. "I'm looking for Cassandra La Rosa," he said. "*Cass An Dra La Ro Sa.*" He emphasised every syllable. "Such a wonderful name. You wouldn't happen to know her flat, would you? I lost my piece of paper."

"I'm Cassandra La Rosa," she said with a smile.

He started. "I had an entirely different picture in my head. I thought you'd be one of those lady executive types. Smart suit. Employ some poor old codger to deal with your trash."

Cassie laughed. "Actually, I have to confess, that's more me than this is. You got me at a bad time."

"Me too. Bad hair day." He looked at her, very directly. "Your Denise totally intimidated me. You have exquisite taste, she told me."

"You're the artist ... the sculptor?" said Cassie uncertainly.

"Darcy Diamond. Don't laugh – it's my real name."

"I thought you were going to phone me first," she said.

123

"I did too," he said seriously. "But I didn't." He followed Cassie as she started to walk along the corridor. "So? Exquisite taste?"

"Taste of some description, I hope," said Cassie lightly.

They went into the apartment. He looked around. "With a name like that you'd have to live in the penthouse."

In the morning brightness, she saw his face more clearly – lively, intense, and weathered.

"Fucking fantastic," he said softly, as he took in the expanse of harbour.

Cassie remembered that the gallery owner had recommended Darcy Diamond with a covert warning, almost a nervousness, stressing the quality of his vision. That, she remembered, was why she'd wanted to commission him. Vision. The term, overused in business, had seemed appropriate in relation to art.

"Could you wait while I have a shower?" she said. "Then I'll make some coffee and we can discuss this."

In the shower, she felt oddly embarrassed to be naked, with a man in her living room. It felt strangely intimate and intrusive. Dressing, she felt embarrassed again, getting into her work clothes, as if she was becoming someone else, as if his opinion of her mattered. But when she came out into the living room, he barely glanced at her. He had his drawing pad, some photos and photocopies from books spread all over the dining table, covering the papers she had been working on the previous evening. Quickly, she made the coffee and brought it to the table, with cups and a plate of fruit.

"Dream client," he said. "I'm caffeine dependent."

She moved her papers out from under his mess of photos. He grabbed the drawing pad and turned to a new page, so she only got a glimpse of what he had been sketching. It had intrigued her.

"What were you drawing?" she asked. She was excited by this, commissioning the piece, but more than that, by this strange man. She had been attracted to his face and, despite his oddities, to his whole being. The attraction felt so unusual to her that it took her a moment to identify the feeling.

"Fantasy," he said quickly. "You wouldn't want it. I'll sketch what you want."

She felt annoyed, but poured the coffee and sat down. "I designed this interior myself," she said. "I knew exactly what I wanted, and I worked on it for nearly two years."

"Your secretary told me – exquisite and definite taste." She wondered if he was being condescending.

"Except . . . I had wanted an abstract piece. About a metre high, for that corner. Simple, smooth, beautiful wood, but I'm beginning to think . . . maybe some other input. Another idea." She tried to formulate what was going on in her head. "I like this flat. I like what I've done, but it's beginning to seem a little self-contained, a little, I don't know, almost self-indulgent. Maybe in danger of drying up."

He smiled at her. "Self-indulgent?" he murmured as he doodled on the pad, a hint of mockery in his voice. He had dark, deep-set eyes, and untidy dead-straight black hair, unusual in a man of his age, which she guessed to be about fifty. A fifty, she thought, who had lived. Unlike her way of living, something dissolute, but also enviable. Darcy was a creator, a weaver of webs. Her life ran on straight lines.

"What I hate," he said, "is when people want suggestions."

"Why did you draw something then? It was for this apartment, wasn't it? I could tell that."

"No, no, no. It was for my own amusement," he said.

"So why can't we talk about it?"

He clasped his hands round the mug. She noticed they were a little like her father's hands – big, but finely proportioned. "Because of what happens when people start from my drawing. I don't like doing it that way. Okay, say I've sketched an idea. Then, the client – say it's you – you tell me you love it. Then you tell me you want it a foot shorter. Then you want me to take off the top and make the sides different. And in the end, if I do that, I make something that I consider hideous and doesn't work."

"What if," said Cassie, "we negotiated those things? So if I wanted it shorter, we could change it in a way that was okay with you. So I'm not simply saying do this, do that, but we're working on it together, as a combined creation."

"Doesn't work," he said stubbornly.

"You won't even consider it?"

"I did consider it. My last job. Broke my heart."

"Broke your *heart*?"

"Work of art," he said shortly. "Deeply personal."

Cassie felt annoyed. "So, even though I'm commissioning you, at more money than I'd pay in a gallery, you won't actually design anything for me?"

"I'll work from your brief," he said calmly. "Design from your brief."

"What if I don't have a brief?"

"Except you do. A person like you, an apartment like this. You do."

She felt childishly frustrated that he wouldn't show her the sketch. She wanted it, wanted to see it, touch it, consider it. It was ridiculous.

"I want an abstract modernist piece for that end of the room," she said icily. "The light hits it in the morning. And it has to fit given the height of the table. I don't want something poking its nose over the top of the table."

He laughed. "Its little abstract nose. I could make it a cute little nose." He didn't notice that the idea was amusing him, but not her. "A Pinocchio nose, a lying, cheating dissembling little nose."

Cassie produced a magazine. "See how they've done the piece in this apartment. Not that design exactly, but that sort of style."

He sighed heavily. "And you're set on that?"

She had sensed that he would bait her in some way.

"Do you want me to beg," she asked crossly, "to see your sketch?"

"If I did the design," he said, "you'd have to pay me extra for the drawing. Whether you like it or not. If you do, we can talk about it, but *I* have final say." He looked at her, straight in the eyes. "I like sugar in my coffee," he said. "I know thin, rich people often don't have something as crass as sugar in their houses, but if you do, I'd really like it."

She felt like hitting him, but instead fetched the sugar. "Show me your sketch," she said. "I only got a glimpse of it. I feel you're holding a gun at my head."

He laughed. "I'm sorry," he said. "Here am I laying down all the conditions, and you're the client. I am sorry." He was suddenly annoyingly sweet. "Of course you can look at the sketch." He turned the drawing pad over.

The sketch was effortless, so fluid that it made her want to cry. It was abstract, but with a suggestion of flight, totally different from the smooth, modernist piece she'd had in mind. It was baroque, emotive, suggestive. She glanced at him, almost expecting to see elements of the sketch in him. Her money and power dissipated. What he had drawn was fluid, lyrical, beautiful.

"I won't even ask what wood you're using," she said. She extended her hand. "It's a deal."

"I can tell that you are going to be a pleasure to work for," he said, taking her hand in both of his, then dropping it awkwardly. He smiled, a charming, lopsided smile. "I used to sell through galleries," he said hesitantly. "Then, someone told me you don't go through galleries these days, you have cli-ents." He gave the word two distinct syllables. "So I do, but I'm often not good at clients."

"I'd say you were pretty good this morning," she said wryly.

"Okay!" said Anthea. "Most of you have been passing on class work, which is just terrific. In fact, I think everyone will be graded up to a pass." With a little manipulation of statistics, she thought. "So, for the exam, you need to put in just a little extra effort, and I know you'll all pass. And next term, we'll have the war history behind us. We've got a great course on the role of women coming up. Anyone got any last-minute questions?"

A small, enthusiastic girl, dimwitted, but with enough of a crush on Anthea to pay attention, put up her hand.

"Yes, Miss," she said timidly. "What's the difference, like between the First World War and the Second World War?"

Anthea turned back to the board, a familiar despair coming over her, wondering why she was teaching. She had spent two terms on the wars, using film, pictures, charts – everything to make it easy for this class of sixteen-year-olds.

"Yeah." A deep, aggressive voice boomed from the back of the classroom. "I reckon they're the same, because it was like us against the Germans in both of them."

"No, they weren't, Miss," shouted one of her brighter students. "'Cause they didn't happen at the same time. And Gallipoli was the second one, wasn't it Miss?"

Anthea turned to the class again, smiling benignly, reminding herself that next year she was taking the top HSC class for history. She'd protested at being relegated for years to the slow learners, with whom, it was known, she was particularly good. She liked many of them and she helped them, but she needed a change. Maybe from any form of teaching, she thought. Or from my life, she wondered gloomily.

"Ten minutes to bell," she said. "Let's see how many differences we can find between the two wars. We'll put the First World War over this side of the board, and the Second World War over this side. The class sunk into silence and she smiled encouragingly. "Come on, I'm sure we can remember."

The class managed to find three differences between the wars, and she knew better than to bombard them with further information. It wasn't their fault, nor, she reminded herself, was it hers. She collected her books and strode down towards the staff room.

As she walked along the corridor, several students greeted her and she smiled back. But she was glad to get to the staffroom, a haven, albeit noisy, messy and tumultuous.

"Hey Anthea," yelled John Watson. "Cassandra La Rosa rang." He smirked as he spoke Cassie's name with an edge of sarcasm. "She's got a real sexy voice." She hated the juvenile cast of mind of some of her colleagues. No wonder the kids thought John was a dork. She retreated to the other side of the room where there was a phone, and comparative privacy.

"How's your day?" Cassie asked.

"Bedlam plus. Yours?"

"Highly productive." Cassie's days, unlike hers, were always productive. "You want to go and see *Richard the Third* tonight?"

"I can't," said Anthea, knowing Cassie thoughtfully asked her on Tuesdays because of half price. "I'm going to an in-service on language structure. Besides, I think we need a weekend for a major Shakespeare experience, collect the neurones."

"We could do it on the weekend then," Cassie persisted. "I want to tell you all about this sculpture I'm commissioning. The artist came this morning. He did the most extraordinary sketch. He's actually pretty extraordinary himself."

"I'd love to hear about it. Let me check the diary." Anthea always felt bad for rejecting

Cassie. It made her uncomfortable that Cassie needed her more than she needed Cassie. She looked at the pages for the weekend. She was going out with someone to the beach on Saturday, and meeting friends for Sunday breakfast. "Sunday night. No, let's not do a movie. Come to my place. My wonderful tomato soup! We'll talk and you bring a bottle of that fantastic white."

She hung up and looked at her watch, and remembered she was supposed to be seeing one of her students, a slow learner, who had committed yet another delinquency. An end of the road kid, a kid who couldn't come good, who made her wonder if she had run out of resources for this job. She walked slowly down to the room where he was waiting.

He sat in front of her, dumb and sullen. Anthea stared out into the playground, watching the other kids walking up the driveway, pushing, shoving, high-spirited. There was, at a distance, something about the mean energy of adolescence that attracted her. Unfortunately, the kid in front of her lacked even mean energy. Even more unfortunately, his parents had given him the name Elvis.

"What did you do with the books you stole, Elvis?" No-one ever stole books to read them.

"I burnt 'em." There was a hint of pride.

Major indicator of disturbance. Add bed-wetting and cruelty to animals and she was probably looking at a potential mass murderer. Fifteen years ago, Anthea would have worked hard to get through to the kid. Not only that, she would have been open to him. She would have felt her own rebelliousness, her own youth. She wondered if they had gone forever, dissipated into nothing or temporarily submerged in the lonely fatigue. She'd seen Elvis and his manifestations too often. She wanted him out.

"Okay, Elvis. You can't pay for them. You can't replace them. You're not here most days. But the days you're here, starting today, you work out in the gym at lunchtime or after school with Mr Lewis. It's a new program we've got for year nine. If you go regularly, if you participate, it'll change your life. You'll have good friends, a good body." Elvis looked at her, surprised. He liked her as much as you could ever like a teacher. "If you ever do anything else, we'll suspend you forever." She held out her hand. "Good luck."

He took it, limply, lamely. "Might go," he said. Might not, thought Anthea.

Cassie worked for weeks with Simon. She made sure it was a pleasant, easy relationship of which she was firmly in control. They worked long hours, qualifying and quantifying facts and hunches, turning them into graphs and diagrams on the computer in a way she hadn't known was possible. She was eager, curious to learn the technology. He had been plucked from the Melbourne office and brought to work at a top Sydney salary, purely and simply for his mind. He had, apparently, made no deals, owed no-one. He was like someone working for a wage, whereas most executives had built careers on networking and deals as much as on performance. It was attractive to her. She felt he must have considerable integrity.

But she was aware that she lacked Jennifer's skills in attracting personal loyalty. Bayliss was still working against her behind the scenes. She hoped Simon would transfer some of his loyalty to the project across to her. But despite her control, she felt insecure, almost at his mercy because of his technical wizardry. Even worse, at odd times she found herself aware of his looks, a startling young male beauty from some angles, that sent her briefly into an internal flurry of embarrassment. It wasn't the sort of thing that happened to her and she was reminded of what Anthea had said about the sexiness of crisis, the charge of fear and adrenalin.

"Apart from the Asia project," she told him, "I want to look at the relationship of Information Services and Research."

He looked at her quizzically.

"We work well together," she added. "I'd hoped we might work together in the future."

"Sure," he said. "Maybe we could have lunch on that one." The invitation surprised her, but he then produced a piece of paper from the printer. "Taiwan's really interesting. Look at this."

She studied it. "It will change when you factor in the new price structures."

"I'll try it." He turned back to the computer. "By the way, John Anderson told me he wants to see all this as we produce it," said Simon. "He's, ah, telling me that he and Tim are very keen to keep up to speed on this project."

Cassie felt sick to the stomach. "Did you give him the files?" she asked, trying to sound casual.

"No." Simon turned his attention to the screen, and Cassie felt relief flood through her.

"Look, this is confidential," she said, "but we've worked together long enough for me to tell you what's happening. Tim Bayliss is interested in taking the Research Department under his wing. And one way for him to do that is to sabotage this project. I want to be careful not to help that agenda along by giving Tim or John any preliminary information."

Simon didn't look up from the screen. "I told John Anderson that it's pretty meaningless piecemeal," said Simon. He paused, clicking with the mouse, intent on the screen. "Which disappointed him." He still didn't look at her, but she realised he knew a lot more than she thought. "I'll give you an extra password. *Simple*. Remember it. *Simple* Simon."

"I will." She smiled and sat down beside him. "Julian's working on re-structuring. I was thinking that with the ability to predict that this system gives us, I'd like to do some work on the budget for that. We could look at various departments, various economies of scale."

He was still fiddling with a graph on the screen.

"I'd like to look at the breakdown of what goes into Product Development, what goes into Promotions, what goes into Research and into Information Services," said Cassie. "It might even make sense for you and me to combine. Make us less vulnerable to take-over."

"Cool." He smiled at her. "I've been thinking along those lines too."

She handed Simon a page of figures and wandered over to the window, her mind and stomach churning, feeling herself her father's daughter. She had made an alliance, but she still didn't feel easy. Italian, the Italian mistrust,

Italian guts and go, but still held back by her mother's English politeness, the deference to others. Before his retreat home to Italy, her father had worked for twenty years at the fruit and vegetable market as a buyer and seller, his sharp entrepreneurial attitudes honed by the standover tactics of the times. She pieced it together later. He was somewhere in the middle, exacting his tribute, as well as paying his dues, rebelling against those above, resentful of those below, always out for the opportunity to move sideways, cut a slice of profit in a new territory.

He'd been a cog in a system that was part honest trade, part exploitation. In the end, it had trapped him. In the sixties, the stakes had escalated. Marijuana started to bring in big money and the drug scene became part of the world of the markets. It overturned long-standing alliances, introduced new pressures and increased the edge of violence that had always been part of the markets. She had begun to understand then, in her late teens, in a way her mother never had, that her father was trapped. Faced with his black moods, her mother had primly suggested finding another business, while Cassie had watched him, late at night, beer in hand, staring hour after hour at the television. Waiting till dawn, when he had to face it all again. It made sense to her that, when he knew he was dying, he would go to Italy. The men at the markets would demand anything of a man with nothing to lose.

When Cassie had become ensconced in this corporate world, she'd been taken in by the good-guy language, seduced by the veneer of the team spirit. Increasingly, she'd become aware of the game that was played at higher levels. She'd played it herself, like her father, a loner, and now, like him, uncertain.

Her reverie was broken by Denise knocking at the door, with sandwiches and coffee. Cassie thanked her. She should take Denise out to lunch soon. Loyalty. Build loyalty.

At the end of lunch, Simon stood up and looked down at her. "We should go out to dinner. You and me."

"Dinner?"

"Nothing to do with business. Just you and me."

The possibility flashed through her mind, along with the complication. She could see he was physically attractive, but their relationship was basically impersonal. Perhaps he was shy, but she hardly wanted a romantic complication, or the gossip that would follow. Caution won out, but she had to be careful here, keep him on-side. "Thank you. It would have been fun. But I'm seeing someone at the moment."

Inexplicably, Darcy Diamond flashed through her head and then was instantly dismissed.

It was already dark when she got into her car that night to drive home. The wind whipped across William Street in a blur of rain and lights. The Coke sign had its "C" missing. Cassie hated that, the incompleteness of it.

She felt disturbed by the day, by her uncertainty about what she was doing. The success she now enjoyed had once seemed the pinnacle of her ambition. She had simply assumed she would continue to struggle further and further up the ladder. But she had become less certain.

Susan toyed with the idea that she might be self-centred. Her mother had used the phrase about her so harshly and frequently in her childhood that she had blocked it out as too painful. Recently she had begun to think about herself. Even wondering about her own self-centredness, was, she supposed, self-centred. But it was in a different way. When she had been bulimic, she had thought about not being fat. When she was getting married, she had thought about being a bride. When she was pregnant, she thought about being a mother. But not about herself, about who she was and could be.

Almost automatically, quite abstract ideas about herself came to focus on her body, on feeling wrong, fat, clumsy and different. She could feel clever like Cassie, or pretty, as she used to be, but these thoughts were like butterflies flitting briefly through her head. Her most common thought was a feeling of shame, tinged with self-pity. Nick was ruining her life. If he could see beyond her wifeliness and motherhood, she might be able to find her talents, her niche as a person.

There was her sacrifice to her mother. It made her feel closer to her mother, more bound to her, but sometimes she was brought to tears by the emptiness of the relationship and the bleakness of its history. She was angry with Cassie for not recognising her goodness and self-sacrifice. The most genuine thing Susan could find about herself was her love for her children. She alternated between the high moral ground and self-disgust, usually in the form of chocolate cake, leftover lamingtons, or more shamefully, Tiny Teddy biscuits.

She had begun thinking about herself when she gave birth to Jack. Nick had been there at the birth, ecstatic, and had promised to come back in the morning with the girls. By the time he appeared, late the next day, Susan was convinced that her brain had thrown a switch.

She had become furious and neglected, terrified of this new person, whose husband and children were sucking the life out of her.

Since then, she had trudged wearily through her life, until now. She felt on the verge of collapse, with no-one to tell, no-one to sympathise with her. The nurse at the Early Childhood Centre had suggested she had post-natal depression, and hinted she go to a doctor, or a support group. But it had thrown her into panic, just talking to the kindly nurse. If she even acknowledged the great black pit of unhappiness, she would fall apart, perhaps go completely crazy as she had with the bulimia. Julie nagged at her, with her prettiness, her freedom and her closeness to Nick. In saner moments, she realised Julie acted strangely probably because she was so hostile to her. All she could do was try to hold the line. Her friend Maria had told her that everyone gets depressed with kids. She just had to tough it out.

It had grown worse. As her fear of mental illness receded, her relationship with Nick deteriorated. She became restless. The mountain house offered relief, even if it was only in fantasy. She imagined how she would live there. Elin would go to school. She'd join a mothers' group and learn something. She'd find a job in a craft shop. She'd stop eating. She'd stop buying

Tiny Teddies, even for the children. She'd make bean casseroles in winter and carrot salads in summer and bake bread from soya flour that she didn't like. She even made a virtuous shopping list – *brown rice, chamomile tea, acidophilus yoghurt, tofu, leave Nick*.

The fantasy expanded beyond the list. She'd surprise Cassie with her extraordinary yet untested ability to make the roses bloom as their mother had. She'd chop wood and go to yoga and aerobics. She'd learn ballroom dancing and start her own restaurant. Packing up to leave there would be hard, but after that, it would be wonderful.

As she went into the kitchen, Kelly threw herself round her legs.

"I love you, Mummy." Susan picked Kelly up, tears in her eyes. There was an anxiety in Kelly, something that always needed more of her, but also fought against her. She held her now, and the child relaxed against her, rocking into her. Susan was aware of Kelly's happiness. She sat down in the rocking chair, Kelly against her. She wondered who she could talk to. She needed to have a plan, a when and where. It was urgent. She needed a confidante. Nick came to mind – a strange momentary flash of tenderness as the person to talk to. Of course it was nonsense to talk to Nick about the possibility of leaving him.

She had to be practical. But the idea of Nick was still in her, a stab of feeling, a captured moment. She wondered if she really wanted to leave. But he was so unreasonable.

Chapter 9

Cassie and Anthea stood at the edge of the deep green pool, at the bottom of the high sandstone cliff. Above them, the waterfall cascaded down the cliff. They had walked here from the mountain house where Cassie had worked obsessively all day in the garden, cutting back the dead wood in the front hedge and digging a new bed. Now, the late afternoon spring sunshine filtered through the gum leaves, lighting up the yellow bluff of the cliff face.

"Since I stopped smoking," Anthea said, "I'm sure my breathing capacity's worse. We'll probably need to call the rescue helicopter to get me up to the top again." She looked round irritably. "And I've become horribly bad-tempered. But it's true what the Social Scene people said. Men don't notice foul moods – as long as you're thin and have prominent breasts."

Cassie kneeled down and looked into the rockpool. "I might take a holiday this year. Away."

"Away from what?"

"From everything I usually do – Japan, Italy. Not a business destination. A tropical island, but not Bali. No culture, just nature."

Anthea skipped a stone across the water. "You hate sea, unless it's from a penthouse. You wrap up like an Arab from the sun. You don't like resorts. Why would you do that?"

"Think about things," said Cassie. "Relax."

"A new skill?" said Anthea dryly, "to add to your repertoire? It'd be easier to buy the how-to book."

"What about you?" Cassie said resentfully. "You go to these Social Scene parties, which sound totally nerve-wrecking. Teaching's a high-stress job, and you go out all weekend. Maybe we should go on a holiday together."

"Except you won't go in school holidays."

"I'd consider it."

"You've got so much more money than me. I couldn't keep up."

"Don't you want to go?" Cassie was offended.

"Maybe," said Anthea. Cassie never realised that her friend might have other plans. Anthea looked at her critically. "I tell you, you're driving me crazy at the moment," she said abruptly.

"How?"

"The mountain house, gardening, Japanese fucking prints, commissioning a sculpture, Bali, Japan, a resort, relaxation. Christ!"

"Is that all?" asked Cassie coldly.

"No. You expect me to be involved with it. Go along with the latest fad."

Cassie was stung. "They're not fads."

"They are," said Anthea. "You're jumping from this to that to another thing. It's incredibly irritating. That's all I have to say." She sat down on a rock, facing away from Cassie. Cassie stood, hurt and angry, watching the waterfall.

A sudden gust of wind sprayed the water towards them. It hit like rain and they ran for the shelter of the cliff. They stood, breathless and wet, watching the sprays of water.

"Okay?" said Anthea.

"Okay," said Cassie. "You giving up smoking isn't all that easy either." She looked down at their wet clothes. "Like a real wet blanket, actually."

"I know. Everyone at school has made it their business to point out changes in my mood," Anthea said, flicking the drops of water off her jacket. "We're both looking for the same thing. Call it what you like – connection or meaning or peace." She turned to Cassie. "I'm more desperate than you because I've got no money or prospects. Like the poor rellie. Single, middle aged and female." She tapped her fingers nervously on her forehead. "I feel so strung out." She smiled. "So *irritated*. It's awful to think I'm such a tortured personality that cigarettes gave my life meaning."

Anthea's year nine personal development class lounged back, scornful, cynical, curious only when sex was mentioned. Often they were angry, racist or sexist. Yet at times, she felt a certain fondness for the traces of stupid candour that emerged from their comments.

"Mitchell smokes, Miss."

"I don't." A scuffle broke out.

"What we're talking about today," said Anthea, "is what nicotine does to you. If you look at the sheets, you'll see a box, with the effects – six of them. So we'll split into six groups and every group look at just one of those effects in a bit more detail."

"What about the good effects, Miss?"

"What good effects, Jackson?"

"Like when you wake up in the morning and you light a fag. It feels like you can get going. Or like really late at night and you're stressed, and you have a smoke and you feel cool again."

The thought of a cigarette hit Anthea with such force that she couldn't speak.

"Yeah, Miss, what about that?"

"You smoke. I know." Jackson eyed her.

"Okay," she said. "Seven groups. And Jackson – your group comes up with the good things about smoking."

She sat the rest of the lesson, answering queries, occasionally quietening the louder boys, waiting for Jackson's list, longing for a cigarette, fantasising about the whole room lighting up or bludging a cigarette from one of the kids.

She toughed it out to the end of the lesson, and as she walked into the staffroom, she announced loudly that she needed a Nicorette.

"Dull the pain of teaching," someone said. "Anything to dull the pain of teaching."

Everyone laughed. Anthea was struck by the pain of her own years of teaching – the low pay, the horrible conditions, the pitying glances when she told people where she taught, the constant political shifts and changes from on high, the hearty but deadly pessimism of the staffroom. She gathered her bag and hurried out.

She thought of Cassie's job. Although she had never said anything to her, she despised what Cassie did. It was clever and complicated, but selling more building and engineering products to build more ugly office towers was far less useful than teaching difficult adolescents. It seemed wrong that Cassie reaped such enormous rewards. Anthea often felt jealous of her salary, her travel, even her privacy.

She softened, her affection for Cassie re-asserting itself. The worst aspect was how the job stifled Cassie. Schools stifled people too. There was nowhere private, nowhere you could go and be sure of being alone. And the crowd, the jostle of school life, emphasised the solitude in the rest of her life. The predictability of her professional life, year after year, gave her a sense of embattlement, of struggle – to get up in the mornings, to drive through the traffic to school, to teach, to make things happen in the rest of her life. Part of it was being alone, another part was that the longings she felt would never be filled, that the struggle would become more entrenched, making her harder and more remote.

This term, she was struggling through each day and each week, hanging out for Friday night. At least today was Friday. Another twenty minutes, ten minutes, five minutes to freedom.

Tonight. Another trial by dinner. She wondered how many more Social Scene dinners she could do. Desperation versus humiliation. She collected her books, hurried home, showered, perfumed, blowdried her hair, did her eyes for dim lighting, tried on the short black skirt and was glad she had good legs. Dying for a cigarette, she threw down a glass of cask wine, then a Nicorette, then chewed peppermints in the car and gave herself a final spray of perfume as she walked in.

Anthea prided herself now on being able to sum up the company. The men divided into looks and bodies versus power and wealth. Then there were those who were neither – yahoos, loose cannons, who often became drunk and unpleasant. Almost as difficult were the immeasurably sincere and bland men. In the beginning, she'd accepted dates with them so as not to hurt them. Now she refused them for the same reason.

The women, amongst whom she had made some friends, could also be categorised. There were the dollies, past it in their own minds, struggling to keep young, no brain, no perspective. There were the willing, wanna-be wives, who would submit themselves to any degree of boredom for matrimony. Then there was her group – eclectic, a hidden, cultivated desperation and loneliness, running on biological clocks and life views formed back in girlhood. They had grown up seeing themselves paired. Feminism, affairs, disastrous experiences of matrimony had changed their conscious views, but their most basic instincts and image of their lives, woman plus man, remained intact.

The group was standing round the bar. You could always pick the Social Scene group – large, often a little too loud, friendly, something artificial in the tone of the conversation, before you even got close enough to hear the words. Anthea recoiled and looked again. There was Johnny Jamieson, seeing her, smiling in triumph, as if she humiliated herself just by being here. He'd never feel the humiliation, she thought – too bloody arrogant – but he must be desperate. Worse, she felt the old feelings. She'd forgotten her addiction to him that had kept her seeing him, month after month, at short notice or no notice, to be stood up or forgotten, to be brought out when convenient, to be embarrassed or abandoned. She'd forgotten how powerful it had been.

"Hi, babe."

"Hello, John."

He winked and raised his glass. "At least I know I'll score tonight."

This cut the group to silence. Even Johnny realised the remark was unacceptable and smiled at her, ratlike but placating. Mike, the journalist, who had driven her home from her first dinner, was there and a woman she had met before, two new men and two other women. They looked at her in stunned silent sympathy. She searched for a cutting comeback, but she felt the terrible loneliness of it, the falsity and the hopelessness.

"Have a nice night," she said to the group. "I won't stay."

"He ought to go," said one of the women loudly, "and you stay," but Anthea didn't look back, wanting oblivion, wanting a cigarette. As she stood at the pavement edge, waiting to cross, Mike grabbed her by the arm.

"Nice to see you again," she said jokingly, but feeling near tears.

"I should have punched him out," he said. He shrugged his shoulders and put his arm tentatively round her shoulders. "But it's not my sort of thing, punching people." He talked quickly. "I mean, you don't meet pigs like that often enough to be practised in the art. By the time I'd thought it through, my courage had gone, and they were sitting down. You were the one with courage and style."

"He's a karate expert anyway." She began crying. "I'm sorry," she said. "You're not doing a story about this, are you? Because if you are, please don't do this."

"I was never doing a story. My wife left me," he said, "a year ago. My mates told me to socialise, but I've lost the knack."

"Okay, well thanks for coming out. It was nice of you." She smiled wanly, thinking she wasn't a wan sort of woman, not the sort to cry on men's shoulders. She wanted her sassy, black-clad, short-skirted, flirty personality back. "You won't see me again." She managed a smile, more like her own. "Think I'll let my membership lapse."

"Me too," he said. "Want to go for a drink?"

"Not really," she said. "My car's parked round the corner. I'll go home."

"You shouldn't brush it off," he said. "It was too horrible."

"I'm not brushing it off. I'm going home."

"Can I walk you to your car?"

"Okay."

They walked in silence. Wrong time, wrong place, thought Anthea. He's sorry for me, so now he wants to sleep with me.

"You can come back to my place for a drink."

"You sure that's okay?" he asked.

"It's okay." She rallied. "It would be nice."

Cassie rarely received any personal mail, so she looked at the letter with interest.

Dear Cassandra – such grandeur!

The tree grew somewhere in the south-west of the state, tall timber, old growth, that produces a wood which is suffused with warmth and colour. Although I know *little of the particular life of the tree, I sense a joy in it, a movement and wildness that has shaped what I carved, sculpted and formed from it. It is perhaps warmer, richer, less yellow than what you envisaged. (But I'm sure that if you changed your carpet to a deep, almost black green and your walls to a rather richer, pinker tone, the pieces will suit your needs admirably. Just kidding!) However, I hasten to stress that the sculptures are not quite the design we discussed, the wood having dictated something different. Mainly – note the plural – there are now two pieces, not one. (They go together, like cashmere and pearls, no extra charge!) If you would like to come down on Sunday week, 19th, I will give you lunch, caught and cooked by my own fair hands, and we can discuss the matter further. If you sense a faint note of apology in this, you are correct, but it is restrained by the fact that I have spent the $2,000 advance you gave me and have invested it and even more of my time and effort in these pieces for you.*

Nervously yours,
Darcy Diamond.

"Shit," said Cassie. "Shit!" But she felt a shiver of excitement.

She sat down and read the letter again, this time less seriously. It was probably a joke, although possibly true as well. She was serious by nature, and sometimes had trouble with jokes. She had read many years ago that people who laughed got sick less often. This had worried her for years, until she read a contradictory point of view by a doctor who pointed out that people who joked about symptoms often refused to take appropriate action. She had shown the article to Anthea, who had roared with laughter. This annoyed her, especially as she knew that there was a joyousness she was missing out on.

Cassie remembered when Simon had asked her out, how Darcy Diamond had sprung to mind. He'd stayed in her mind since then, his sculpture already in the map of her flat. He was there, just beyond the edge of the map, where he had no business to be, but a stronger presence than Simon, who fitted neatly into the office grid. She liked the edges to be clear. Perhaps Darcy and the blurred edge was just part of her restlessness, her sense of nameless frustration, struggling with life in a new, but undetermined way. When she left teaching in her late twenties, she had felt the same sort of turmoil, the same sense of searching. Then she had battled against her need for security, the need to be good and do what was expected. Against that had been a desire to shine, to expand into something new.

She read the letter again, carefully.

It was awful. Anthea wanted to feel something for this man, but her emotional lock had always come with bastards like Johnny Jamieson. Since that relationship finished she'd wanted something less destructive. Would it be Mike, lying here on her bed, caressing her, telling her he loved her body, against her rising panic, after having cried her eyes out on account of Johnny Jamieson? Could she trust this man? She'd liked him the first time they met, but she had wondered if she would drive him to being a bastard. Probably she would. She had that in her. But as he lay here, gently kissing her, stroking her, it was his gentleness that began to work on her. Usually, a man so intent made her impatient. Usually, she was turned on by his need, his ready excitement at her body, at the fact that she turned him on. She liked fierce, hard kissing, biting, even bruising, but now, she felt herself tingling under his touch. But she also felt distanced from him. Such gentleness wasn't quite her.

"I want you," she murmured, feeling, in spite of her physical arousal, that it was artificial in some way.

"I want you," he told her, and she felt the orgasm building, part of her, ready to explode. She handed him the condom.

"I've got one," he said.

She turned off the light and abandoned herself to him. Maybe it would change.

Anthea looked out the car window. "I'm over the cigarettes," she said. "Finally, after all these years."

"Did this fellow Mike specify a smoker or a non-smoker?" asked Cassie.

"A non-smoker," said Anthea. "Cass, he is a really good man. I should probably write a testimonial for Social Scene, except there's not a lot of passion on my part. I think I've lost the sort of openness I had when I was younger."

"You mean not knowing what you want?" Cassie said cynically. "Who you are?"

"More," said Anthea. "I was critical when I was young, but I didn't really notice bad things in people, because the wanting and the passion was more intense. And there wasn't this great bank of hurtful and hateful memories pressing down on me. I wasn't so *careful*."

"I was *always* careful about relationships," said Cassie firmly, as she changed lanes. "*particularly* when I was young." She softened. "I suppose because my parents were so unhappy with each other. I didn't know how to make sense of relationships, what I wanted, how much I should give."

"I was confused too," said Anthea. "But there was still something wonderful. I used to be able to abandon myself, to be infatuated." She paused. "I *believed* in it. Come on Cass, don't you remember?"

"Maybe I was too uptight," said Cassie. "Maybe I still am," she added lightly. "It seemed painful, not wonderful."

"Wonderful *and* painful," murmured Anthea. "I can't get swept up like that any more. But I suppose I'm more rational. Mike would be good for me, so I'm trying to drop the cynicism." She looked at the map. "Where does this woodcarver live?"

"He's a sculptor. An artist. At Kurnell. Have you found it?"

"Just tucked up here between the oil refinery and the caravan park," said Anthea. "Next left." She held her finger on the map. "Cass, why am *I* coming on this expedition?"

"I thought you might . . . you might –"

"Be bored silly? Like I am by most modern art?" She looked at Cassie critically. "I'm your protection, aren't I? Protecting you against a lecherous artist whom you find attractive against your better judgment?"

Cassie said nothing.

"Okay," said Anthea. "I'll check him out. Look out for you. See if he's a three-star man or a four-star man."

Cassie smiled. "Five-star. You know me."

"Is his stuff any good?" said Anthea looking round at the bleak landscape of scrub and factory sites. "This doesn't seem very arty territory."

"Maybe that's why he's good." Cassie tried to make light of her own prejudices about the desolate landscape. "He's not predictable."

They drove down the long road by the side of the bay. Cassie noticed the contrast between the mangroves and the chain-wired industrial estates. Then they were in the village of Kurnell, past the entrance to the national park, past the Greek take-away. The waterfront was divided into sections by stone breakwaters, so the beach looked like a series of small, private enclosures. The oil pipe snaked its way along an enormous wharf, shining out into the bay. The water stretched tight and blue across the bay, the city in the distance. The houses were like holiday cottages – some new, cheap brick, some old and painfully decrepit. Most, because of the downward slope of the land, did not even have a view of the water. Along the road, dogs and children casually chased balls and each other, like scenes from a long-lost suburbia.

"This is ghastly," said Cassie. But underneath she was excited by it. The designers and decorators she had used in the past had lived in tasteful terraces, ultra-modern apartments, or had back-to-nature rural houses. Like a Jeffrey Smart painting, *this* was art. Maybe. But the flatness, the ugliness of the landscape began to work on her. Maybe not. "I wonder why on earth he lives out here."

"It's wonderful," said Anthea. "I think it's wonderful."

"But all this industry. And these junky little houses." The possibilities of Darcy were in doubt again. "Look, here's the number. God, what a hovel."

Darcy Diamond's house had a hedge of honeysuckle in profuse springtime bloom, untidy and rambling. The lawn, on the other side of the hedge, was green, full of bumps and ridges, as if it was the site of an old mine. Wisteria ran lush along the back fence, twining up into an enormous mulberry tree. Some cast-iron pieces, either of junk or very modern sculpture, were scattered across the lawn, which was divided by a free-standing hedge of cape jasmine with long shoots of orange flowers sprouting from the top like a punk hairdo.

To the side of the house, a cat sunned itself on an upturned runabout. The house was an old wooden cottage, side verandahs turned into fibro add-ons and sleepouts, faded, peeling brown paint, a traditional front verandah with broken-down cane chairs and weathered cushions. It would have stopped there, minimally comfortable, with old, seaside charm, except that from the exterior of one side of the house rose an imposing wooden staircase. It was made of a rough, weathered wood, but it was formal, elegant in its proportions, with a carved rail. It rose to a wooden cabin, perched on poles, one side almost resting on the branch of the mulberry tree. It was like something out of a fairytale. Cassie watched as Darcy seemed to materialise from the branches of the tree.

"Welcome," he said, "to my home." And bounded down the stairs.

"It's great," enthused Anthea.

"Unusual," said Cassie briskly. "Do we come up to see my pieces, or are they down here?"

"Not so fast, not so fast. Remember I asked you for lunch."

"Don't worry about lunch," said Cassie quickly, "we're in a hurry." She was nervous. Whatever she had thought or dreamed on the receipt of his letter didn't tally with this reality.

"I can smell it," said Anthea. "We're starving."

Darcy opened the front door of the cottage. Inside, the dividing walls had been removed and the uprights replaced with tree trunks, so the house was one large room, looking like a forest. Rugs hung in some of the areas where the walls had been, and creepers, made from all sorts of odd materials, hung from the ceiling and wound around the tree trunks. On one, orange fungi appeared to be growing but on closer inspection the fungi turned out to have been made from inflated, amputated rubber gloves. An enormous collage dominated one wall. It was incredibly detailed and intricate, consisting of hundreds of pictures cut from magazines and books and embellished by sketches. Birds soared out of chimneys, cheeses and coffee and fruit lay piled on a picnic basket, legs ran upside down, lions roared from the corners, zebras galloped through the clouds and the Harbour Bridge spanned a roaring torrent. It flowed seamlessly, humorously, effortlessly taking leaps of imagination. One of the tree-trunk supports was covered in carvings, a series of interlocking hearts and tiny stick-like animal and human figures. Some were in comic strip form with hearts in their speech bubbles. At the bottom of a tree was a carved suggestion of a dying animal. Another tree trunk, intricately and realistically carved, had a horse head being devoured by a lion. The floor was also painted in a leaf-litter pattern, in one corner rising to a small mound, which proved to be simply a trick of the paintwork.

"I lived here as a child," said Darcy. "And one of my sisters always wanted us to make it into one big room. It was such a poky little house." He laughed. "Mind you, when I demolished all the walls, she claimed she'd never said any such thing." He looked at Cassie. "You'll be pleased to know the bathroom is still walled, although the bath itself is open to the sky. Now, will you stay for lunch? I caught some excellent bream out in the bay yesterday."

"Thank you," said Cassie. She was stunned by this creation, this world of a house, so rich and eclectic, unbound by conventions.

Darcy went into the kitchen area and began chopping herbs. "The pieces I've made for you," he said, "I think I should tell you, apart from there being two of them, they are very different from that sketch you saw."

"Different?"

"If you don't like them, you can cancel the commission."

"How are they different?" Cassie was nervous, but animated.

Anthea sat down and watched the con-versation with a twinge of jealousy. Somehow, whatever was going on between Cassie and Darcy made them larger than life. It prickled her, putting Mike into a smaller perspective, as if she were seeing herself with him through the wrong end of a telescope. She felt jealous of Cassie – so cool, in a way Anthea never was, and because of it, annoyingly desirable. Anthea knew that *she* could easily fall in love with such an improbably romantic, eccentric character as Darcy. Almost, she thought, a collector's piece. Mike, by comparison, seemed dull and prosaic. Cassie, she could see, was alternately attracted and then scared off by Darcy's eccentricity, as he hummed his way round this extraordinary house, dressed in shorts, thongs and an old check shirt, loose over his flat stomach. If Cassie could ever give in to her obvious attraction to Darcy, thought Anthea, it would change her forever.

"I've been over-excited by you coming," he told her. "I hardly get any visitors. You've been in my mind ever since that morning we met. I'm probably in love," he added in a mutter.

Cassie smiled politely. A little more than politely, Anthea judged.

"It would never work," he went on. "You're an arch capitalist, I'm stuck here in the worker's paradise, maintaining the rage." He sliced the shallots into elaborate curls and tasted a piece of cheese. "Trotsky. Leon Trotsky and the ice pick. That's my beef."

"You don't know I'm an arch capitalist," protested Cassie.

"I certainly hope you *don't* have socialist principles," said Darcy. "That would destroy any possible integrity. Can't stand those rich bastard socialists, stacking up their squillions and salving their consciences by voting Labor. Your beauty is in being the *other* to my socialist, an ice maiden to my warm heart."

There was a growing intensity between them that made Anthea embarrassed, except that she was also curious.

"I'm not an ice maiden," Cassie said.

"Ice is a beautiful thing, easily shattered."

"I'm not easily shattered either." Anthea could see that Cassie was a little lost in this play.

"It's a great thing to be easily shattered. I wish I could be," said Darcy. "Truly great artists need to have the ability to be shattered, and then, to re-assemble. That's what makes art – not just modern, but classical too."

"Cassie's into Japanese art," said Anthea. "Do Japanese artists get shattered?"

"Being Japanese is about being shattered," said Cassie quickly. "The whole culture is about that – and then re-assembling." She wondered why she had agreed to lunch.

Darcy laid the food out on the plates. Exquisite, Anthea thought, like a chef's cuisine. Rustic, masculine cuisine, but with small touches of delicacy.

"So, do you get lots of commissions?" asked Cassie.

"Enough," said Darcy gloomily. "I should be more friendly to gallery owners, get an agent and launch myself properly. Become a presentable artistic figure. A large and respectable part of my income actually comes from making prototypes of environmentally sound wooden puzzles for tourist shops." He poured the wine. Cassie noticed the glasses were cut crystal, not matching, but very beautiful. "Eco wood carving."

"I wouldn't have thought eco wood carving *could* be very eco," said Anthea.

"As long as it's beautiful," said Darcy, "and made out of pine."

"Do you make any money?" asked Anthea. "Or is this like me teaching? A labour of love?"

"I defy the capitalist ethic," said Darcy. "I'm a believer in serious leisure. I'm not one of your worker bees." He shot a quizzical look at Cassie. She was not sure if he was mocking her. "But I make an elegant sufficiency," he added, "which continually surprises me."

"I like working," said Cassie defensively, "because the money tells me how good I am at it. Because work teaches me things."

"Things about the world? Or about yourself?"

"Both. I'm a different person than when I started in this job. I've changed a lot, improved myself."

"Improved your *self*?" Darcy's voice took on a slight tone of mockery. "I went through a stage of *self* improvement, but I am a seriously lost cause. Then I decided to improve other people. But they all went away. Live and let live."

"Easy to do if you live alone," commented Anthea. "Too easy."

"I like living alone," said Darcy. "A danger neither to myself nor to others."

"I don't like it," said Anthea, "but I've done it so long I sometimes wonder what it would be like not to do it."

"There's got to be a value in it," said Cassie, "being a person who lives alone. You can do things, be things, that otherwise wouldn't be possible. There's got to be some meaning in it."

"Bit of social variety," said Darcy. "Marrieds, singles, old, young, queer, this, that. There's no meaning in anything much. We're variations, all of which seem very important, but probably aren't."

Throughout lunch, Cassie and Darcy badgered and argued, agreed and disagreed, insisted then desisted, as Anthea looked on. They began to laugh and joke, the sense of being strangers retreating, an intimacy between them that made Anthea less and less relevant.

"When are you going to show me the work?" said Cassie as she finished her coffee.

"You don't have to have them," protested Darcy. "You don't have to take them. The only thing is that I'd prefer they stay together. Like a Tupperware set." He was speaking very quickly and nervously. "They're a combination of art nouveau and organic modern." He hastily stacked up the plates and put them under the tap. "Come upstairs while I'm drunk enough. I think you have probably both had enough to drink too."

He led them up the outside staircase, and with a wild, grandiose gesture, opened the door. There, carved from a section of a tree trunk, was an abstract, but recognisably female form, reaching out, eerily beautiful, its lines inviting touch. Parts of it were sanded smooth, but they blended into the natural finish. Some of the areas left rough provided a suggestion of clothing. The other piece was a bird, wings spread, echoing the gesture and form of the female piece, but harder, wilder, the jagged mouth almost vicious.

"This?" gasped Cassie.

"This," replied Darcy, a hint of pride in his voice.

"You're right," said Anthea dryly, "it's different." But she could see it was good. She walked out onto the little balcony, to leave Cassie and Darcy alone.

"It will look good in your apartment," said Darcy as Cassie moved round the piece. "I didn't forget its place. And remember, it isn't quite finished. Don't panic, just look. Look."

"They are wonderful," said Cassie, running her fingers along the female figure. She could see he was shaking and she felt a sense of oneness with him in the creation, knowing, suddenly, that he had created it for her. This was what people meant when they talked about *falling* in love. She certainly wasn't *in* love, but she had the distinct sensation of falling, the force and energy of him and his sculptures, made for her, drawing her in.

"Let's forget this for a moment," he said awkwardly. "This is all too charged for me. Let's go for a walk."

"Okay," said Cassie. "But I do like them. I do want them." She stroked the bird piece. It was all too intense and she wondered how this feeling had occurred, but it kept happening. She made no move to stop it, to get away.

They all left the sculptures and walked along Kurnell Beach, collecting hundreds of orange-coloured pearly lustrous shells, which Darcy wanted for some reason. Later, walking miles up to Cape Solander, they went along the cliff tops, above a wild sea. It was like no other afternoon – sober and sedate on the outside, but containing something wild and passionate below the surface.

They watched the sun set across the bay, and then, exhausted, retreated with hot chips and beer to Darcy's upstairs room to watch *Dr Zhivago* on TV. Darcy insisted it was the only place where the TV would work and he draped a long lead up through the mulberry tree. He pulled a couch out of his workroom, and they sat, squashed, rugged up in his fishing jumpers, drinking whisky, the TV precariously suspended in the branch above.

"It's a great movie," said Cassie.

"My favourite," said Darcy. "It has the rare quality of pleasing moderate social democrats like me and arch capitalists."

"And romantics," added Anthea from the other end of the couch.

"But not bloody Stalinists," added Darcy.

Chapter 10

To Susan, the idea of leaving Nick was not quite real, but nevertheless all-encompassing. She was pricked by the drudgery and demands, the sadness and loneliness of her marriage. She felt as if she couldn't bear the relationship a moment longer, yet it continued to stretch interminably in front of her. Yet the thought of Julie taking Nick, half real in her mind, aroused her to a pitch of jealous rage.

Gradually, the idea of leaving was taking her over, swamping her, with rushes of desire and dreams of peace; an "if only" dream, somewhat like her adolescent bulimia, an idealised state always about to be realised. This power of it frightened her and to counter it and make it practical she bought a notebook, in which she would list pros and cons, means of escape, methods of withdrawal. Still, she couldn't make a decision. She had bought such notebooks as a teenager, meticulously recording weights and measures, calories and exercise, a goal etched in the front of the book in elaborately scrolled handwriting. Now, she could not even formulate the goal.

New school uniforms for Elin – $37.

Gumboots and gloves for Kelly – $20.

Warm underwear for me – $80.

This last item she crossed out.

The money should not be in dispute. The move should be accommodated by a slight re-arrangement of their finances. The more she worked on the figures, however, the less they looked like a re-arrangement, and more like serious expense, escalating to the realm of breathless extravagance. Although Susan had always prided herself on her accounting abilities, these figures did not add up, even with the lima bean casseroles the children hated, no chocolate cake, with no big Nonna and Poppa family dinners. She wondered about getting a full-time job. But she could never abandon Jack. If she did, it would also mean abandoning her mother too, and Kelly on the days she didn't go to preschool, and Elin during school holidays. The more she thought about it, the closer she grew to tears.

Finally, the black notebook was full of figures and she put the children to bed, threw herself crying on her own bed and waited for Nick to get back from the surgery. By the time he came home, her tears were exhausted, and she was left with a dry, red-eyed rage.

She left the notebook where he would pick it up.

"What's this?"

"I was doing calculations – to leave here." She hesitated, wondering whether she should come out and tell him she was leaving. "To go and live in the mountain house. We can't afford it."

"What the hell are you talking about?"

She sat up, hating the feel of her extra weight pulling her down. It detracted from what she had to say. "I feel that I have to leave you. But we can't afford it."

"Leave me? Why?"

A man from a different marriage, she thought.

She felt tears coming back, the familiar sensation of wanting him to feel sorry for her. "Because I'm so unhappy." She wanted to tell him this, to share it with him, for him to put his arms round her, to meld together the way they used to.

"So you give me a notebook. And tell me we can't afford for you to leave. Shit!" Nick banged his hand down on the dressing table. "I can't afford a holiday in Noumea and now, we get the next alternative, you can't afford to go and live in that shitty mountain house." He leaned across the bed, menacingly angry. "We can afford it. You work out what you need, how much it will cost and you fucking go, because I've had this!" He picked his jacket up off the bed, pulled some clothes out of the closet, and walked out the door. She heard him go down the stairs, the car starting up and then backing down the driveway. She would have been reassured by the drama of a door slamming or the theatrical squeal of brakes, but the silence he left was empty.

"Cass, I need to go up to the mountain house and I've lost my key. Nick and I have separated and I can't afford to live up there, but I *can't* stay here. The whole family has descended on me."

"Susan, what's going on?"

"I'm . . . unhappy."

Cassie sighed. She wanted to ask Susan if there had ever been a time when she was happy. Susan, she thought, was always projecting her problems onto other people, never dealing with them. "When did this happen?" she asked, an edge to her tone.

"It's been going on for ages. Since Jack was born. Nick won't talk." It sounded lame, and Susan wished she could describe her desperation.

"Nonna's here, begging me to go down on my knees to make Nick come back. Every time I refuse, she grabs Jack and says the rosary over him. His father's been yelling at me, threatening to take the kids away from me. Even his sister rang me up and gave me an earful. We've always been good mates."

"Why exactly did you separate?" Cassie asked. "When did it happen?"

"I've been planning to go up the mountains," said Susan, as if this gave her some credibility, "but when I told Nick we couldn't afford it, he walked out. And the whole family walked in."

"Susan, did you think about this? Have you two talked it over?"

"No, I told you, that was the problem. I'm sure he's taken the keys."

"Suzie, this is your marriage. You have to talk about it." Cassie felt the potential upset to her own life from Susan's marriage break-up. She had felt a sense of relief when Susan married Nick, at having someone else to deal with her sister's moods.

Susan began to cry. "You don't understand. There's no way to even start talking."

"There's always a way," Cassie said firmly. She had an image of Susan, on the other end of the phone, hysteria rising, losing her grip on reality.

"Please. Spare me the lecture. Can I just have the key? And maybe borrow some money?"

Cassie was furious. This was why she had had less contact with Susan recently, sensing a resurgence of her potential for drama. All her childhood, all her adolescence, Susan had been crisis after crisis. "This is simply about effective communication," Cassie said coldly.

Jack pulled himself to his feet, knocking his head against the coffee table. He began screaming, and with her free hand, Susan picked him up and put him to her breast. He drew back, howling. "Hang on," she said to Cassie. She put him over her shoulder, patting him, and picked up the phone again. "I'm here," she said tearfully. "I just need the keys."

Cassie took a deep breath. She thought of her own dreams for the house, of the muddle of Susan's plan. "It's my house and you can't have the keys. You can't live there."

"Mum was going to leave it to me," Susan reminded her.

"If she still had it." Cassie felt resentful at Susan's claim on the house. She had always been more attached to it than Susan and she had made a large financial sacrifice to buy it from her mother. Susan had never acknowledged how much responsibility Cassie had taken for their mother. "We needed that money for her to be properly looked after," Cassie reminded her. "And we agreed on it." Cassie felt safely distanced from Susan now. There was no point in buying into an argument on the house. "It's not a practical family house, anyway." Cassie tried to soften her tone.

"Your friend Anthea suggested it. And you said, when we made that arrangement with Mum, that Nick and I could use the house as if it were ours."

"Let's forget the house for the moment." Cassie took a deep breath. "You and Nick need to sit down and talk about this calmly. Use those techniques in that book I gave you last year." She tried to sound encouraging.

Susan put Jack down. He crawled quickly to his Nonna, who had appeared in the doorway. Kelly and Elin sat determinedly at the dining-room table, colouring in, heads down in fear. Susan looked at them, realising that they were waiting for her to do something. These were her children, and her poor confused mother-in-law. Nick had gone. She, Susan, was the adult.

It was an unfamiliar feeling. She was a grown up, responsible adult. She didn't want Cassie's help. She didn't want the keys to the mountain house. Here, with the children, she wasn't exactly free, but she was freer. It was what she wanted, but without having to move. A sense of calm descended on her. It was such an enormous, unfamiliar calm that she thought she might be dying or going crazy. She shut her eyes and waited, but nothing happened. She still felt calm.

"I never read the book," she said into the phone. "I don't have time for those sorts of books." She felt her anger with Cassie rising. "You don't know about real people. You always get the answer out of one of those stupid books about fixing your life, or your job. Or the universe, while you're at it."

"I could come over," said Cassie, feeling alarmed.

"Don't! I need fewer people in the house –" Susan looked darkly at Nonna – "not more." She put the phone down.

She knew her secret life with chocolate cake and Tiny Teddies and leftover puddings was drawing to a close. She looked at Nonna again.

"He will forgive you," the old woman whispered, clutching the rosary, "if you sorry."

"I'll take you home," Susan answered. She turned to the girls, desperately sad for them, wanting to protect them from this adult mess. "We'll get Macca's, just tonight, and then we'll all have a spa before we go to bed." She picked up Jack and shepherded the two girls out the door, her mother-in-law following, grumbling.

The night was bright and cold, and Susan imagined how, after the spa, she'd climb into bed alone. She could watch the stars all night. She could go on a diet, be in control again. There would be her and the three children. And no Nick.

There was a bruised silence broken by occasional difficult communications, but no move towards reconciliation between Susan and Nick. Susan explained to Elin and Kelly that she and Nick were having a holiday from each other. Elin looked at her knowingly and despairingly, Kelly blankly. Jack looked expectantly at the front door at night; in puzzlement at his parents' bed in the morning.

I'm coping, thought Susan. I'm coping.

She dug out her old calorie counter and put herself on a diet. She felt a stiffening of herself, a resurgence of an old pattern. She tossed it round in her mind, knowing the history of her misery, but she felt she needed the steel of her dieting self. Grit, determination. Except she had to be careful. There was a fine line for her between grit and determination, and hysteria and yelling. She had a feeling there was something she was missing, but which didn't bear examination. Under her determination was a fragile and delicate balance.

She thought of Nick, which she did intensely and often. She distracted herself by reminding herself that she had a life to lead. But he came to mind painfully.

She dropped Elin at school and Kelly at kindergarten and drove slowly past the surgery. She saw Julie going in, with a cake box. She felt a stab of furious jealousy. While it didn't seem to be in Nick to be unfaithful, she was sure it was in Julie. Julie caught sight of her and waved, uncertainly. She didn't wave back, but drove on to a shop selling exercise equipment. She went in, and bought a new expensive treadmill on Nick's credit card.

At home, she dragged the heavy treadmill out of the car, battling a squirming Jack, and collapsed, near tears, her sense of grit gone. Jack fell asleep on the breast and every time she tried to ease him off, he started to whimper. She sat there, trapped, and then picked up the phone.

"Nick."

"I'm with a patient."

"Have you and Julie started having little tête-à -têtes over morning tea?"

"What? Susan, I have to go." She hated him calling her Susan. It was so cold. It had always been Suze or Suzie.

"I saw her with the cake box. Don't lie, Nick."

"It was for Mrs Young. Her teeth are going and she comes in all the time. Julie noticed it was her birthday, so we decided to do something for her."

"Oh sure, dentists giving out cakes."

"She's ninety. It was the only thing we could think of."

"We?"

"Stop it!"

"I don't want you home."

"I don't want to come."

"I'm getting over the post-natal depression."

"What are you talking about?"

"I'm getting over the post-natal depression I had when Jack was born."

"You never mentioned you had post-natal depression."

"Because you would have thought I was crazy."

"So what am I supposed to think now? I'm hanging up, Susan. This is too much for me."

Darcy's house stayed in Cassie's mind, along with his laugh, his face, his remarks, his jibes, the woman, the bird, the collage. He was a vibrant image, overlaying all her maps. She went into work and felt it was separate from her, rather than her most central part. She waited, knowing he would call.

He did call. Cassie repeated the experiment of visiting him, this time without Anthea. Darcy asked her if she would like to come and check the final detailing on the work. He offered a bushwalk across the headland. Low key. No rush, except the excitement she felt.

But without Anthea, there were long, difficult silences; both of them blurting out the beginnings of remarks across the other; difficulties about who went first along the track, who followed. Then Darcy fell into an instructive role, lecturing Cassie on the different plants and their role in the ecology. He knew about the structure of leaves, the insects that left trails eaten out of wood, the eggs attached to seed cases, the seed cases that looked like insects, the variety of heath birds, the geology, the history of the place. Cassie began to long for the difficult silences.

"I'm talking too much," he said.

"Yes," she said shortly, wondering why she had come, retreating from the whole idea of him.

"Nervous, anxious to please, scared."

"Scared of what?"

"Rejection. I may as well say it. I can see it in your face already."

She smiled. But she had distanced herself, deciding that they were so far apart in the way they lived and the way they thought that the attraction she had felt was irrelevant.

"We're worlds apart," she said firmly.

"That's part of it."

She wondered what had happened to all her dreams of him. She had woken to see Darcy as he really was – someone totally foreign to her. "Different lives." Her voice took on the reassuring tone she used with junior staff. "Which means we can have a great afternoon. Maybe a friendship. You'll come and install your pieces in my flat when you're ready. We'll have coffee. Have you ever thought of having an exhibition?"

"I'm working on a solo exhibition, but sometimes making a living takes over. So the exhibition is up in the air. Painful. I've been stuck on it for years."

She was frustrated by his tentative approach. "I could help you organise it." That made sense to her. A friendship with an organised connection between them.

"You don't understand. It's not like those trade exhibitions at Darling Harbour."

"I know," she said coldly.

"It's an ideological compromise," he explained. "A good exhibition and you get taken seriously as an artist. It also sucks you into the corruption of the art scene, whereas now I happily live on the underbelly of capitalists." He picked up a leaf and ran his finger down the side. "See how this creature lays his eggs down the *edge* of the leaf. I accept that position." He picked another leaf, with two large bulges. "They're living *in* there. Off the fat of the money tree. Not me!"

Darcy liked money. He liked good food, wine, the best materials, entertainment, even fine glasswear. Despite his love of leisure, he obviously worked hard at times. Cassie lived in a world where money determined the standard of living, the exercise of power, even personal worth. She had become accustomed to the trappings – the clothes, the other possessions, the patterns in the lives of those with money.

The afternoon went nowhere, but in the week after that distancing, prickly conversation, Cassie was unable to let go of him. Darcy drew her back, so she felt as if the darker, unexplored edges of her map were closing in around her. It was more than friendship, more than difference. She rang.

"I thought we could do the headland walk again," she said, "but right to the end."

"Great," he said. "Saturday." They made the arrangements quickly.

On the headland, she looked out over the sea, deeper and bluer than the harbour. Further, stronger, wilder. She imagined the tide, waves drawn in, smashing on the shore. Her mind spun. There was something about him, something in him that she craved, that went beyond his facetious politics, into his art, his soul, his being. Why shouldn't she have a relationship with him?

"If we had a relationship –" she began.

"You and me?" he asked, surprised.

"Wasn't that what you were . . . ?"

"I thought you'd politely missed the point," he said impatiently, ". . . organising an exhibition . . . worlds apart . . . great afternoon, good friends?"

"I was backing off."

"But now . . . *if* we had a relationship –"

"We could." She was unsure now.

"Creative tension." He sounded certain. She didn't know what he meant.

"Creative tension?"

"We spark off each other," he said enthusiastically. "Not dependent on each other. You don't need me. I don't need you. A buzz out of our differences. We fight, argue, pursue lines of enquiry, diverge, come together. That's, of course, if we like each other too. But I've had a sense of liking you from the moment I met you in that lift." It occurred to Cassie as he spoke that his mind was not unlike hers, organised and enquiring, but running along different lines.

"I like you too," said Cassie. They had come to the edge of the cliff. There was a sign warning that children were likely to topple over. Darcy leant against it. Instinctively, Cassie went to pull him away.

"It makes me nervous."

"Me risking my own life?"

"Is this what a relationship might be like?"

"Better. Sex makes things better. Sharper. More poignant. More involved."

"I'm not interested in sex yet. Not until a lot of other things are in place."

Darcy sunk to the ground, leaning up against the sign, his head in his hands. "Are you not interested in sex . . . until? Or basically, not interested at all?" He groaned melodramatically. "First we're friends, organising exhibitions. Then there's a relationship in the air. Now the nitty-gritty. No sex." Cassie blushed. She was "normal" and "rational" when it came to sex. She had never been confused about sex in the way Susan had been in adolescence. Susan had gone with boys just for the sex, muddling it with notions of love, with a drive for sexual pleasure that seemed at times to dominate her whole being. Even as a child, Cassie remembered the horrible embarrassment of five-year-old Susan masturbating in bed at night, sucking her thumb at the same time. She had stopped only after their mother caught her and beat her with the hairbrush. And Anthea. Anthea talked openly of a need for sex, about sexual predilections which Cassie found too distasteful to explore.

Cassie felt sexual attraction with Phillip and more recently with Simon. It was part of what she felt for Darcy. But there was no sense of urgency, not even a cogent sense of any need which had to be filled.

Anthea had had arguments with her lovers about sex as her desire waxed and waned, ignited by new passions, dampened by boredom. Susan had had sexual counselling after Kelly was born. But Cassie's desires had been even, spaced and defined. The real issues were personal space, personal habits, schedules, mutual support, separate money.

"Sex is an important part of relationships," she said primly.

Darcy laughed. "If we lay down here and started making love, you'd be more worried about falling over the cliff than having a great orgasm."

"I'd be worried about someone coming along the path. And I wouldn't want to lie down on a stony path anyway."

"The sun in your eyes, dirt under your nails?"

"Exactly," she said. "We understand each other."

"What am I to understand?" he asked. "Poor, desperate love-struck fool that I am."

"One minute I feel a whole lot better than I ever did," said Susan despairingly. "The next moment I'm in tears." She and Cassie were standing at her clothesline, folding the dry clothes and putting them into the basket. Jack played with the pegs, while the girls chased each other hysterically round the lemon tree.

"What did you expect?" asked Cassie.

Susan had expected Cassie to be nicer and kinder to her; she'd expected Nick to come back to her a changed man; she'd expected to lose more weight than she had; that Jack would have weaned himself by now. But the look on Cassie's face told her that it wouldn't be a good idea to expose her expectations.

"To be less emotional," she said. "But I'm not."

"You've made a very serious decision," said Cassie, folding Jack's overalls. "You must have known you'd be emotional about it. Unless you hadn't really thought it through."

"I did think it through," said Susan crossly. "Not in the way you would, because I think differently. But I'm not a complete flake."

"I know," said Cassie patiently. "Now, why don't you leave the rest of this and the kids with me." Cassie had decided her reaction to Susan's separation had been extreme. It was Susan's life, and as her sister, she should help her. At least Susan had given up the crazy idea of moving to the mountains. Perhaps, thought Cassie, Susan might even become more independent without Nick. "Go out, and buy what you have to buy. Have a cup of coffee. Don't worry about the time."

"Okay." Susan resented Cassie's distant kindness.

She backed the car down the driveway, knocking the wing mirror, remembering the last time she had done that it had cost eighty dollars. She couldn't think about it. She couldn't tell anyone. It would be more ammunition for Nick and Cassie, proof she was crazy and unbalanced.

Automatically, she walked into the super-market and started pulling packets and cans off the shelves into the trolley. She hadn't made a list. She knew she would forget something. She could feel the tears starting. She'd become one of those women who had a nervous breakdown in Woolworths. She'd have to take Prozac, she'd become agoraphobic. She put on her sunglasses.

Susan tried to summon back the feeling she'd had the night Nick left, the fleeting sense that she was an adult, in control. She put a box of diet drinks in her trolley. An adult, she told herself. However much she might feel she wasn't, she was, in reality. She would be alright. Maybe.

Darcy took Cassie to see the chemical factory at night. "It's free and it's spectacular," he said. "But environmentally unfriendly."

Visually everything meant something to him – the flames against the night sky, the billows of white smoke, the lights of the trucks in the depots, the chimneys silhouetted against the sky. In his mind, it was another world, full of demons and beauty, shapes and forms.

"That's why we have night," he said. "Black and white. So we're more aware of form."

They drove back to his house, and walked over to the beach. "In summer I swim in here at night," he told her. "Naked in the night. Inky water. It's wonderful."

"What about sharks?"

"Water's full of them. I'm terrified. That's what makes it such a thrill."

She sat down on a rock. She felt relaxed. "We could have whatever we want," she said. "We don't have to please anyone else, fulfil any expectations. I can decide if I want sex. You can decide if you want to wait for me to decide. I can decide how often we meet. Or you decide something different and we negotiate. We can decide if we want to see each other every week, or twice a week, or three times a month. There's no reason we can't negotiate all that."

Darcy burst out laughing. "What a deeply spontaneous, romantic, throw caution to the wind, woman you are." He stood up, put his hand on his heart and faced the sea. "I am ready," he intoned, "to make whoopee any time, any place, that Cassandra La Rosa desires me. Until then, I shall hold my peace. God help me!"

Back at the house, he pottered in the kitchen, as Cassie toyed with her wine and talked to him. The awkwardness was gone. Two friends, but with an undercurrent of erotic potential. He often referred to his childhood in the house, the house his father had inherited from his grandfather, the house he had inherited from his father. His grandfather had been a painter, an academic painter of mediocre talent.

"He's in the gallery," explained Darcy, "but not hanging. Only in the basement."

"Was your father an artist too?"

"Booze artist."

"So why don't you exhibit? You don't want to be left in the basement, surely?"

"It's a long haul. Working on stuff. It takes time." She sensed she'd struck a raw nerve.

"Is this how you've always lived?"

They sat outside, on the porch of the little upstairs room, looking out over the bay. "People think I built it for the view," said Darcy. "But it's a grown-up version of a childish dream of spying on the neighbours." Cassie noticed a group of children climbing out along the breakwater. The youngest climbed bravely into the darkness after his older siblings.

"I bummed round Asia and India for about ten years as an idle youth," he went on. "Did terrible damage to myself and others. Drugs and dissolution. When I got back, my parents had died. I'd been told, but I hadn't taken it in. Sisters married. They were good, though. They kept the house for me. They hate it down here. They like those suburbs with the big gardens and avenues named after the English aristocracy. But they knew I should live here." He stroked Cassie's knee, the first real physical contact they had had. She touched his hand lightly. "Different from what you were doing in the corporations," he added.

"Not until I was in my thirties." She looked at his hands. Big, but supple and strong. Finely made, sensitive hands. "I've been such a good girl all my life. It would never have occurred to me to do anything bad like drugs."

"Sure," he said. "So you just sold out to the military industrial complex. Well, the industrial part."

It seemed so facile she couldn't take it seriously. Besides, by now, she felt the inevitability of the attraction.

Chapter 11

The relationship with Darcy progressed for two months, sporadic, emotionally intense, but physically restrained. "Your call," he told her. "Better that way. Unless I go mad first." Cassie liked this stated hiatus, the calculated pacing of her emotions. More than anything, she liked the agreement that the experiment was hers to control, the sense of the relationship building slowly. She continued to work long hours, called him almost every day but saw him only once a week. She had moments when she liked her power, but it was double-edged, making her more intensely and emotionally attached, ultimately more bound to him. Some mornings, when she woke in the placid light of the apartment, she was convinced that she must be going crazy, but at nights, she felt shivers of excitement at the thought of Darcy, at the unexplored possibilities. And however drawn in she was, she held herself apart, aware of their differences. She made herself think rationally, supposedly clear of emotions, to analyse what she wanted and why, what degree of emotional investment she should make. She made lists, drew diagrams, thought intensely. She had a sense of him observing her, sometimes impatient, sometimes amused.

Anthea considered the process idiotic, arguing that there was no insurance against mistakes in relationships, that attempts to modify the progress of a relationship were like trying to control a tidal wave. "Mistakes," Anthea often told her, "are life's major experiences. Practise them for when the truly devastating happens."

Cassie sat on the end of the bed. She didn't believe Anthea. She had seen her parents make mistakes and then compound them, never learning anything. To her, a relationship was like an investment, to be carefully weighed up.

She often thought about when she and Darcy would make love. She wanted it first in her bed, her territory. She had toyed with the idea of asking him to dinner, to see a movie, to install her sculptures, which, he insisted, still needed some finishing touches. These would be artificial devices, to bring him to her, instead of her visiting him, which had become their pattern.

She longed for him with an intensity that was new to her. But some shyness, and a need to settle this in her own head, meant she still waited, afraid of being too bold, too explicit, too exposing of herself.

When she arrived on Saturday morning, she often found him carving some piece of wood, tinkering with his collage, repairing the house, doing his washing, or simply arranging shells. He read a lot, and religiously went to films on cut-price days. "Practising to be a pensioner," he explained, knowing how it irritated her.

"I can't understand why you don't do more," she said, frustrated. "It's not as if –"

"Not as if I have no talent," he said and put the kettle on. "Talent needs brooding time."

"Don't you get bored?" she asked.

"If I get bored I look at the sky. It's full of clouds and smoke from the chemical factory and pollution and aeroplanes. It's fabulous. I bet *you* never look at the sky."

"Of course I do," she said stuffily, remembering, as a child, watching the clouds race over the tops of the pine trees against the intense blue of the mountain sky. She wondered if she had ever really looked since that time long ago. She made a resolution to look some time soon, and then told him proudly that she had watched the sunrise one morning.

"Like watching the opening titles and missing the show," he told her. "It's on all day. And there's a night-time session as well."

"Doesn't it worry you that everyone else is out there working, and you're watching the sky?" she asked.

"It'd hardly be worth having it up if no-one bothered to watch," he said. "Think of it as me working on an exhibition if that makes you feel better. Maybe the exhibition will be about futility." He smiled at her. "I'm a curiosity. Soon, tourists will flock to see someone like me making tea in a teapot and drinking it sitting on my lawn. It will be an extraordinary sight, because everyone else will be doing the twelve-hour day in offices. They'll put me on postcards."

She was silent, knowing better than to set him off. And after all, as a sculptor, he was respected, successful. Maybe it was the peasant in her that ached at the waste of time.

Her own work, however, felt different now. He caught the trail of her discontent and unravelled it further. She fought against any loss of her belief in DMC Dolan, but she saw more sharply the contrast between the ideology and the reality of corporate life. She wanted to see it as a game, but the game now seemed devoid of real meaning and passion. The corporate vision and the sense of mission she had embraced with fervour now eluded her. With the Asia presentation coming up, she worked as hard as ever, but against Darcy, her mother and her dreams for the mountain house, it had become a balancing act.

"Tell me what you do all day," said Darcy.

She told him about the research. "It's complicated," she explained. "Because if you configure things different ways, you get different pictures. So it's like trying to see it through other people's heads, other perspectives. Predicting what will be important, what won't be, what will be real."

"You see, that's what I do, too," he said excitedly. "Search for an ultimate truth, which is reality. Or God. Actually, God and reality are one." He looked at her slyly. "Tell that to the board of directors."

"There are relationships and politics too," she said. "I'm not so good at the politicking. It's hard to make friends, because at some point, you get into a power play. I stopped making friends, which was stupid. Now, when I'm thinking about it again, I don't seem to be having much success." Darcy was the only person she could admit this to.

She explained to Darcy about Simon, about her difficulties with him. "I'm working on this plan with him to incorporate what he does into my department. That way, we protect ourselves from an outside take-over. But I can't quite figure him out. I don't know if he's super dumb or super smart."

"Be careful of him," said Darcy.

"I think we should go out for dinner," Simon said one morning. They were working in her office, graphing out some projections. "Give us a chance to unwind. Look at the bigger picture out of the office."

She blushed, and was annoyed with herself for it. She supposed it was because, despite Darcy, she still found Simon attractive. "Sure," she said. She'd set the ground rules, make sure he had no sexual expectations. It would simply be an extension of the work relationship. "Monday's a good day for me."

"Any particular restaurant?'

"I'll leave that to you." She looked out over the Harbour Bridge thinking that she should have suggested dinner. "I think it's a great idea. We're working so hard, it'd be good to get to know each other a bit better. As friends."

"Exactly what I had in mind," he said.

"I was wondering if you'd heard anything more around the corridors of power about the restructure?"

"Not really."

"I thought people might tell you things – because you're new. It might be an advantage to us when we work out the fine details of what we would like to happen with the new structure."

"I'll see what I can find out and we can discuss it over dinner. Our future plans."

"Tim Bayliss has been wining and dining Julian, but I'd rather present him with a solid plan about the money they can save by bringing Research and Information Services together," said Cassie. "Julian's more interested in facts than in flattery."

"Like you," said Simon dryly. He studied his organiser. "I forgot I'm going to Brisbane next week. And Monday's booked up. What about Tuesday week?"

"Sure," said Cassie. She usually dropped in on Susan on Tuesdays, but she could put that off.

Susan had changed her life in a serious way. Serious and deliberate. She had got rid of all the junk food. She had moved her head into a different space. She'd had the experience before, where she made her mind up about something and it happened. It seemed silly, but she felt she could decide her fate. Her physical fate was first on her agenda. She would become trim. This she judged differently from the thin figure she had strived for when she was bulimic. They had warned her then about dieting, but all she planned to do now was eat sensibly.

She had sacked the cleaner, which meant she saved money and burnt up extra calories on housework. The house was tidy, almost spooky, she thought. By eight o'clock the children were in bed. And the phone was off the hook, to stop Nonna's constant calls. And Susan was on the treadmill, in front of the TV. If Nick made a fuss about the price of the treadmill, she'd pay it off with the cleaning money. Last week, deciding she needed a social life, she'd invited Maria and some of the other mothers from school over for a children's clothing party one of them was organising. They'd all got very drunk and bought far too many clothes. It was fun, but this quiet TV life was bliss.

She had given up the idea of lima bean casseroles, but they all ate healthy kiddie food – fish fingers, custards, mashed potato, little slices of carrots frilly around the edges. The children had moderate helpings of icecream with Adora Cream wafers to follow. Jack had weaned himself and insisted on drinking from a cup. Having wanted to wean him for so long, Susan now felt suspicious of Jack's timing. His rejection of her, at the exact time Nick left, seemed like a gesture of solidarity with Nick. In general, Jack had become more like Nick. He learned to walk, strutting around the house, bellowing from wherever he found himself stranded, demanding food out of the fridge, treating her, she thought, like an Italian Mama, which also involved the compensation of long and passionate embraces. But the whimpering, demanding, difficult baby had gone.

Sometimes, she wanted all the people she was independent of to know just how independent she had become. When Cassie had called to cancel her visit, she had told her firmly that it didn't matter. She was fine, okay, in control.

It was eight o'clock and Susan had just put the children to bed when there was a knock on the front door. Susan looked through the peephole. Nick stood there, in jeans and the Fairisle sweater she had knitted two years ago. He looked thoroughly miserable.

"You agreed not to come unless we arranged it first," she called.

"I was worried something had happened. Your phone's engaged," he shouted.

"It's off the hook to stop your mother. I'm fine. Go away."

"I've driven all the way over here," he said plaintively.

"Daddy," said Elin from the stairs.

"Come in," said Susan angrily.

Elin catapulted herself into Nick's arms, but he walked into the living room like a stranger.

"I'm okay," said Susan wearily. "The kids are okay. This isn't a good idea."

"Seeing my kids?"

"Coming over unannounced. We were all settled."

"Yeah, I'm pretty well settled on the spare bed over at my parents'," said Nick. "Dad has his tools in the cupboard, but the bed's clear, and I keep my clothes behind the door."

"You left," said Susan.

"You were going to leave – run off to the mountain house, remember?"

"We've got to talk sensibly." She shot a look at Elin. "Privately."

"Everyone thinks you're crazy. My whole family –"

"Surprise, surprise!"

"Your own sister."

"You talked to Cassie?"

"I rang her. I didn't want her thinking it was all my fault."

"Very thoughtful. So that's why she thinks it's all mine," retorted Susan.

"I told her you were upset, and she said you'd always been pretty emotional. You don't need to get paranoid about it."

"I'm not so sure. You've got Julie on side and now my own sister." Susan thought it was amazing how all these barbs had been lying unspoken beneath the surface of their relationship. She started to take Elin from Nick. "Come on sweetie, Daddy's going now. Up to bed."

"No!" screamed Elin.

"Okay," said Susan evenly. "Daddy will take you up to bed and sit with you till you go to sleep."

"Oh shit," said Nick.

"It's called being a parent," she said sarcastically. "I'm watching TV." She walked out of the room and into the lounge room. She switched the TV on and then got onto the treadmill. She was too tired, but she wanted Nick to see, when he came downstairs, just how well her new life was working. She was thinner, better organised, more in control. But harder. She'd always tried to avoid being hard. She had disliked her mother's hardness, which she was sure Cassie had inherited. She had wanted to be warm and flowing, but she had hit a streak of nastiness. She wanted payback and revenge. She wanted to show Nick, show Cassie, show the mothers at school who thought she was not as good as them. Stuff niceness, she thought.

"We need you," said the Matron, "to come and sit with your mother. She's hurt her other leg and she won't let us dress it."

Cassie had an image of her mother's painfully ulcerated leg. "Maybe you could ring my sister," she said. "I'd like to help out, but I'm tied up all morning."

"Of course we tried her first." Cassie felt a stab of guilt at the Matron's tone, firm, like a school teacher's. "She's engaged." Cassie felt a stab of irritation at Susan's new habit of leaving her phone off the hook. "Maybe you could tell your boss it's an emergency," the Matron went on. "We'll actually need you every second day this week. I wouldn't ask you, but it is important." The blackness of her mother's illness loomed in front of her.

"I'll organise it," she said evenly. "Unless there's an alternative way of doing it."

"We could sedate her," said the Matron. "But as you can imagine, it's very confusing for these patients. And there's a danger of a fall, because she won't stay in bed afterwards, unless we tie her in."

The picture of her mother tied to the bed was too painful. "Of course, I'll come," said Cassie.

"Yes," said the Matron slowly, "I knew you'd hate anything that would endanger her."

Cassie wondered how much further the Matron would push her guilt. She felt weary, defeated and unreasonably annoyed with Susan.

"I'll be there by ten o'clock."

"Doctor doesn't come till eleven."

Cassie almost cried. She was no good at this game. "Okay, that's fine. I'll be there." She put down the phone and went out to Denise's desk.

"I'll be going out at ten-thirty, back about twelve."

Denise looked at her apologetically. "Julian just rescheduled the meeting for eleven-thirty."

"I'll be a little late." She went into her office and closed the door. She made some notes and fired off some memos. She quickly filed a rough end on one of her nails. Her skin was dry, looser than it used to be. She'd noticed it the other day when Denise was in her office. Denise was young, with plump, smooth skin. She, Cassie, was ageing. When she was old like her mother, there wouldn't even be a reluctant daughter. There would be no-one. She'd be an old woman, on her own, her life, her very soul unaccounted for. Even now, her life felt diminished.

She collected her things and looked round the office, with the imposing, self-important luxury. Even the view, she never had time for. It was an occasional view, not a scene like Darcy's beach at Kurnell, to be studied and enjoyed. She stood, staring at the Harbour, but thinking of Darcy's collage. He'd told her he had done it just for fun, like the carved tree trunk near the bathroom, like the little sketch books he carried every-where. He worked in a way she couldn't

understand, constantly, but unpressured by anything outside himself. He had no competitors, no
time frame. He was as solitary as she was, but
spread his spirit wider.

She hurried to the door, dropped a folder on
Denise's desk and rushed for the carpark lift,
Darcy still in her mind.

"I haven't propositioned anyone before," she
told Darcy, "which is silly at my age. But I'd like
you to come over."

He laughed nervously. "That puts the fear of
God in me."

"Will you?"

"Will I? Won't I? Will I? Won't I? Won't you
join the dance? Of course I will. When?"

"Tonight?"

"Presents a slight problem. The car – you
could come down here."

"Darcy . . ." Cassie felt as if she was going to
cry. "Yesterday. I had . . . a day . . . my mother
. . . I went to see her."

"Tonight? You need me tonight. It's blowing
down the phone lines. I'll be there."

"How?"

"By bus."

"You want a Cabcharge?"

"If I live in squalor, it's by choice, a man of
independent means. I'm coming by bus."

"You don't have to." Her heart was beating fast. He did have to.

"I know. I could fund a taxi myself. More people-watching on the buses."

Cassie thought it was a long time since she'd been anywhere by bus.

"Be there. Eight."

"See you."

No skyrockets, no women's magazine G spots igniting. But there was passion. And a quality of intimacy Cassie hadn't felt before. She had never seen sex as something particularly intimate in itself, but something that people who were intimate did with each other. A part of intimacy, not an act of intimacy. But with Darcy, she felt intimate with every part of him, body and mind. And she let him have her in the same way, softer, closer under his touch than she ever had been. Everything in the room, the darkness, the music, became part of him and her together. Physical and emotional boundaries dissolved. Later, they lay in the darkness, looking out across the harbour lights.

She could feel tears in her eyes, as he became aware of them too, tracing the moisture across her face with his finger.

"So," he said gently. "Life at the capitalist big-top got to you? Why me? Why now?"

"It was bound to happen eventually. Anthea was right. All these boundaries and parameters I was working out had nothing much to do with anything."

"What made you realise that? Not Anthea, I hope?"

"No, my mother actually."

"Your mother? I thought she didn't really know you."

"She does and she doesn't. Usually, I visit as the dutiful daughter. But yesterday they asked me to go out there and help calm her while they dressed her leg." She smiled. "Which was hard to cope with."

"What happened?"

"It made a difference my being there. They could do the dressing. And just for a moment, I did have a feeling of being her daughter again. Probably Susan has never lost it. Anyway, I felt connected to her again."

"Well connected? Did it feel good?"

"Took away the guilt and the angst for a moment. Yes, it was good. It was like being a child. Not having to worry who you are."

"I'm all in favour of that."

"It was so intense. I was comforting her. I suppose that's why Susan does it, because it does connect you. But it was strange, the childlike feeling. And after that, I wanted you. So I rang you. Another connection . . ."

He laughed. "Is that what we just did? Made a connection? Like plumbers and electricians do?"

"Connecting our bodies and souls."

"Ice maiden was the wrong term for you. It implies coldness. But sometimes . . . I think you do feel fragmented . . ." He hugged her tighter.

"Is it *so* important to get these metaphors right?"

"Nope." He stroked her hair. "But if you put yourself under all this pressure, you can get fragmented too often. Changes who you are." He ran his fingers lightly over her back. "Be careful." He stroked her as she went to sleep. In the middle of the night they made love again, slowly, sleepily passionate. Later, near dawn, Cassie dreamed of a map of the village where her father was born. It was like the maps drawn for children with landmarks and houses sketched into its narrow twisting lanes, the market place drawn with its cobbles, the church, with the priest's house beside it. She imagined herself following the map, down to the church where her father's funeral was being held, but when she arrived, she found him there, and she walked, holding his arm, to the altar. She whispered to him in Italian, asking him if this was how Italian funerals were done. His laugh rang out through the church. "No funeral," he answered in his dialect. "You're getting married."

In the morning, Darcy had gone. He left a frame about a foot square. Between the spidery, cracked, mirrored back and the glass, an orange shell was mounted on its thin edge, so that from the front, it appeared like a sliver of orange, but from the side, it could be seen, with its reflection, like a pair of wings, delicately veined with the imperfections of the mirror.

"This is you," he had written on the frame. "Amazing."

Chapter 12

"I can't understand why you're so het up about Susan," said Anthea. They were sitting in the white-tiled steam room of the Korean baths. "She's just left her husband, or he's left her. People do it every day."

"Susan doesn't just talk like a stream of consciousness," retorted Cassie. "She acts like one. It comes into her head and she does it. She's always done it."

Anthea laughed. "I think it's called spontaneity."

"Which is fine," said Cassie, missing the irony, "when you're sixteen or so. When you haven't got kids to worry about. Or a marriage at stake."

"Maybe it was brewing for a while."

"I doubt it," said Cassie. "It probably occurred to her when *you* told her to go and live in *my* mountain house."

"Okay." Anthea smiled. She was sweating, her face pink. "I'm beginning to think I may have had my share of Korean steam baths this lifetime," she said. "You want to have a shower?"

Cassie got up and gathered the towel around her. "But why did you tell Susan to go and live in the mountain house? It started off this whole idea of leaving Nick. And now Nick's not there, she spends her life on a treadmill. Losing weight is pretty dangerous territory for her. She's even told the retirement home that I'm the person to contact about Mum."

"Good on her," replied Anthea. "She probably needs a break. It's hard for you, but given what you're paying *you* can tell the hospital to go jump. She has to pay in good works. One of the terrible costs of having no money of your own. I know."

"It's not that. I can't really talk to her about Mum. I've hardly said anything about putting up all the money, but then she throws hints at me that I've somehow cheated her. And that I'm not doing the right thing by Mum."

Anthea turned on the shower and stood under it, luxuriating. "This is nice. This bit."

"She's crazy," Cassie persisted, "changing her life on a whim."

"She's growing up," said Anthea. "I see kids doing it every day."

"You're not fazed by it because she's not your sister."

"That too," said Anthea.

"Besides, she's behaved like this all her life," protested Cassie.

"But this time, it's having an effect. You said yourself she's cleaned up the house. Not that I think that's a particular sign of maturity."

"Nick's going to get sick of waiting for her to apologise. And then she'll end up breaking up a perfectly good marriage."

"Depends on whether it was a perfectly good marriage." Anthea got out of the shower and sat down, wrapped in towels. "Look, I didn't realise there was this demarcation dispute about the mountain house. So I'm sorry I mentioned the idea of her living there. But whatever you say, I don't think she is being frivolous. She acts dumb and you let her. But apart from the Daffy Duck role she plays with you, she's pretty bright. Maybe even as bright as you." Anthea let the remark sink in. "And bright people don't throw husbands out for frivolous reasons, even if it looks like that."

"Maybe you're right." Her relationship with Susan had always been a minefield.

They dressed in silence, and went downstairs to the restaurant. It was a difficult silence. Cassie remembered that when she had been seeing

Phillip, there had been changes in her relationship with Anthea. Then, it had been a question of organisation – time for him, time for her, so the friendship could be kept separate from the relationship. With Darcy, it was different, because the relationship with Darcy was intimate in a way it never had been with Phillip. Her intimacy with Anthea, although largely unspoken, now shifted position. She saw it, schematically in her mind, left of centre.

"New phase," said Anthea, picking out a tray of sashimi. "For you and me. That was part of us bickering about your sister."

Cassie looked at Anthea with admiration. "I was worried we'd lose the thread."

"Me too." They sat down and Anthea went on. "With Johnny Jamieson, it wasn't as if he and I were ever going to grow old together. I mean, most men wouldn't even lend me the bus fare home. And now, you and me both, we're looking at something different. Which will make the relationship between you and me different."

"Does it make you sad?" asked Cassie.

"There are compensations," laughed Anthea. "Mike isn't what you'd call too intellectual, but he's pretty damn keen in bed."

Susan stepped off the treadmill in a lather of sweat. She had just walked ten kilometres. It was two in the morning. She rushed upstairs and jumped on the scales. It registered one kilo down on the previous day. A flood of relief. She went into the darkened bedroom. The three children sprawled across her bed, the blankets kicked to the ground. She covered each of them and kissed them, and went out onto the balcony, where the spa was bubbling and steaming. Quickly, she took off her sweaty clothes and slid into the warm water. She lay there, looking up into the sky. It was cloudy and she could feel faint spits of rain on her face.

The problem now was that she couldn't rest. She was in control, but she could not rest, and she was lonely. Cassie was angry with her. Nick was furious. Nonna was giving her the silent treatment, which was, in fact, welcome. The old man roared at her. The kids loved her, but they missed Nick.

She had the childish feeling that she would like someone to explain the situation to her. When she had been in hospital for bulimia, they had made the group of emaciated girls tell each other what was wrong with them. Everyone had been able to pinpoint other people's problem – distorted body image, starving to death, terrified of life – but she still remembered the shock when someone had told her that she was too thin. The old fear of fat, the fear of being locked up in the hospital flitted across her consciousness occasionally now. Then, Susan had known her father was sick, but she never knew he was dying. Before he left with Cassie, he seemed to her to be uncharacteristically angry, rather than sick. When they got news of his death it was a year before she believed it.

Her mother had been angry with Susan for needing to be hospitalised. Cassie had accused her of making trouble, and had not understood until much later that she had been ill. In the face of it all, she'd been good, put on weight. But she'd never really recovered her heart until she met Nick. Nick who had loved her, who had wanted her, who had liked her. Tears of self-pity coursed down her face.

She was fearful and breathless. Maybe she wanted him back. But if he came back she wanted him loving her as she was now, not who she used to be. But some days she hardly knew who she was herself. And she wanted him how he used to be, before he became so serious, so intense, so remote and such a dentist! It was too confusing. She needed an intermediary. Maria at school was too hard, too definite. Cassie was too sensible. Her own mother had never been good at any of this. Susan felt a stab of pain at her desertion of her mother. In the morning, she'd ring Cassie's friend Anthea.

"How often do you think we should see each other?" asked Cassie. "Now that it's a real relationship?"

"Often as we like," said Darcy. They lay on the sand, the breakwater protecting them from the wind, the afternoon sun streaming down. Darcy had collected hundreds of the delicate orange pearly shells.

"What *are* these?" Cassie asked. "I mean they're lovely, but I don't understand the obsession."

"They're part of the home of a very small version of your basic Tassie scallop," said Darcy. "The shells wash up round about this time every year. I've always wanted to do something with them."

"What on earth will you do with so many?"

"There's a fellow over at Ramsgate, used to be a surfboard maker. Does wonderful things with fibreglass. I'm thinking we could work together and embed them between two sheets, without losing the lustre."

"What would you use it for?"

Darcy lay back, squinting at the sun. "Don't know. Needs light behind it." He laughed. "I'll probably end up knocking out that back wall.

Make a wall of translucent orange shells. Beach variation on the stained-glass theme."

Cassie sighed. "I don't know why you don't *use* some of these ideas. That's very marketable."

"Someone undoubtedly will market it. And there will be machines trolling up and down the seabed finding these shells and pressing them into fibreglass moulds till every shower screen in the land has orange shells embedded in the shape of seahorses." He paused and let the sand run through his fingers. "And won't that be wonderful?"

"I don't mean mass-production. I mean the top of the art market."

"Stop thinking about money for five minutes."

"It's not money," she said. "It's giving you a profile."

He ran his finger down his forehead, down his nose to his chin. "Ape forehead, bumpy nose, movie-star chin. I've got a profile. I don't want another." He sat up and kissed her. "My exhibition will give me a profile."

She didn't believe in the exhibition. There were no carvings in progress, no sketches, nothing. She decided to ignore his comment. "So, how often do you think we should see each other?" she asked again.

"You never stop."

"I don't want to argue about it. I want to define it."

"I don't mind arguing. I hate defining."

"Guidelines?"

"You worried about too much or not enough?"

"Both." Cassie smiled at him. "I want some framework. So I feel secure."

"An illusion of security. No passionate relationship is ever secure."

Cassie sat up and looked out along the breakwater. She could see the white sand, the wall of rocks and the waves, breaking gently. It was idyllic, picture-perfect. She looked beyond to the tankers out in the bay, the industrial hardware of the place, the planes taking off which would soon be roaring above them.

Her mother's influence and then her father's death, when she was barely twenty, had made her wary of intimacy. She'd been so close to her father as a child, but it had meant she'd walked a knife edge, aware of her mother's disapproval of the closeness. And in the end, he'd asked so much of her, drawing her to him, till she'd felt as if she would die with him. She had dealt with the pain in Italy, away from her mother and sister, feeling that her grief was different from theirs – Susan's more childlike, her mother's modified by the estrangement that had already taken place. Although nothing had been said, it was clear her mother regarded Cassie's taking her father to Italy as a betrayal. Now, there were moments she felt a closeness to her mother, other times a cold withdrawal. Emotional chaos. Intimacy and death, descending on her.

"Do you worry about dying?" she asked Darcy.

"All the time," he answered flippantly.

"Really. Do you?"

"There's nothing else to worry about, is there?" he asked.

"I've always thought if you got your life organised –"

"What, that death would take care of itself? It's the other way round. Get your death organised and life takes care of itself. All those years in Asia, I was railing against death. If I couldn't kill myself with drink and drugs and dangerous social acts, then maybe I was immortal. As a kid, I dreamed about my impending death constantly. What if a car hit me? What if the house fell down? What if the dog bit me and it turned septic?"

"Nobody thinks like that!"

"I see the old codgers making their way along the street, stopping for a cough and a smoke on every third paling, and I thank God I stopped smoking. At the same time I'm thinking there's not much anyway between them and me, between me and meals on wheels and the old glory hallelujah."

"Darcy . . . you don't really think like that?"

"I'm getting it under control. Such a thought only occurs every ten minutes or so. Death is what life is."

Cassie sighed. She looked at the sky and lay back against him. "I thought *I* was getting morbid," she said.

"You're not in spitting distance."

Anthea wondered how much emptiness you had to put up with in a permanent relationship. Did it get better, or did it get worse? Did you find things to fill the emptiness, or did love grow to fill it? She remembered her lonely, desperate singleness with a certain fondness, which seemed so insane that she couldn't possibly admit it to anyone. Mike was crazy about her. She made him laugh, which pleased her. But the sense of sexual interest she had felt in the beginning was now starting to wane. She reminded herself there was nothing wrong with him. He was attractive. He was intelligent. He had a good sense of fun. They liked the same music, although not the same films. She should be falling more in love with him, not feeling an increasing sense of distance. He was a chance, a better chance than she'd had in years.

"This car's a mindless extravagance left over from my marriage," explained Mike, as he and Anthea drove away from the school in his Jaguar. "I hardly ever use it, because the bike's easier round town. Christ, when I think of the money I made and wasted."

"I can't understand why financial journalism made you so rich then, and now it hardly pays the rent," said Anthea.

"Temporarily rich. In the eighties, every man and his dog subscribed to financial newsletters. Now, the market's a whole lot leaner, the institutions do newsletters for free. I'm going to have to do something else."

"Such as?" asked Anthea.

"Financial consultancy for one of the big firms. I've had a few offers."

"Great." Anthea looked out the window. "I had an offer from a North Shore private school today. Which was flattering. But I said no, of course." Since she had been seeing him, her discontent with work had fallen away. She felt more enthusiasm for school life than she had for a long time. She didn't know whether she had shifted her discontent to him, or whether she was happier because she'd made some sort of commitment to him.

"Really? I can't believe you. Don't you get sick of teaching out here?"

"The travelling?"

"That. And it's pretty grotty. Social problems. All that."

Anthea sighed. She knew his views were different from hers, but it shouldn't matter. After all, there were lots of people who didn't understand why she was committed to an underpaid, difficult job. Cassie regularly told her she could do much more. Anthea suspected she meant more money. Mike didn't appreciate the value of what she did either.

"I get sick of the problems sometimes," she conceded. "I went through a bad patch at the beginning of the year. But I get more sick of the fact we're so under-resourced. Most of the kids are great, though. Better than a selective school or being in a posh area."

"Better?" He laughed. She was still drawn in by the warmth of his laugh. "How could it be better?"

"I was in a selective school, ages ago – back when Cassie and I were teaching together. It suited her because she really cared about the kids doing well. Results-oriented. Whereas I like to see them grow up. Change. Really take life on."

"You're a saint." He leaned over and stroked her knee. "This place I've booked, you'll love. A big warm double bed in the middle of the woods."

"Does it worry you that I'm eight years older than you?" she asked suddenly.

"No. Not at all."

"What about it being too late for me to have kids?" Anthea blushed, an old shame and grief at her lack of fertility. "I know it's a premature question, but it occurred to me that if we were serious and then you woke up and decided you wanted kids, you'd wish you'd married Miss Fertility 1997. And break my heart." She really meant that he would have wasted her time, but she could hardly admit that.

"I thought about it too," he said. "The woman's more important than the kids." He looked across at her. "I don't want to break your heart." At that moment, she felt a surge of affection for him. But as they drove up into the mountains, she wondered if she wouldn't rather be at home, by herself.

"I can't come down to Kurnell during the week," said Cassie briskly into the phone. "It's simply too far. I don't know why you don't come up to the apartment."

"The car," groaned Darcy. "Doesn't travel well out of its territory."

"It travelled down the south coast on your camping trip last week. That must have been a hundred kilometres or so."

"It's not an urban car," said Darcy.

"Darcy, grow up!" Cassie tapped her pencil on the desk impatiently. Darcy, who charmed her with his eccentricity on a slow Sunday afternoon, had become irritating on a Monday.

"I'm not the one who needs to grow up," he said. "You're constantly in crisis mode." His voice sounded petulant.

"I've got a lot on at the moment." She felt impatient with him, but she hated this division between them. She could see, in her mind's eye, a collision, their falling apart, the ice maiden shattered, Darcy fading away into his dark intensity. Beyond this she was sustained by their intimacy, the coming together of her heart and his.

"I'll come down tonight," she said. "This is important."

"Don't treat me as a crisis," he said coldly. "Don't come down here in your business suit with shoulder pads and the rest. Don't do that."

"I want to discuss it. I want to come." Why shouldn't she wear shoulder pads? "Do you want me to come?"

"Okay." She knew he was standing by the phone, sketching on the wall, as he always did.

"I've just drawn a prawn risotto," he said. "It'll be on the table at seven."

The clock on the office wall showed six o'clock. Outside, Cassie could see the smog enveloping the city, the haze lit by the last rays of the sun, the stream of lights pouring along the freeway and over the bridge. She should be leaving, but there was a pile of correspondence on her desk she had to look at.

The phone rang. "Simon here. Jennifer wants to come to dinner with us tomorrow to discuss the restructure."

Cassie took a deep breath. "I think tomorrow's a chance for you and me to wind down and put things in perspective." She paused. "In fact, I wish you hadn't mentioned it to her. I don't think it's appropriate for her to come."

"Not appropriate?"

"There's no reason for Jennifer to know what we're doing. It would simply create more fuss about the whole thing." Cassie heard her voice take on the tone she used to use on the junior grades when she was teaching, that she sometimes used on Susan. Jennifer always made her react like this. She tried to soften it. "Please ring her and put her off nicely," she added.

"I think it's a good idea actually," Simon said, "to put her off. She works . . . very differently from you and me."

"I suppose she does," said Cassie, relieved. "But don't tell her that's the reason. Explain that we're so busy running our own show, we don't need more input."

The phone rang again. "It's Matron Alexander, from your mother's retirement village," said Denise.

"Put her through . . . Hello, it's Cassie La Rosa."

"Ms La Rosa. It's Matron Alexander. I know you're busy, dear, so I've just got two things. First is, your mother's leg is healing well now."

"That's good. Thanks for letting me know."

"Your mother slept all yesterday and today. The only thing is that now, she's very restless, and just a little bit distressed. So, we were wondering if you could pop in tomorrow. I don't know whether we've hit a new phase, but I think she has been asking for you –"

"My mother wants me?" Last time Cassie had seen her mother, she seemed unable to speak.

"General distress. Muttering things. It could pass, or it might be a new phase."

She could see the light flashing for call waiting and she ignored it, but it increased her sense of urgency. "How bad is it?"

"There's a slight neural deterioration."

"When you say she's been asking for me . . . ?"

"After your sister left, she started saying your name. That's all." Cassie's heart jolted.

"Is she still calling me?"

"She just said your name." Matron's voice was measured, as if Cassie was having trouble understanding her. Cassie could feel the tears in her eyes. "She's dozing now," the Matron went on. "We won't wake her for tea."

"I'll come by tomorrow."

"You could come tonight."

"No." There was no way to explain the need to steel herself for this. The image of the sore on her mother's thigh, the fine white skin with the ugly cut and the varicosed veins traced across the surface, came to mind. "I'll be there tomorrow. Thanks for ringing." She tried to recall the easy, everyday things about her mother – her white hair, her still-pretty face, the way she held her hands together like a good child. Cassie looked at her watch. Darcy's darkness. She was aware of her body, tight with tension.

As she walked to the carpark, she tried to organise her thoughts logically. She was having a disagreement with Darcy. She didn't have to panic. They had different methods of conflict resolution, that was all. As she drove, she tried to do a chart in her mind. Advantages.

Disadvantages. There was a computer program where you used a diagram of scales to try to balance out the pros and cons of any situation. Benjamin Franklin had supposedly thought up the technique, and then someone had developed it into a decision-making package. In Cassie's mind, Darcy jumped from one side of the scale to the other with maniacal glee.

Although it had started to rain, she drove confidently. Darcy's house had been incorporated into her map, and she knew the way without having to think about it. It sat there, in one part of her brain. In the other, she decided to think seriously about the relationship. The real disadvantage was that Darcy lived at Kurnell in the charming but ridiculous house and . . . she couldn't think of anything else. Then she remembered his remark about her shoulder pads and her resentment began to rise.

She got out of the car and knocked on the door. He opened it.

"Shit!" he said mockingly. "Them's some shoulder pads."

"Don't! Or I'll go."

"I feel like you've put me on notice." He looked at his watch. "And you're always late when you come to see me."

"Not very."

"An hour." He was tense too.

"Sorry."

"You're not sorry. But come in anyway. I've eaten the risotto."

Her head was swimming. His hostility was as obvious, simultaneously, as his pleasure in seeing her. The bundles of advantages and disadvantages began to move in her head, changing sides and weights. She sat down in one of the wicker chairs and he sat opposite.

"What we have," she began, "is important. Important in a way I can't even work out. Except I've never had it before."

He looked at her, the dark eyes not quite so cold. "Me too," he said.

"I'm a person who likes to know where I stand, what the boundaries and conventions and rules are. I respect your personal space, and I need you to respect mine. But at the same time, we need to create a safe space for intimacy."

He began to laugh, then stopped and then started again. Every time he looked at her, he began to laugh. She felt like crying. He took her hand, and began to laugh again. Finally, he stopped, went to the fridge and got them both a glass of wine.

"I've never had a proper relationship," he said, "so I claim no expertise. But this isn't real language. It's out of a book, I know."

"Maybe," said Cassie stiffly, "but those things are important. And I want to talk about them. And I have had relationships."

"But obviously not lasting ones." Darcy sighed. "And not true love. You told me that."

"I wasn't pulling rank," she explained. She wanted to stop all this. "I've had a shit of a day," she blurted out. "I need to be here. I want to be here."

The sound of the rain intensified on the tin roof, and the garden was illuminated by a flash of lightning. Then came a crash of thunder. The lights went out, the cottage dark. Darcy wrapped his arms round her. She held herself tight against him and cried on his shoulder. He kissed her and stroked her back, massaging her spine.

"We're stepping into a fucking great void," he said. "Some enormous black hole, with no rules or boundaries or conventions. And I'm as shit-scared as you, so the only thing I know to do for both of us right now is to get into bed and make love, and hope that two people as idiotic as you and me can get through this somehow."

Chapter 13

"I was bulimic," Susan explained, "so I'm always having to watch my weight." She pushed up the speed arrow on the treadmill and took a forkful of caesar salad from the bucket attached to the front bar. "This treadmill is fantastic," she added. "It tells you how many calories you're burning, so if you're eating something like a caesar salad or chocolate biscuits, you get to eat it and burn it off at the same time."

"Amazing way to run your life," said Anthea dryly.

Susan glanced at her, wondering if she was making fun of her. "It's not totally sane. Cass probably told you I'm nuts. Well, I am. I'm not like her. I have a lot of trouble controlling anything. That's why walking on a treadmill and counting out calories makes sense. If it doesn't get out of control, it's good for me. I needed to lose the weight."

"If it doesn't get out of control?" asked Anthea.

"Everything has the potential to be out of control. Every single thing can turn into an obsession." Susan's voice was higher, lighter. "I can't make things happen the way Cass does. I just have to hope like crazy that they happen right."

"When you were bulimic, was everything out of control then?'

"Long time ago." Susan spoke with difficulty, increasingly puffed.

"Yeah, but what happened?"

"Everyone was furious," said Susan, tapping the speed arrow down so she was walking more slowly. "Dad had cancer. Mum was having a nervous breakdown. Cass was dragging Dad back to Italy so he could die in his village." She wiped her face with a towel. "It should have been a fight between those three but Mum and Cass were mad at me." There was a slight hint of triumph in her voice.

"Have you worked it out? What it was really about?"

"The psychiatrist in the hospital had this theory that anorexics and bulimics were very controlling, manipulative people," Susan said, getting off the treadmill and unhooking the salad. "But I've been thinking back to all those girls and I realise that we were very fucked up kids. No control."

"I agree. From what I've seen of eating disorders."

"What do you think I should do?"

"What about?"

"About Nick."

"About Nick," said Anthea. "Do you know what you want?"

Susan threw herself back on the sofa and looked across at Jack who was asleep in the playpen. "Maybe I made a mistake. Maybe all this discontent I feel doesn't have that much to do with Nick. But I couldn't think it through while he was around. The thing is that even though Nick and I have problems, I'd need a hundred years not worrying about him to get myself together."

"So you want him back?"

"Maybe . . ." She hesitated. "I want him to understand that I've changed. But maybe I should be able to accept that he's changed too, except I don't like what's happened to him. Somewhere in my head I want him back as he was, when he really did something for me."

"What *did* he do for you?"

"He made me feel good about myself. He believed in me, so it made it easier for me too."

"I'm not sure relationships work like that." Anthea realised she'd said it in her schoolteacher voice. Personal development: Module 4. But Susan was an adult, a woman with three kids, a marriage that had lasted longer than any relationship she had ever had.

"I don't think so either," said Susan. "He's changed. I've changed. So in theory, I should simply ask him to come back, except I don't know if he'll come." Jack lifted his head and looked at her sleepily, about to cry. Susan went over to him and picked him up. Anthea felt a pang of jealousy at the weary automatic gesture she used. Her relationship with Mike had stirred the old desire for a baby, and she often felt a despair at the unstudied gestures of mothers and babies. Susan sat back on the couch, Jack snuggled against her.

"Maybe you need another aim," said Anthea. "Not to do with Nick or the kids or calories."

"What else is there?"

"What do you enjoy?"

"Nothing much at the moment," said Susan. "People tell me I must be wonderful with kids because I have three of them, but that's not true. My friend Maria told me to get a job, any job, but it's so complicated."

"I didn't mean a job," said Anthea. "I wondered what you like doing. What you can really lose yourself in."

Susan laughed. "Nick's accounts."

"Is that good or bad?"

"It's good. I love making them balance, but I also do things like graphing the billings. Now he knows what months you can expect more patients, and that the overall practice is growing, but he needs more capital. I think so, anyway."

"Have you ever thought of doing a course?" Anthea asked.

"You should see my HSC results," said Susan. "Pathetic!"

"You could do TAFE, or mature age at uni," said Anthea. "Study accountancy."

"I love numbers and money. I always have. But how on earth would that help me and Nick? It's such a mess."

"Doing something totally unrelated often does help," said Anthea. "I get kids to do it all the time. Don't ask me why it works."

Susan sighed. "Nick is very determined not to understand all this. He's so convinced it doesn't matter how you feel. You're just supposed to do it anyway."

"Forget Nick. You're going round and round in circles about him. I'll help you find a course. You already know some of the things you want to happen in your marriage. You know where you're at, approximately. You won't stop thinking about it. But if you do accountancy, it'll take you out of that."

Susan passed Jack to Anthea. "Mind him a second. I'll make us a cup of tea."

Susan went into the kitchen and Anthea picked a book up off the floor for Jack. But he wriggled off her knee and followed his mother.

Cassie was surprised at the restaurant Simon had chosen. It was much smaller and more intimate than the "corporate" restaurants where she sometimes ate with colleagues. She liked it. It was the sort of place she felt comfortable in, the way she felt comfortable when she and Anthea had dinner together. Simon, it seemed to her, was much less oppressed by the corporate style than she had been when she started working for DMC Dolan. She had tried to adopt the style of those above her, whereas he had his own style.

"Do you like the company?" she asked. "Is working at DMC what you want?"

"For now," he said, "but I'd hate to end up like our friend Bayliss."

"So what's your game plan?"

"Get some experience. Maybe work overseas. I've learned a lot in the last few months. Especially from you." He looked at her, intently. His foot brushed against hers. She felt confused. She had simply wanted to build a more personal relationship, but it felt as if he were coming on to her. She wasn't sure of the signals and pushed her chair back a little. He was attractive, but she didn't want any complications. She wasn't like Anthea or Jennifer, who both enjoyed sexual adventuring. At the same time, she wanted to be able to deal with this without her usual primness.

"What I like about a big company is that you're always being challenged," she said. "Constant change and movement." She paused. "It's hard though, because you're always collecting scalps. Moving up at other people's expense." She was thinking aloud, not realising till this moment what a strain this aspect of her life was. "I'm not sure I'm a natural predator," she said.

"More a gatherer of fruits and berries?" he said.

For some reason she told him about her dream for the mountain house, her desire to become passionately immersed in the garden, to start growing things again. As she talked about it, she felt her frustration at her continual procrastination, of always putting work first. He told her of his passion for car racing. She smiled to herself, thinking that there was a very different dimension to their desires, but also more confident now that they could be friends in the working environment. They went on to discuss the outlines of the restructure, laughing at Bayliss's naked ambitions.

"I'm glad we didn't ask Jennifer along," he said, standing up after they had paid the bill. "It was really nice getting to know you." He took her arm as they went out of the restaurant. It made her uncomfortable, but she told herself that it was only a continuation of the friendliness that had developed over dinner. She wished she was more experienced – in friendship, and in love. They came to her car and she got her keys out of her bag.

He leaned on the roof of the car and looked at her intently as she opened the door. He put his hand on her shoulder. "Hey," he said. "Remember what we said back at the office. Getting to know each other a bit better. Future plans. Let's not leave it half done."

There was no mistaking his meaning. "I told you, I'm seeing someone." It was true, but she also wanted to say that she didn't want him anyway.

"That's cool," he said. "You and me – when I suggested it before, I wasn't thinking of anything serious. Just dinner. Then perhaps satisfying lust and curiosity – plus friendship."

Cassie laughed, trying not to be offended. "I'm too old-fashioned. Very serious about relationships. Know the type?"

"The C word?"

"C word?"

"Commitment – mortgages, marriages, children. All that."

"Just the commitment," said Cassie. "I can do without the rest." She got into her car. "See you tomorrow."

She drove, feeling affront from Simon's approach and frustrated with herself. Finally, down by the Woolloomooloo Wharf, she felt overwhelmed, stopped the car, and leaned wearily on the steering wheel. Although it wasn't late, the area was almost deserted, only a few drunken yells coming from a distant lane. She looked out over the wharf, a cruiser blocking a full view of the harbour. But above, the full moon hung in the dark sky. She thought of how Darcy would look at this scene, noticing the lines of the ships, the depth of the darkness. She felt a longing for him, a weariness with her job. Once the presentation was out of the way, she would be able to schedule her life into a more reasonable timetable.

She thought about Simon. She had to get on with him, even though she had been offended by his approach. Maybe she took things too seriously, but that's how she was as a person. It was hard to work out how much of what she felt came from the inhibitions imposed by her upbringing, her mother's strict, puritanical beliefs, or from her inherent reserve. After the presentation, perhaps things would become clearer.

Jennifer rattled a bag of coffee beans as she stood at the door of Cassie's office. "Gourmet coffee for you and Denise. A bribe to get in the door."

"You don't need a bribe," said Cassie, "it's only that we've been flat out. But we do like coffee. Come in."

"I want to talk to you about the restructure again," said Jennifer, sitting back in Cassie's recliner. "Don't panic, I'm only sounding you out."

"I've been working on the Asia project," replied Cassie evenly. "I know this whole restructure business is rife with rumour, but my view is that Research has always been quarantined. So I'm not really expecting things to change."

"Except you're cuddling up with Simon."

Cassie winced at the terminology. "I'm working with him on the Asia report and I have seen a way we can rationalise staff. At the moment, a lot of the technology he has access to is under-utilised."

"I wouldn't trust him," said Jennifer. "He's gone off to Melbourne this morning. God knows what he's up to."

"I don't really need him this week," said Cassie. "He's got something to finish off down there, so it seemed a good opportunity."

"You and I would make a much better team," Jennifer persisted.

"We've got very different styles. And Research and Promotion – there's no natural reason for any sort of combination."

Jennifer threw up her hands. "The natural reason is that Bayliss and Anderson are going feral, the Board is up on its hind legs demanding cuts, and Julian's running scared. That makes me see a hundred logical reasons for Promotions and Research to get into bed together."

The thought flashed through Cassie's mind that maybe Jennifer would outshine her. Besides, despite what had happened with Simon over dinner, they had come to an understanding about the restructure. They had a solid proposal. The politics of changing horses at this stage was too much. "Julian told me this is fairly minor," Cassie said, "to improve efficiency."

"Sure," said Jennifer. "Remember last time we improved efficiency we lost over two hundred people from Sydney alone. Tony Stephens, who had been Julian's golden boy, got done over."

"I don't think Research can get done over," said Cassie. If she was less uptight she would probably talk to Jennifer and work out some strategies. Her father had always made alliances, done deals. But in the end, he had been betrayed. Cassie wondered if she was more like her mother, closed, remote, wanting to do things on her own. With Simon, her age and experience gave her an edge. "If it comes to the crunch, I'll support you," she told Jennifer.

"You'll cut and run," said Jennifer matter-of-factly. She looked at Cassie, assessing her. "You know, Cass, there's no-one who talks more about team work and the morality of business than you do." She paused. "It makes an interesting contrast to your actual modus operandi."

"I'm sorry you feel that way," said Cassie, "but I'm sure there's nothing for you to worry about." She added, "I don't think there's really much more for us to talk about on this one though."

"Up yours," said Jennifer, and walked out of the office.

Darcy roared with laughter when Cassie told him the story. "Up yours, Miz La Rosa. You people are fucking unbelievable. I mean, doesn't it worry you and this woman that you're behaving like this? The last time I took that sort of fight seriously was in kindergarten."

"Maybe that's because you've removed yourself from the real world," said Cassie. She liked the cut and thrust of their arguments.

"As would any sane person." Darcy picked up a prawn head and sucked it with relish. Cassie closed her eyes and tried to forgive him. "What I can't believe is that you take this shit seriously."

"It ultimately involves a lot of money," said Cassie.

"Oh, God!" Darcy laughed. "Well, that makes it dead serious then." He put his hands in an attitude of prayer and bowed his head. "I didn't realise it involved money."

They were sitting in the garden, sheltered by the hedge of honeysuckle. The small aluminium table wobbled unsteadily on the uneven lawn. Darcy poured more wine into the two plastic cups as the wind started coming through the hedge. He put the wine bottle on the newspaper wrappings and Cassie put her sweater around her shoulders. It seemed wonderful to her that she felt so much at home here, so much part of the strange little backyard. She peeled another prawn and dipped it into the chilli sauce.

"I like money!" she said passionately. "At the moment, I actually need it to look after my mother. But despite what you think, it's not the bottom line for me."

"What is?" said Darcy, leaning forward intently, suddenly serious.

It felt comforting to her that they could be different, and still be more united than most couples she knew. As a child, she'd longed for her parents to be more similar, to share more. But the problem hadn't been their differences. Cassie saw now that it had been their mutual intolerance of the difference. Her mother had wanted to make her father into a handsome and slightly exotic English gentleman, matching or exceeding her own genteel country background. Her father had wanted to make her mother into a small, delicate but impassioned Italian woman. As a child, she had wanted to modify both of them, to bring them together. But they both stayed stuck in their positions, set against each other.

"The bottom line is a sort of game, an inter-action, a contest with other people. Sometimes, it gets too serious, but if you can take it as a game, it's fine." She reminded herself that she needed to remember the game-like aspects of corporate life. "The corporation provides a structure – for that element of human nature to play out in. And to produce things at the same time," she explained, "in case you're worried about the social good."

He was delighted with her argument. "And some people really get to screw other people?"

"It's not particular to corporations," she told him. "Look at us."

"True," said Darcy, stroking her leg. "Such a lot of human energy goes into being truly awful to other people. The time and energy we all spent on petty hatreds, thinking up cutting remarks, crime, wars, hating billions and billions of other people whom you've never even met. Staggering. The whole sum, the extent, the sheer ferocity of being horrible. Staggering. Good is just a mosquito bite in comparison."

They left the glasses and the newspaper in the sudden summer rain and went up the wooden stairs to the upstairs room. One half of the room was his workshop. Cassie liked to make love surrounded by the smell of wood shavings and varnish. She sometimes thought of her primness with Phillip, her lack of knowledge, her lack of discrimination. Now, she liked the movement and sense of her own body, alone and with Darcy's. She loved to hear his sigh of longing for her, hers for him. She loved to touch and caress every part of his body, to explore with a ferocity which amazed her. She had orgasms which left her shivering with pleasure, that involved every fibre of her body, which bound her to him. It wasn't that he was a better lover, but that they were, in reality, lovers.

In only one respect did they differ. "I'm all over the place," she told him. "It's like blowing a flute. I reverberate, it shudders through me, emotionally and physically, for days after. Sometimes, I have to let it quieten."

"Bad simile," he said. "Flutes shudder and reverberate, and you keep playing anyway. Adds to the richness of the tone." He leaned over and caressed her breast. "But I take your point."

She had begun to see they shared an ideological undercurrent – an anarchistic sense of life having no great or defined purpose, but itself a force that required search and pursuit, questing and pondering. She had attempted to answer the questions by finding rules, he, by eschewing all rules.

Invariably, Cassie woke early in the mornings, while Darcy still slept. When their relationship began, in winter, the mulberry tree had been bare of leaves. Then she could see right out into the bay, and make out the fishing boats returning in the semi-darkness. She loved to watch the sun lighting up the bay, its surface disturbed by birds diving for food. As the weather warmed, the leaves on the mulberry tree unfolded pale green, gradually thickening to a dense blanket, so there were only tiny glimpses of the bay. She still sat and watched the day begin, Darcy asleep beside her. She looked at him and then lay back, gazing up through the mulberry leaves to the eggshell blue of the sky.

Darcy opened his eyes and looked up at her. "Whitebait fritters, maple syrup pancakes or love?" he asked.

"Pancakes," she said. "Lemon and sugar."

"I love you," he said and pulled her under the blankets. She realised that it was the first time he had said it to her. And that he was embarrassed.

Chapter 14

The Korean baths seemed hotter than usual and the air was thick with steam, mixed with the smell of the massage oils, soaps and creams. Pink and sweat-soaked, Anthea and Cassie sat naked in the spa.

"Mike wants to move in," announced Anthea.

"Do you want him to?" asked Cassie. "Is it too soon?"

"If it's not soon, it'll be too late," said Anthea. She wriggled, as a jet of water played into the small of her back.

"I thought you were crazy about each other," said Cassie. She got out and rubbed herself with a towel and sat on the edge of the spa. "He seems really nice."

"He is. It's part of the problem. Too bland for me, maybe."

"He didn't seem bland."

"Maybe he's not." Anthea shrugged impatiently. "There are a lot of things to consider. I mean if we were living together, would I still come here with you every Thursday night? Or, would I stay home with him and watch the new 'Seinfeld' and the 'Ab Fab' repeats?"

"I don't know," said Cassie impatiently. "Is that really the big question?"

"No," said Anthea. "That doesn't matter."

"What does?"

"When I met him, it was madly, deeply, almost first sight."

"I remember."

"He felt like that too."

"It hasn't lasted?"

"About five minutes. Well, a few weeks. Little things annoy me. He thinks my job is okay but he can't understand why I don't work at a private school. He thinks westies are fundamentally different from people who live in Balmain." She smiled at Cassie. "Your sort of reactionary social views."

"You and I get along okay. Even though we disagree about loads of things."

"Yes, and I don't know why we are such friends. Maybe because we accept each other. Maybe because we've known each other a long time. Maybe because we're women."

"Mike is a nice guy. You're not really thinking of ending it with him, are you?"

Anthea sighed. "Yes I am. But for once, I'm thinking about it before I do. Because for years I've gone round wanting this very thing, hoping for it, telling myself not to be too choosy and generally teaming up with men who were hopeless jokes. And now, I've got one who's serious, who's ninety per cent right, and I'm quibbling about the other ten per cent. Except, it really does niggle me."

"You won't change him."

"I know. So I've got this strange dilemma between Mr Ninety Per Cent and nothing. Your sister is a contrast to us – I'd guess she had about fifty per cent of what she really wants. And now, she thinks this separation was a mistake. Poor Susan."

Cassie gave a sigh of exasperation at Susan's name.

"Maybe I'll grow to love him. Remember that hideous cat I got fond of. And I hate cats in principle. At least I like men."

"Have you told him?"

"Don't be crazy. Not a time for baring the soul. Do you feel anything like this about Darcy?"

Cassie thought, and then smiled at Anthea. "Before, I've always wanted someone I could

253

agree with, who was like me. But Darcy and I are very different. And happy about it."

Anthea got to her feet, wrapped the towel around her head and stood straight and naked. "You and I are magnificent women. And Darcy knows just how magnificent you are. I've seen the adoration in his eyes."

"That's different from love," said Cassie. But he had said he loved her. Once.

"We have to medicate your mother more heavily now," said the Matron, "otherwise she wanders off down the bush and hurts herself. It's not very nice, you know."

"What do you mean, 'not nice'?" asked Cassie, aware of disturbing possibilities, remembering the cut on her mother's inner thigh.

"In this form of dementia, people aren't always themselves," Matron said primly.

"What exactly does she do?"

The Matron looked at Cassie directly. "She mutters about her boy down in the bushes. She giggles and yells and screams gibberish. I don't know what she does down there, but she's done this injury on the inner thigh again." Cassie realised that the Matron was watching her for a reaction. "People read all sorts of things into these happenings. But I'm sure you understand that her mind has been deteriorating. Inhibitory mechanisms no longer work. Other parts perhaps stimulated. This behaviour has no particular relationship to the person your mother was."

Cassie looked down at her mother. Her eyes were closed, but her hands clutched at the blanket. Her face, in Cassie's memory always a mask to the world, characteristically expressing a quiet, polite concern, now looked deeply aroused, flushed, full of fleeting thoughts and feelings. Small sighs and moans escaped her. A lifetime of enforced politeness was falling away. The struggle to be and feel something else was happening, but too late, too unstructured, dissipating into nothingness, except the embarrassment of those around her. Cassie felt a reverberation in her own mind, the parts she had restrained, the feeling, sensual parts of her.

"What now?"

"We'll transfer her into the nursing home section," said the Matron. "It's in the building with the wisteria on the right as you come in. The Wisteria Home."

"Is she dying?" asked Cassie bluntly. She felt cold with fear.

She saw the look of affront on the Matron's face. "Physically, she's very strong. Dementia lowers life expectancy, but it's not life-threatening. She's only in her seventies."

"So if she got over what's troubling her, this distress, this restlessness, could she go back to her unit?" Cassie was thinking out loud. Each new stage of the illness unsettled her. She longed for some retreat from the relentless progress of the disease.

"She's been borderline for semi-independent living over the last few months. Hopefully, we'll get her off the medication, or stabilise her at a lower level, but she'll deteriorate in other ways."

"You'll arrange the sale of the unit?"

"We've got a buyer. In fact, there's the question of the furniture your mother brought with her . . . if you could perhaps think about what you'd like to do with it?"

Cassie nodded. She wondered whether she should kiss her mother before leaving. She looked unkissable, but the Matron, standing there, seemed to demand it. She took her mother's hand from the blanket and, suddenly, her mother reached out and clasped her. As Cassie pulled away, terrified, her mother made small animal groaning noises.

"I'll be off," Cassie said, and fled.

She drove to Susan's house. Susan opened the door, her long hair piled up on top of her head. She was wearing shorts and a tight-fitting T-shirt. Cassie had wanted Susan to get her life together, but the change in her was unsettling.

She wondered whether she was jealous of Susan, or whether she was still afraid of any dramatic change in her sister.

"I want to talk about Mum."

Susan raised her eyebrows with an "about time" expression. "Come in," she said. "Nick's taken the kids for the day. I'm studying, but I was just about to have a coffee break."

Cassie followed her into the kitchen. There were no piles of dishes, no mess of kids' toys. The computer was on the kitchen table, a pile of books beside it.

"What are you doing?" she asked, wondering how Susan had become so tidy, so organised and so together. Despite herself, she was impressed.

"I bought myself this accountancy package," said Susan calmly. "I'm transferring Nick's accounts to this new system and developing a business plan. It's only theoretical, of course," she added. "Just to learn."

"That's great," said Cassie, sitting down. "I've got some books I could lend you." It was out before she saw the look on Susan's face.

"Anthea found me some books," said Susan smugly. "She's been great."

"Good. I'm glad." Cassie felt jealous. Anthea was her friend, not Susan's.

"So how's the separation going?" asked Cassie. "Do you think it's permanent?"

"Don't know," said Susan.

"Don't know? Aren't you being a bit sanguine? Considering that apart from you, there are the kids."

Susan set two mugs down on the table and poured the coffee. "I don't want to talk about my marriage. You don't know the answer, I don't know the answer, Nick doesn't know the answer."

"I do think communication might have something to do with it. Or rather the lack of communication."

Susan burned, silent for a moment, then took a deep breath. "I read those books you gave me. Or some of them. Bits of them. They talk about active listening. About not patronising people. About . . ." She paused and looked at Cassie sardonically. ". . . About empowering people to deal with their own problems, which most of them are perfectly capable of doing. I think you should read the books before you foist them on me."

Cassie reddened. "I only gave them to you to try to help," she said. "I actually came about Mum."

Susan sighed and moved the mouse round the table. "So, you've been to see her?"

"I've been seeing a lot of her," she said, aware that Susan already knew. "But she's got much worse."

"Well, I'm back on deck now. So it's okay. You can get back to work." She clicked impatiently on the mouse.

"I'll keep seeing her," said Cassie. "I'm trying to do the right thing and not feel guilty about what I don't do, because there's no point in that. I find it really hard balancing all this – what's right and what's wrong, what's appropriate and what's not. I don't know what the right thing to do is with someone losing their mind. I can't guess what she thinks and feels and experiences. I'd rather be dead than lose touch with the world like that."

"Babies are like that," said Susan. "At a very basic level. That's how I think about it. They go forward, not backwards. But that's the only difference."

"Look," Cassie said, "I just don't find it that easy. I agonise over it a lot." She was silent then as they both sipped their coffee. "Maybe we should stick to the practicalities. I came over to tell you that they have to move her to the nursing home section – the Wisteria Home."

"I know she has to move," said Susan, getting up from the computer, "but I want to move her to the Sisters of Poverty, down at the end of Randle Street."

"The Sisters of Poverty?" There was a shudder in Cassie's voice.

"Where she should have gone in the first place. Or come to me!" said Susan indignantly, all her energy directed at Cassie. "Then maybe none of this would have happened. That bloody garden mausoleum out in the middle of nowhere. Any sane person would lose their mind." Tears came to Susan's eyes. "I want her back here. I asked them. They can take her when they've got a vacancy."

"The Wisteria Home is the best nursing home facility in Sydney."

"Sure! Send you mad in comfort and style. I should never have let it happen."

"It's a disease. It's nothing they did."

"She hated that place. She hated it when you took her there. You seem to specialise in taking decaying parents off to harebrained places. Did you ever think that Dad saying he wanted to go to Italy to die was just another stab at Mum? That, in the end, he might have been better off here? Or that the Sisters of Poverty – I know it's an embarrassing name, but maybe it would have been great for Mum to have me there every day, and she could have come to us for meals and at least had some sort of life. You're so full of solutions, Cass, you never see the problems. Or that the solution might be something else, like actually taking care of her."

"I took care of the money," she said. "And the arrangements."

"And I never got to have a say because I had no money," said Susan.

"It wasn't that; it got to a crisis point so quickly." Cassie was weary. She looked at her sister. "If you want to move her to Sisters of Poverty, that's okay. Do you want me to organise it?"

"They're letting me know when they have a bed," said Susan sharply.

"How are the kids?"

"Elin's a mess. The other two are okay."

"Is Elin . . . because of you and Nick?"

"She hates it. Poor babe."

"So how do you handle it?"

"I let her cry, and wet her bed and sleep with me and be upset. I let Nonna gossip to her and Nick and I tell her things. She's confused and it's too much for her." Susan's voice rose. "But I've got this new idea that you don't talk people out of things." She looked angrily at Cassie. "You don't find solutions and rationalise them, and hide little truths. You just let them be."

Cassie was shaken by Susan's outburst. There were things that Susan, as the younger sister, hadn't known about their father. Things even their mother hadn't known, hadn't wanted to know. But there was a sharp truth in what she had said. He had taunted them all with going back to Italy, played with it, dangled it in front of them, until Cassie had bought the tickets and made him go. She began to wonder now if she had done the same with their mother, organising the sale of the mountain house, buying the retirement unit, installing her there and trying to bury the distress. She *had* lectured Susan on her marriage, nagging her to use all the communication devices that she failed to use on Susan. Cassie wasn't used to being so wrong.

Her life seemed so unsettled and fluid that her ways of coping and managing were in danger of disintegrating. At times, Darcy felt like part of the disintegration. It was as if he had drawn her into a dream world, a world like Susan's, of disorganisation, where lines and boundaries were unclear. It had changed her, until she could no longer quite recapture her old self. After her conversation with Susan, she wanted to retreat into her own space, to feel a separate person.

"I need a week off," she said when she rang Darcy. "I have to prepare my presentation and work on any contingencies for the restructure." She was confident Julian would accept her plan to integrate Information Services and Research, whatever he did with the Promotions Department and New Products. "So I can't see you this week or next weekend."

"Sure," said Darcy sarcastically. "I wouldn't want our sex life to interfere with presentations and restructuring at good ol' DMC."

"It's important to me."

"I know," he said reasonably. "But I could come for a night."

"I don't think so."

"You're locked in. I can hear it in your voice. Something's happened."

"I had a blow-up with my sister. And things are happening with my mother. I'm over-extended."

"Maybe I could unwind you?"

"Darcy, when we started this relationship, do you remember the things I was worried about?"

Darcy sighed. "Yeah . . ."

"I wanted things defined, to know where we both stood –"

"*I'm* standing here next to the phone."

"They are serious things. To me." Cassie had wanted to tell him exactly what had happened with Susan, but she thought he would take Susan's side and not understand how painful it was for her.

"That's the problem," he said. "That they are so serious."

263

"Problem?" She felt a stab of fear and irritation.

"Defining and structuring and deciding where we stand. We've had such a good time the last few months because things have been undefined, unstructured –"

"We've had a good time being in love."

"That too." He laughed, dismissing the word "love".

"Darcy, I need this week."

"Okay," he said. "Have it. I'll get on with thinking about my exhibition."

She sighed with exasperation. She hated this fantasy, this lie about the exhibition. He had even admitted that he hadn't made a single piece. "Do that," she said. "Think about it."

She suffered sexual frustration, sexual need. She could feel it, setting alive every part of her. She imagined his hands caressing her, hers caressing him, a blush of a remembered orgasm rising to her face. She pushed it aside relentlessly in a determination to finish and polish the Asia project. She rallied and bullied her staff. She avoided Tim Bayliss and John Anderson.

She smiled at Jennifer in the lift. "After the presentation," she said, "we'll all have lunch. I've heard Julian thinks Simon has done an excellent job."

"Yes," said Jennifer stiffly.

"If I can help," said Cassie, "let me know." She had done a mind map and a self-analysis questionnaire after her discussion with Susan. She had realised Jennifer would regard her invitation as insincere, but she made it anyway.

At first, she was furious with Simon for being in Melbourne, but then she decided that, as the presentation was virtually complete, it was probably better. It put him more in the position of a protégé, rather than a colleague.

"I really need my six-monthly review," Denise reminded her. "I thought –"

"I thought I would have had time too," said Cassie apologetically.

"It's been ten months," replied Denise. "Twelve for most of the staff."

"I'm sorry. I'll prioritise time for all reviews straight after the presentation," said Cassie. "It's the best I can do."

"Everyone's talking restructure," Denise said. "I'm going to be at a disadvantage if I haven't been reviewed."

Cassie felt a sudden guilt over all the time she had spent with Darcy. Late staff reviews were bad management on her part. "Has there been talk?"

"There's talk all the time."

"You don't need to worry." She hesitated, wondering how much to tell Denise about the restructure. "I'm seeing Julian again this week."

"He's not seeing anyone."

Cassie felt defeated. She tried to smile at Denise. "Don't worry about things. It'll be okay." She went into her office, wondering if she was trying to reassure herself or Denise.

"You look terrible, Cass," said Anthea. "Like I feel."

"I'm tired. I'll be okay after this presentation." They sat on Anthea's balcony in the late afternoon, watching the weekend sailors coming back to their moorings in the bay.

"Darcy?" said Anthea tentatively.

Cassie sighed. "I'm not seeing him this week, because I have to do this work." She looked out to the harbour. "I've never needed anyone so much, and I've never known two people as incompatible as me and him."

"Incompatible? You were telling me how well you got on –"

"He doesn't believe in time management." She looked at Anthea's dubious expression and smiled. "Okay, I know it sounds crazy, but could you live with someone who takes an hour to eat breakfast and believes in siestas? I mean, really. What are the long-term options? I live in the city and he lives in the tree house?"

"Maybe that's the way you'd have to do it."

"He's got this fantasy about having an exhibition."

"How do you know it's a fantasy?"

"He's been thinking about it for years – getting his courage up and his ideas together."

"Some things do take years," said Anthea. "Look at Susan. Just beginning to grow up."

"Under your expert guidance."

"Do I detect . . . ?" said Anthea.

"I know it's irrational," said Cassie, "but it complicates things."

Anthea laughed. "You actually sound like her right now." She leaned over and hugged Cassie. "Sisters and friends don't really mix. It's intriguing for me to get to know Susan. I see things about you I didn't know. But even though I like Susan, we don't have a lot in common."

Cassie felt a surge of relief. "It seems childish being jealous of your sister."

"We're all childish now and then, thank God," said Anthea. "You and I have a very long history." She sat down again. "Now tell me about Darcy."

"Maybe all this uncertainty started before him, but he certainly didn't help. Sometimes, I'm not sure I even see the point of my job any more."

"I've never seen it," said Anthea.

"I know," said Cassie impatiently, "but it matters more when I don't."

"What would you do instead?" asked Anthea.

"It's just a phase," said Cassie. "Maybe it's good I'm not so single-minded. But you certainly don't just throw away a hundred grand a year."

That night, Cassie lay in bed, the curtains drawn, encased in the comfort of the flat. Outside, the rain was falling. She could hear it on the roof, but it sounded different from the rain falling on a house, where it could not only be heard on the roof, but on the ground, on bricks, on grass, on the tin shed. At Darcy's she could hear the sound of the rain on the leaves of the mulberry tree, soaking into the grass. She felt a pang of longing for Darcy. Arms in the night, as Anthea always used to say. A warm bum. Until now, Cassie had always got what she wanted. Or maybe, she'd made it her business to want what she could get, careful not to want beyond that. When they were children, she had been the one who made do with what there was. Susan was the one who wanted, who pushed and took, fought and screamed and finally collapsed with wanting. Susan, who was never content, with Nick or herself or the children. Susan who had never been contained. The disorganisation of it appalled Cassie. Now her own wanting was coming out.

Darcy was still unknown. Unknown in how much he loved her, why he loved her, how much he would sacrifice. She shut her eyes and tried to run the presentation through her head in preparation for the morning.

Chapter 15

The map was in her head – the route down William Street, then along George to the laneway where she turned into the underground carpark, the walk to the lift, reception on her floor with its black marble, the spiky bird of paradise floral arrangement, the company logo etched into the brass behind the receptionist. She stopped in her office, took the final presentation out of her briefcase and walked down the corridor to the conference room. Cassie felt a quiet confidence. It was simple, straightforward. The presentation, then a discussion of the restructuring options.

She pushed the heavy door of the conference room and was surprised to see that everyone was already there, except Julian. The chatter stopped. Eyes avoided hers. The greetings were small and guarded. People moved uneasily on their chairs. She looked around the room and positioned her chair so she could use the overhead projector. Simon had taken a seat on the other side of the table and made no move to sit next to her. Something had happened, but it was too late to do anything. Her heart started pounding.

"Enjoy Melbourne?" Cassie asked Simon, determined to keep her voice from shaking.

"Got a lot done," he answered coolly.

Jennifer drummed long nails on the table. They heard Julian coming along the corridor, barking instructions to his assistant. He came in quickly, put his folder on the desk and sat down.

"Roll it, Cass," he said, not looking at her. "We've got a lot to cover."

Something had clearly been decided without her and Cassie wondered how she could do the presentation. The restructure had gone against her. The palace coup had taken place. They knew and she didn't. She could feel her stomach churning.

Jump or be pushed, she thought. Somewhere, she had made a grave miscalculation. She thought of Jennifer's luncheon invitations. Maybe it was Jennifer who had done her over. She couldn't let it rattle her. A weak presentation would leave her more vulnerable. The report had all the facts and figures. She could perhaps salvage something in terms of credibility and courage. Some old sense of fight surged through her.

"Okay," she said. "Everyone has the summary document, so I'm expanding on the main recommendations in it and looking at ways of implementing them." She looked at Simon and smiled. "As most of you know, Simon has been working very hard on this report. I'm sure he's kept at least some of you in touch with our major conclusions." The sarcasm was for Simon, but he showed no reaction.

The presentation took almost forty minutes. She did it without a hitch. It was probably a useless exercise, but she was proud of herself. They all watched her with admiration, not for its contents, but for her cool. She finished, to polite but muted applause, and sat down.

Julian leaned back in his chair and surveyed the table, his eyes languidly half closed. There was a complete silence as everyone waited for him to speak.

"There's a positive slant in a lot of the material Cassie has presented," he said. "Good detail. But it isn't really up for debate." He sat up. "What is important is what we come up with when we compare these possibilities with a straight export strategy. In that context, setting up in Asia doesn't offer us a lot." He turned his back on Cassie and faced the others. "Instead, we'll be aggressively pushing some export targets that Simon has been exploring. What he's got is very forward looking, very exciting. Simon will give you the full report next week."

Cassie's head spun. She hadn't expected it to be this explicit. Simon had done it in Melbourne, setting it up earlier, perhaps cutting her out when she'd refused him. The dinner, the proposition, had been part of a power play, under the guise that he was the new boy. She'd bought him – hook, line and sinker. She had only herself to blame.

"The export possibilities are considered in my appendix," Cassie protested. "They are actually the baseline of this report, because we believed we could do better by setting up there. Which is what my figures, also worked on by Simon, actually show."

"Yes, but Simon looked at new possibilities, not just the figures we had," Julian answered.

She knew it was useless, that she was doomed, but she refused to back down. "Simon was working under my direction here. As head of Research, I should have been overseeing those figures."

Julian took off his glasses and glanced back at her. "Technically, yes. But there were a couple of meetings you missed where it came up." Cassie thought of the useless, hopeless visits to her mother. But she would have been shafted anyway. Simon was the new favourite. "But yes," Julian added vaguely, "I don't know why that didn't happen." He made it sound as if it was her fault. "Of course, I wanted to keep them confidential, because there are some very exciting possibilities here. Sorry, Cass." Conciliation to the vanquished, she thought as Julian turned back to the others.

"Simon will now be heading the Information Services Department which will take in parts of the current Research Department," Julian went on. "The whole area will be overseen by John Anderson. That will give us the management expertise and link Research to New Products, which will become entirely John's responsibility. And we're devolving Policy into something bigger, with the Policy Unit headed by Tim Bayliss. Jennifer stays with Promotions, of course, which will integrate most of the Legal Services people. The whole thing's a lot more dynamic. We get considerable savings in downsizing plus improvements in efficiency."

Cassie was waiting for her name. Julian reached over and poured himself a glass of water. "We're also devolving a lot of the basic research interstate. Cassie will be in charge of co-ordinating the results from these state bureaux. That's it folks." Julian rose hurriedly and left the room.

Cassie made a quick calculation. John Anderson, until now always Bayliss's shadow, had engineered this. She'd overlooked him as a shaker and mover. In her mind the danger had been Tim, but Tim had been dead wood. In a year, Tim Bayliss would be fishing on the Gold Coast. Simon had done the deal with John. Simon got up, collected his papers and made his way to her side of the table. "No hard feelings, I hope."

She didn't answer and he went out. She felt revolted by him, his dishonesty, his sleaziness. She felt angry with herself for ignoring these aspects of him, for not trusting her gut feeling.

Tim Bayliss and John Anderson left, amicably ignoring Tim's defeat. Probably, thought Cassie, Tim had sold out for the promise of a very large retrenchment package. Cassie, wanting desperately to be alone, waited for Jennifer to leave, but Jennifer sat, looking at her across the table.

"You still don't know why this happened, do you?" asked Jennifer.

"I should never have trusted Simon." She felt intensely humiliated. Bitterness swept over her at the unfairness of it. Her spectacular fall from grace would be gossiped about and analysed for weeks to come. The last thing she wanted was consolation from Jennifer.

"Simon wasn't your problem," said Jennifer. "The world is full of creeps like Simon. Let me tell you something. You probably don't remember when you and I started here and my Danielle was just a baby. I was half mad with not knowing how to handle the job and the kid, and the bastard husband who walked with the property settlement. That woman Margot, who is the accountant over at Florentas now, took me along to a support group for women in business. They were so wonderful that I asked you to come along. You turned your nose up."

"I don't see what it's got to do with this."

"It's got bloody everything, Cass." Jennifer strode over and shut the door. "And I want you to listen. I don't know if you'll take any notice. But listen, will you?"

Learn from the opposition. It was taped to the inside of her desk. "I'll listen."

"When you came here, you looked at the people at the top, you looked at how they operated, and you decided to be one of them with a bit of female charm thrown in. And you never thought about what they were doing, if it was good or bad or whether they might be complete arseholes."

"Look," protested Cassie, "I know. We talked about Bayliss and Anderson. And you warned me about Simon."

"Did he try his 'C word' line on you?" Cassie winced at Jennifer's directness.

"Okay, but he didn't tell you about his own big C word, did he? She's called Lizelle and she's out there in the suburbs with his wedding ring and his baby. That's what I call basic research, not all your facts and figures."

Cassie felt as if she'd been slapped, but Jennifer continued. "You could see that what Bayliss does has a limited future. You went beyond the Bayliss game. You hooked your wagon to this corporate crap, the soul of the company, the good of the whole – as long as you were at the top of the heap. You've played by their rules, even if you can't quite stomach playing their game. And you shut out people and experiences and all the stuff which women are so good at. You couldn't see or understand what a creep that Simon is."

Jennifer looked at Cassie, exasperated. "You ignore people, Cass. You don't even know that your Denise is wetting her pants to work for me because I talk to her like a human being. And that your staff have come begging to me to get you to do their evaluations. They know you remember their names and their birthdays, because you've got a reminder system on your computer. But they know you don't give a shit about anyone's career except your own." She came over and put a hand on Cassie's shoulder. "Go home. Have a nervous breakdown. Find out who you are. And if you ever forgive me for saying all this, ring me. For Christ's sake."

As Jennifer left, Cassie could feel a muscle spasm, clenching her stomach. Tears came to her eyes, the harshness of Jennifer's words ricocheting round her head. She took a deep breath and looked at the booking sheet. There was another meeting in fifteen minutes. She lifted the phone and dialled Julian's number. There was enough despair in her to collapse her completely, but she was determined to say what she felt to Julian.

"Why did you let me do the presentation, when it was all decided?" she demanded.

"The room was booked."

"Very droll. You wanted to see me humiliated. I don't know what you've got against me, but I didn't deserve that. I've always been loyal to you."

"Cass, you're upset, imagining things."

"So, are you serious about this research for the other states?" she asked sarcastically.

"Are you?" he countered. She could imagine his smirk.

"No. Of course not. I'm resigning."

"I could make a few phone calls on your behalf." Julian's tone was conciliatory. "I mean, this is just one of those things. Part of the general downsizing we're involved in. Nothing personal. You always go by the rule book, Cass.

You've got a good head, but it gets a bit deadly. And you let things slide with your staff. Always leaves you wide open."

It had enough truth to sting. She'd done some great things for the company, which would now be forgotten. The Asia project had been excellent.

"Do you want me to ring round? See what's going? Sound out a few people?" Julian seemed more like himself, but she was too angry to respond to his human side.

"You were wrong about export being an alternative. There's no comparison," she said. "And you're wrong about letting the Asia project slide. It was one of the best pieces of research I've presented."

"Maybe, maybe not," he said coolly. "I've got another meeting, Cass, so just tell me if you want me to call in a few favours on your behalf."

If she accepted his offer, she'd have a job in a week, but she'd be indebted to him forever. She hated the hypocrisy, the shuffling of discarded or burnt-out executives. She'd do something else, find another life. She had a sudden image of herself, alone, in the mountain house, running through the lawn of daisies to the big row of pines at the bottom of the garden. Then lying under them, looking at the sky. It must have been when she was four, just before Susan was born. She'd been there alone with her father, without the constraints of her mother. She remembered sitting in the pine needles, the wind whispering above her, the smell of pine, the red tips on the leaves of the eucalypts in the bush beyond, the late afternoon call of the currawongs. She had felt specially and distinctly herself.

"I don't think so, Julian."

"You're asking for a redundancy package?"

"Yes, if you can . . ." she stuttered. The idea of money caught her by surprise, a sudden panic. What would she live on? How could she pay the mortgages? Pay for her mother?

"I could swing something for you. Not enormous. Come back to me in a week."

Mechanically, she walked down to her office and collected her things. She attempted to log on, to send an e-mail to all her staff thanking them, but her password had already been changed. She took some company letterhead. She'd write from home, do good references. She felt a stab of guilt about Denise, but Denise had almost certainly done better in the restructure than she had. She went out of her office. Denise wasn't there. She looked round. All her staff except the most junior had gone, presumably to be redeployed. She'd seen this happen to others and had never imagined it could happen to her. At least there wasn't a security person there to escort her from the building.

She couldn't face the lift and she walked down the fire stairs to the basement. Her car was still there. All that meant was that it would be part of her settlement. She got in and drove home, and entered the flat. For a moment she was disoriented by the brightness of the midday sun shining in the windows. She rarely saw the flat at this time of day.

Her mind was whirling. She hadn't deserved this, not all of it, but she had always said that corporate life was not fair. Her anger was dissipating into despair, feeling the shame, the humiliation of it, wondering what she would and could do. Darcy. She had to ring him.

She noticed there was a message on her machine and pressed the play button.

"Cass, I've gone coastal, which is a bit like feral but wetter. I thought I'd give you some space. I'll ring you when I get back in a few weeks. Bye, my sweet other." She started to sob, wondering if she would still be his other.

She sat, staring out at the harbour, unable even to ring Anthea. She needed to collect herself first. She knew Anthea's sympathy would be tainted by her distaste for Cassie's job. Normally, it wouldn't have mattered, but at the moment she felt hypersensitive, stripped of every defence.

Her job had defined her as a person. A success. Wealthy. Privileged. Woman in a man's world. Somebody. The sting and the shame of Jennifer's remarks stayed with her. She could never ring her now, despite the fact that there had been genuine friendship and truth in what Jennifer had said to her; a truth that extended back into her earliest memories of herself. But they were truths so much part of her that she had no idea how to be different. She had always taken the rules and obeyed them, but she had never seen before how much her solitude had blinded her to other people and situations.

She had been sitting for more than an hour, when the phone rang and she picked it up automatically. It was Susan. Wearily, she explained what had happened. "Don't worry," Susan said airily. "You'll get another job, Cass. And you won't have to pay for Mum. They moved her today."

"What do you mean?"

"Sisters of Poverty. A bed came up."

"You moved her from Wisteria House? To there?"

"I told you I was going to. I know you didn't think I would."

Cassie had a horrible picture of the nursing home, the giant fibreglass figure of madonna and child next to the entrance of the red brick complex. She remembered the grey linoleum corridors, the smell of reheated food, the vacant stares from the rows of beds. But she felt resigned in the face of Susan's triumph, and a guilty relief that it was no longer her responsibility.

"I hope they look after her properly."

"They're taking her off all the drugs. The sister told me she doesn't need all that medication."

"We'll see." Susan had chosen this. It was now up to her. At the same time, it hurt that Susan didn't notice her distress.

"I'll be able to visit her in the mornings, after I drop Elin at school," Susan went on enthusiastically. "They've even got a little child-minding centre. Not like that bloody mausoleum."

Cassie ignored the dig and made one of her own. "I thought you couldn't leave Jack."

Susan laughed. "Actually, it was Jack who couldn't leave me. He's come into his own. I study while he sleeps. And he loves the sandpit. I can clean up the house while he plays there. It's amazing. He and Kelly play together better too. Different boy." She paused. "You sound upset. I guess you're pretty devastated about the job."

"I am. Very."

"I'm sorry," said Susan, "but you'll get another. For sure."

Cassie wished Susan had been more understanding. But perhaps Susan really did believe that Cassie could cope with anything. After all, Cassie had never given her any indication that she couldn't.

After the phone call she felt a sudden claustrophobia, a need for open space. Without changing, she went down to the carpark and drove out. Not thinking of where she was going, she found herself on the road to the northern beaches where she used to go with her father. He had been frightened of the big seas, but at the same time convinced of the health benefits of salt water, and he taught her to swim in one of the sea-water pools. She couldn't remember which one it had been, but the moment she arrived there, she recognised it. Her eyes filled with tears again, recalling her father's indulgence, his pleasure in her, his delight in her pleasure when she had dogpaddled across the pool for the first time. Then, it had been crowded with children, the hot summer wind bringing whiffs of coconut oil. Now, the pool was deserted. She walked down the concrete concourse and then took off her shoes and walked along the narrow edge of the pool. She looked out at the sea, the waves crashing dangerously close.

But the danger gave her a sudden sense of freedom. If she had stayed with DMC Dolan, she would never have been able to do the things she had been putting off – working on the garden, seriously doing a course, changing things in herself. Perhaps this would even remove some of the strains in her relationship with Darcy. The hurt, the humiliation, the despair were still there, but she felt more her father's daughter, discovering his love of life, his pleasure in simplicity.

She drove back to the flat and rang Anthea, who was on a school excursion, not due back till late. Cassie left a message and, still restless, went out for a walk. When she returned there was a message from Anthea. "Hey, Anthea here. Come to dinner at the Fish Cafe. Eight o'clock. I've got something to tell you."

Anthea kissed her. "I've got something *big* to tell you," she announced, her face shining with happiness. "I'm pregnant. Ten weeks. It's the most amazing thing in the world. I thought I was menopausal because my periods had stopped, but I'm pregnant. I got the test results today. The baby is okay. Cass, I'm so happy."

Cassie felt a stab of envy, not at the pregnancy, but at the perfection of Anthea's happiness. "That's great. They've done all the tests? It's really okay?"

"It's really okay and it's a girl. I thought I might call her Rosa, after you."

"That would be wonderful." Cassie smiled at the idea. "When is she due? How does Mike feel?"

"Due at the end of May. And he's over the moon. About the baby, not so much about calling her Rosa." Anthea led the way into the restaurant and they found a table near the window. "We'll live together. Maybe even get married, although I can't really see the point. That's more his idea."

"And you don't feel, um, like you did about him before?"

Anthea rubbed her stomach. "I can't wait for her to show." She took a bite of the bread the waiter put down on the table. "I have thought about Mike. He's very romantic about it, but I'm being practical. With a baby, I'm sure I can make it work. We're good companions and I like him. Mostly. I think it is better for the baby, but if it's really a disaster, I'm sure he'd still be a good father. I want her to have two parents, not like me, growing up with no dad."

Anthea produced an ultrasound that looked like a black splodge on grey stripes. "Like an in utero school photo."

"It's fabulous," said Cassie. "What about your job?"

"I get three months paid maternity leave, plus up to a year not paid, plus long service. Because of my dates and holidays, it's nearly two years. But I'll eventually go back to teaching. Mike wanted me to resign and cash in my super, and use it to start a business for him. He promised me I'd never have to work again."

"That would be bigger than getting married."

"Exactly what I told him. He can't believe that I like teaching. I'd be crazy to stop, anyway. I'm in the old scheme for super. It's like owning a block of flats." Anthea paused and looked idly at the menu. "Let's have a curry. She caught the waiter's eye and ordered the curries. She smiled at Cassie. "You're not jealous are you?"

"Definitely not."

"Haven't you *ever* wanted babies?"

"Flashes, moments when I've imagined it. But when I think about it, no. Everybody assumes all women are baby hungry, but I'm really not. Lots of women aren't, even people who have them."

"Darcy?"

"Terrified of kids. The idea of his own, anyway."

"Odd," said Anthea. "Very odd. So what's your news?"

"I was fired." Her voice was deadpan, but she felt the hiccough in her throat as she said it. She tried to hold on to the sense of freedom she'd felt at the pool, but other feelings crowded in.

"Fired? You were fired? I can't believe that." People at adjoining tables looked round at Anthea's outburst, then turned away in embarrassment. Anthea put her hand over Cassie's and lowered her voice.

"Fired? I'm sorry. I can't believe it. Why on earth?"

"Palace coup. Reshuffle. Miscalculation on my part. Lots of things."

"You don't seem upset enough."

"I don't want to cry in a restaurant." But she could feel the tears. "My Asia project was good." She shrugged, trying to make light of it. "And I hate losing the money." She took a sip of her drink, and with a deep breath went on to tell Anthea what Jennifer Keen had said.

"Isn't it the kettle calling the pot black?" Anthea protested. "It would have had to be true of her too. If she'd got to your level."

"No," said Cassie tearfully. "It's something about me. Doing what I'm told. Rules and regulations. Set paths."

"Tunnel vision?" said Anthea sympathetically.

"Exactly. Except it is unfair because people *liked* me for that. I was bright, single-minded, got things done. But maybe it protected me from things in myself." She sighed. "I always had the illusion it was expanding me, but probably, it was just the opposite. When I'm not feeling upset, I'm angry that I wasted all that time."

"You're well out of it." Anthea took her hand off Cassie's. "Bastards. You can get another job, Cass. This won't blacklist you, will it?"

"I could get another corporate job. I'd have to go down the ladder a bit. But I think I need something different." She felt hollow as she said it. "I need to change."

"Stop trying so hard," said Anthea. "You're always improving yourself."

Susan sat next to her mother, who was asleep. Sitting here, tending her, gave her a feeling of peace in the same way that looking after her children as tiny babies had done. But it was intensified with her mother. There was a sense that, finally, she had pleased her mother. It had been a long journey. Throughout Susan's childhood, her mother had sung Cassie's praises, not directly comparing the sisters, but making her approval of Cassie clear, her disapproval of Susan just as clear. When Susan had married, her mother had been delighted, not with the choice of Nick, but with the arrival of babies. For the first time, Susan had seen a softer side to her mother.

"I wish I could have spoilt you and Cassie like this," her mother had told her, cuddling Kelly after she was born. "You weren't allowed to in those days."

Sometimes, it seemed to Susan that she was mirroring the form of her mother's life – no career, children, a home-maker, an Italian husband. Yet from an early age, she had vowed not to repeat her parents' mistakes. She had longed for love, warmth and harmony, with what she now recognised as a naive simplicity. These abstract visions, of herself and Nick, she now suspected of preventing her dealing with reality.

She took a notepad from her bag and began to write. She did a draft of the letter first, and then, with a sense of satisfaction, wrote her final copy in a neat and precise hand.

Dear Nick,

I want you home. The kids want you home. We all love you. You and I have a lot to work out, but I am sure we can do it.

However, before you step in the door, I have a few conditions.

1. Your Mama has been thoroughly horrible to me. There's no way she's ever going to accept it was as much your fault as mine, but I will not be forever cast as the scarlet woman. Tell her!

2. Your sister, my sister, your brothers. Call them off. Tell them the truth, or at least enough so they know you are as crazy as me. Okay, I wanted to leave, but it was you who walked out that door. You were as unhappy as me in this marriage. You refused to talk, and have made no attempt at reconciliation.

3. Admit these things to yourself. Forgive us both. I have, I think. Let us each try in our own way.

As you have seen, there have been some changes round the house. These seem to have simply happened – I've got thinner, I'm not food-obsessed, I'm fit, but I only do treadmill five times a week. I was on the point of going back to being neurotic about food, but instead, I've gone the other way, and in other areas of my life too.

I used to think you were having a relationship with Julie. Now, I don't think so. I used to be paranoid about the mothers at school. That's gone! It's because I am happier.

Why am I happier? Because I've spoken my mind to you and to my sister. With you, and with her, I've always felt like the kid and you were the grown-ups. Now, I feel equal.

I'm studying accountancy, as you know. I will eventually get a job, or start a business. I'd like your support. This isn't a condition. It's an ask.

Love, Susan.

She took a photo out of her bag. It was an old faded one from their honeymoon in Italy. She was wearing a pair of his shorts, baggy, tied around the waist with rope, and the briefest of bikini tops. He stood behind her, smiling at her. It made her sad, to look at them like that. They'd been so young, so hopeful that everything they had grown up with wouldn't affect them. Nick was determined to leave his parents' peasant poverty, their parents' sense of having lost their home, and his own fears and insecurities. She'd wanted to forget her feeling of being unloved, second best. She kissed the photo and slipped it into the envelope with the letter.

Chapter 16

With no job and Darcy away, for the first time in years Cassie had time.

Time to think about how her job came to an end.

Time to visit her mother, to feel the grief of her life, to witness Susan's motherly patience with her.

Time to wonder why she lacked Susan's patience.

Time to pick Elin up from school.

Time to shop for baby clothes with Anthea.

Time to feel the confusion of the corporate years.

Time to think about the garden.

Time to appreciate Darcy's sculptures.

Time to long for him to come back.

Time to worry about her future.

Time to realise that there was not one other person who would phone her.

She studied her books of Japanese prints. She studied line, design, colour and detail. She studied the people and the landscape. She wondered what lay beneath, what had been felt, what had been said. She wondered if this was the way Darcy saw art, that he could become as immersed in it as she had been in corporate life. She wondered idly if he, like her, lacked the skills for ordinary, everyday life.

She imagined how her life could be with Darcy. She imagined it more easily than she could imagine a new job or a new path in life, which worried her. But she could see, in her mind's eye, the two of them shopping together, going to a Tuesday night film, taking Elin and Kelly away for the weekend, having dinner with Anthea and Mike, waking up together, going to bed together, making love, having time.

She pulled herself away from the vision when it became too intense, and instead remembered snippets of her mother's life. In school holidays, when the mountains were full of holidaying families, her mother had developed innocent, curious friendships with people at picnic grounds and lookouts. When the time came for anything deeper or more significant, she withdrew – "not quite our sort" was her phrase of dismissal. Cassie remembered her own withdrawals as a child, at university, as a teacher, except for a while, when she had been drawn into Anthea's circle. Then, in business the withdrawal had seemed necessary, part of what had made her successful, but in the end with fatal corporate consequences. She wondered if she were capable of being different now.

She waited, suspended, until Darcy's return.

Darcy arrived early one morning, unannounced, excited, smelling of the sea.

"I went whale-watching. I got a commission from some conservation group. To record mothers and babies coming up the coast."

"Did you get that close?" she asked, when she saw his drawings, amazed at the detail, the sense of intimacy between the mothers and babies.

"Partly works of the imagination," he said. "Black shadows off the coast was all I saw a lot of the time. Luckily, I had a book of wonderful nineteenth-century drawings."

"Did you enjoy it?"

"Cold," he said, and hugging and kissing her. "And missied you. And afraid, having left you."

"Did you leave me," she asked uneasily, "or go see the whales?"

"No, no, no. I went to see the whales." He looked at her, smiling. "They offered me *money*." He hesitated. "I can use it to cast some pieces for the exhibition."

They drove to Kurnell and walked down to the beach and then sat beside the breakwater. The sand was damp, and the wind whistled at them through the stones. Cassie had been hoping that when he came back, the pieces of her life would fall into place again, that there would be an answer – an answer to what had happened, what should happen, an answer to life. Not that he would provide it, but his presence might stimulate it. He didn't even ask what had happened with her presentation and she kept putting off telling him about her job. She blamed him for not remembering, not acknowledging what was important to her. He seemed more like an ordinary man, not the magical mystical man who inhabited her fantasies.

"I got scared when I saw you lost your job," he said at last, as they lay on a dry spot of sand. "That's why I stayed away so long and didn't ring."

"You bastard! You knew, and you didn't ring! And you didn't even mention it till now!"

"Well, neither did you." But he looked apologetic. "I thought you'd be all caught up in grief and anger, and justification and fear. And then I'd get caught up in it too. I don't cope well with that sort of thing. So I did the most cowardly thing and stayed with the whales."

"I can't believe this. I was upset, really distressed. And because of that, you stayed away."

"At times, I really am the cowardly lion."

"How did you know I'd lost the job?" she asked angrily.

"*Sydney Morning Herald*. I read it for the Thursday film reviews. Sacking of Cassandra La Rosa caught my eye purely by chance. No, that's not true. I was missing you. I saw the DMC Dolan new Asia strategy and I thought it was you. Then reading between the lines, I saw you'd been given the boot. Panicked."

"I hate you, I really hate you." Cassie began to cry. "I needed you so much."

"That's what I was afraid of."

"Is this how it's going to be whenever I have a hard time? You're going to run away?"

"You ran away from me when you were having a hard time." He held up his hands. "Okay, you said you needed space and time. You put it better. But maybe you're not so different from me."

Cassie was silent.

"I am sorry, Cass. Really sorry. Forgive me."

She nodded and he put his arm round her as they started walking back to the house. "One of the whale watchers did a whale dance on every headland. Not a very good dance. I did a lovely little drawing of her, which was really a drawing of you. Dancing. Home free. My Cass."

In the morning, Cassie slept as the sun streamed into the upstairs room. She slept as power boats zoomed up and down the bay. She slept as a party of children on a school excursion climbed over the breakwater, in search of shells. She woke, to find Darcy watching her.

"Ten o'clock," he said, looking at his watch.

"Maybe some people live like this."

"You and me?"

"We could. I decided last night to sell my apartment."

"I like that. A woman who deals in real estate in the throes of passion."

"Post passion. A feeling of peace." She had been thinking of it since she lost her job. Even before, with the dream of moving up the mountains. But it was Darcy's return that decided her. "If I sell the apartment, I get rid of both mortgages, and have a little money over. I don't really have much choice, unless I rush back to a job in the corporate world. Or take out an enormous loan."

"Where will you live?"

"Here and there."

"*Here* and there? This here?"

"If I'm invited."

"Cass, I don't know."

She sensed resistance and felt a stab of disappointment. The dream she had built up when he was away wasn't going to happen. Suddenly, everything was more tenuous and fragile. Both of them, him and her, were too difficult, too prickly, too solitary. "I'm not moving in. Weekends, like I've been doing." She felt suddenly vulnerable, without a real base.

"What are you going to do? I mean with your time?"

"You don't need to panic about my leisure time. I won't bother you." She sat up. "I thought you were in favour of staying out of the rat race."

"I am. If you have an end. My end is art."

"No serious end for me," said Cassie. "Just being instead of doing."

"I see. Basking in Cassiness. Being Cassie. Going with a Cass flow."

"You don't have to be sarcastic."

"You could become alternative. Grow herbs."

The mountain house and its garden was in her mind, but she wasn't going to risk telling him her dreams now. "I thought this might happen. I'd stop being the other. The ice maiden. Make you feel threatened."

"I don't feel at all threatened," he said.

"Do you take me seriously?"

Darcy ran his fingers through his hair and looked at her intently. "My dear, you're always serious."

"Are you serious about me?"

"I'm serious," he said off-handedly. "But I don't want to go into that because we'll get back into your rules and regulations and the stupid fucking boundaries and constraints. And in no time you'll be down here bullying me with shoulder pads again, and the whole thing will go sour." His face was becoming impassioned. "You shouldn't have left that job!" His voice became plaintive. "I didn't mean that. It's just we've changed the focus here. I don't want to be a job substitute. I've a great need for freedom, Cass."

"So do I," she said. She tried to keep her voice reasonable as she got out of bed. New territory, she thought, feeling she'd had enough new territory. She pulled on her jeans and jumper. "Ring me when you want," she said, kissing him. "I'll be at the apartment." She was gratified that he looked as miserable and confused as she felt.

It was getting late and the cicadas were just starting to drum in the trees outside Anthea's flat. Anthea stroked her stomach. "I love it," she said. "It's begun to move. Just fluttering." She looked down. "Hey, baby. Your first Christmas."

"Do you get sick?"

"I did. A few times."

"Susan got sick all the time. But you could never tell with her because she had been bulimic and with Elin, she was terrified of getting fat."

"Is she okay?"

"Yes. She's waiting for Nick to make a move. Less drama than is usual for Susan. That accountancy program you suggested has really got her going. And visiting Mum. She likes doing that. I mean, she gets satisfaction out of it. I go, and I get screwed up. I can't do it the way she does."

"God, I couldn't either. I think you're both saints. Thank God my one remaining parent is hale and hearty and living in New Zealand."

"I suppose that's why Susan's got three kids and I never wanted any. Basic caring instincts. But then, she *is* more self-centred than me. I know most of what goes on in her life, but when I told her I'd lost my job, she didn't seem to understand that it actually mattered to me."

Anthea smiled to herself. Cassie and Susan were sometimes much more alike than either of them would have believed to be possible. "You doing okay? Apart from the sister hatred?"

"It's not hatred. It's just frustration. I'm okay, though. The redundancy came through. I get to keep the car plus the thirty thousand. And I've got holidays and long service."

"Thirty thousand isn't much in a job like yours."

"Less than half a year's salary. Not a lot." Her voice contained a note of bitterness. "For what I gave."

"Best years of your life." Anthea chuckled. "You ought to sue for wrongful dismissal."

She was about to remind Anthea that corporate life wasn't the public service. If she sued, no-one would ever employ her again. "Maybe," she said. "But I'm more concerned with what I am going to do. I'm thinking of finding a business."

"Coffee shop? Milk bar? Suburban butchery? Art gallery?"

"I thought seriously about art. But I want to keep that as my pleasure. Something practical. Mass-market, but not too mass. Rural-based."

Anthea looked at her and smiled. "The Italian peasant ancestry. I knew it would come out one day. What's it to be? Pigs? Goats? Alpaca? In a city apartment?"

"I'm selling the apartment and moving to the mountains."

Anthea groaned. "Your beautiful, beautiful apartment. It's you, Cass, your heart and soul. I can't believe you're serious."

"It's money. But more. I want that garden. I want to connect. I want some place where people live for a long time, and I'm part of it. Not just hello on the stairs." She looked at Anthea. "Did you know you are my only real friend?"

"Yes," said Anthea.

"Don't you think that's sad?"

"Not for me." Anthea laughed.

"I'm serious. A single real friend, one sister I don't get on with so well. It's lucky I adore the kids."

"You left Darcy off the list."

"When I lost my job, it changed the whole balance of things," said Cassie slowly. "I decided to give him some space. So I haven't seen him for a while. We still talk on the phone."

"Is that all?"

"I'm not sure. I was his other, the ice maiden. But he's the same as me in lots of ways. I'm not really the other at all."

"Cass! You're crazy about this man. I think you should be more upset. I think you *are* more upset."

"I am. I'm upset about Darcy. I'm upset that I don't understand about myself, let alone anyone else. I'm upset I don't have more friends. I'm upset about my sister. I'm upset about my mother. I'm upset about selling the apartment. I'm upset about losing my job. I'm upset I'm forty. I'm upset I have money troubles. I'm very upset!"

"No need to snap," said Anthea wryly. "That was good, Cass. Spontaneous, without thinking. And you got it in one."

"I am desperate about Darcy. I can't imagine being without him. It's as if he's opened some closed door for me, and I'm scared he's going to slam it back in my face. Not out of spite or hatred, but because he's . . ." she paused. "He's like me, I suppose."

Anthea struggled out of her chair. "Mike has bad taste in TV, he doesn't like food that's too spicy and I have a horrible feeling he owns a pair of ugg boots. The ultimate pain. But having caught a glimpse of the great existential loneliness, I'm going to give this domestic bliss a try." She put an arm round Cassie. "Take care."

"Is Daddy coming home?"

"I hope so. Eventually."

"Will he bring me a present?"

"No, it's not that sort of coming home."

"Sarah's dad brought her a present when he came back from America."

"Daddy's at Nonna's. It's not like a trip."

"It is. They were getting a divorce."

"Did they? Did they get a divorce?"

"He got another woman."

"Good as a divorce."

"Has Dad got another woman?"

"No." Susan remembered her paranoia about Julie. Somehow, she knew now that Nick would not be unfaithful to her, that he was at heart monogamous. "I'm trying to get him home. I know you miss him, chicken."

"Not too much."

"Don't lie."

"Why did you make him go if you want him home?"

"Don't kick, sweetie. You'll wake Kelly."

"Why did you?"

"We had a fight and it went wrong so he went. Darling, I want to go to sleep now."

"Dad said not to listen to Nonna."

"You do what Daddy says then."

"Is Nonna wrong?"

"Go to sleep."

Susan stroked Elin's hair as she wriggled her way to sleep. It seemed to her that she had a stronger grip on reality than she'd ever had before. Even the way she wanted him back was different – not to fix the marriage, to make the world right, but because it was the right thing for all of them. A random thought entered her head that – seeing as she had eaten dessert – she should get up and run it off on the treadmill.

"Dumb," she said softly.

"What's dumb, Mummy?" asked Elin, sleepily.

"I used to be, chicken."

A large Christmas tree dominated the ward, decorated with crepe-paper streamers and cheap tinsel, with a skewed gold star pulling the top over to one side. In the recreation room beyond, Cassie could see an old man throwing a child's large, coloured ball to a frail old woman, who caught it slowly, and then bounced it back to him. It was hot, and the smell of institutional chicken wafted out even to the verandah, where she sat with Susan and their mother. Their mother desperately clasped a tray with a piece of cake and a sprig of tinsel in one corner.

"You remember the Christmas when Elin was just a baby?" Susan said. "And she crawled into the Santa sack." Her mother looked at her vacantly. "And the time Nick dressed up as Santa and Kelly went ballistic and wouldn't talk to him till after New Year."

Their mother squinted at the sun, but resolutely held the tray. It had been less than a year, Cassie thought, since their mother had stood in the garden at Susan's for Cassie's fortieth birthday, vaguely aware at least of who was who, conscious in some way of her own being. Even back at Wisteria House, she'd had a brief moment of some sort of sensual or emotional awakening, which seemed significant to Cassie, even though the hospital had written it on their records as "disinhibition". Now, there was an absence, even the smallest manifestations of personality fading. Cassie had spoken to the doctor last week, wanting to know, for her own sake, how long this would go on. Days, weeks, months, or years? There was an impropriety in a daughter asking such a question. The middle-aged doctor, who made his living from people like her mother, did not have an answer. But he smiled at her in pity, for her lack of love.

Cassie had been a good child, and for the most part, a dutiful daughter. But at no time had she sensed any joy from her mother at her being. Her mother had cooed and gurgled over Susan's babies, but Cassie had never had a sense of any such indulgence in her own childhood, except with her father. She had been attached to her mother, but had given up wanting or expecting warmth from her.

"We'll have to go, Mum," said Susan. "We've got to get lunch."

"Turkey," said Cassie.

"And pudding," added Susan.

Cassie couldn't bear it. "Let's go. Now." She leaned and touched her mother's shoulder. "Happy Christmas."

She and Susan walked slowly up the hill to Susan's house. Susan had agreed that the children could spend the day with Nick and their grandparents. She had taken them there, joined in the festivities, but had declined to stay, begging off, using her mother as an excuse. Now, the rest of the day stretched ahead of her and Cassie.

When they got to the house, Susan insisted on a Christmas lunch.

"Why don't we go out somewhere?" asked Cassie. "Buy some prawns, sit by the sea." She was thinking of Darcy, who stubbornly refused any Christmas celebration. He didn't believe in it, claiming he'd never had a good Christmas, that it was a conspiracy on the part of big business. She had given up on the idea of spending Christmas with him when he dubbed Christmas a capitalist plot, but she longed for his back garden, under the cool of the wisteria, peeling prawns, drinking, getting a video, making love.

"No, no, no! I've got a turkey hindquarter," said Susan, with determined gaiety. "And a David Jones' pudding and frozen brandy sauce." But once she had cooked, they sat, barely eating, saying little, the yawning gap of the children's absence between them.

"Mum seems okay down there," said Cassie generously. "And it's good you can see her when you want."

"I feel comfortable with nuns," said Susan. "More than that bitch of a matron."

"I know what you mean," said Cassie.

"I'll work on the accountancy program this afternoon," said Susan, clearing away the two plates. "I won't have any time when we're up the mountains."

"You could bring the computer. I'll mind the kids for a couple of hours a day. Give you some free time."

To Cassie, it felt like a generous offer, but Susan looked at her blankly. "You're coming up too? I didn't know that."

"I'll be living up there – when I sell the unit. I need to think about how I want to organise the house."

Susan looked at her. "I suppose so."

"I wish that you didn't think that I stole the house from under your nose. You remember that night I tried to show you the figures, and you wouldn't look. I could show them to you again."

"It's okay," said Susan. "I don't think you've diddled me. I mean, we're sisters."

"So what is it?" asked Cassie. "Why are we fighting?"

"It's Christmas," said Susan. "Everybody argues."

Cassie went over to Susan. "You're probably right." She kissed her sister and hugged her lightly. "I'll be off now. Don't fret too much for the kids. Happy Christmas."

Happy Christmas, she thought to herself. At least it was a beginning.

Chapter 17

Each year of her childhood, Cassie had gone to the nursery with her father to choose the tomato variety she would grow that year. Sometimes, if they were early enough, they raised the plants from seed. Cassie had loved this part – the precision of the mixture to go in the seed box, the careful sieving and raking of the soil, the laying of seeds into the tiny furrows: then finding the delicate balance of sun, water and shelter from the wind. She remembered a few disasters, when the seedlings emerged with telltale signs of fungus, and her father, enraged, would go back to the nursery for a full-scale argument.

These arguments always took place in Italian. Cassie never quite knew how she came to learn Italian, but the understanding of it came naturally to her during the arguments. On the occasions she went to the markets with her father, she could always follow what was going on, except when the more obscure dialects were spoken. But for some reason, until much later, she never told him that she had this window to his world, a window not always innocent. She knew, for instance, that he had a woman at the market with whom he made assignations. There were secret transactions of money, the dropping of bundles of notes. Later, when he realised she understood, he would be a little more careful, but he also trusted her, as "one of us". He never asked her not to mention things to her mother, assuming he was quarantined by his native tongue and the bond this gave them. She sometimes felt a vague sense of guilt about what was kept from her mother, but it seemed as if her father's world was separate, with different rules. She preferred not to think through all the implications of what she witnessed.

After buying the seedlings, her father would sometimes take her down to the beach and buy them fish and chips. They sat on the grass, viewing the crazy Australians swimming through the waves. He told her then about Italy, the fluctuating fortunes of his boyhood under fascism, his fighting in the war as a reluctant sixteen-year-old, his capture, and being sent to England as a farm worker, where he had met her mother. Her mother, who was two years older than him, was engaged to an Englishman, who went missing at the beginning of the war, but whose loss she refused to accept.

Finally, at the end of the war she understood her fiancé was dead, but she still would not consider Guido La Rosa as a husband. He persisted, and five years later, after a spate of passionate letters, he won her. She agreed to emigrate, perhaps, Cassie thought, to escape the public shame of marrying a foreigner. The story was never told in full, but over the years, she pieced it together, from remarks made by both parents, from recriminations made during quarrels, from old photos, old letters. It seemed to her that their unhappiness with each other came from their fundamental differences, their inability to establish rules for communication and behaviour.

Darcy's caustic remark about growing herbs had sparked these childhood memories. She decided to grow something in the apartment, as practice, a talisman for her future. Since her return from Italy, she had always lived in apartments and her plants had been bought, never grown. The nursery she went to now had only Kwik-gro variety seeds and no proper seed boxes. In despair, she bought a tub of parsley. She placed it next to the photo of the Italian garden, but she knew it couldn't grow here. She thought, apart from the picture, how easily she had discarded her love of growing things, as if she were discarding the past. Real cultivation would have to wait till she got to the mountains.

The apartment felt strange to Cassie now. When she was working, it had been a hobby, and then a refuge, a defined space of her own, a place where she was no longer on public display. Now that it no longer served that purpose, it felt lifeless, except for Darcy's two sculptures. The books that she had so long wanted to immerse herself in kept her occupied, but she missed feeling a sense of purpose. Her map was shrinking, disintegrating.

Her daily rituals had revolved around work. There, she had used the corporate personal trainer. Now, she joined a gym, and decided to go at six every morning, but there seemed little point in going so early. By nine, the gym was filled with women working off their post-baby tummies and at lunchtime, young men struck poses for each other. She stopped going. There were no business breakfasts, no rushed lunches, no working back, no use for her personal computer. She even missed the drive up William Street each night, the familiarity of the flashing Coke sign.

She studied the paper, the corporate advertisements. Still smarting and angry, she nevertheless longed for something new and exciting, that would jump out at her. But she knew the hidden meaning of the advertisements and the profiles of the companies as well as she knew the row of unused, immaculately tailored clothes that hung in her wardrobe. There were jobs she could get, but they would be more of the same, and she couldn't face that. She worked through her pride, her anger, her fear, but all the same, she couldn't do it. She gave up reading the paper, and the flood of business magazines and newsletters gradually stopped arriving in her mail box.

Poverty, which when viewed from a six-figure salary had seemed quaint, suddenly became frightening. She worried about her ability to live without money. As her parsley withered, she lost her confidence. She thought of translation work, even of teaching again, of buying a restaurant, of becoming an adviser or consultant to a government department, but she had no motivation. The books that used to inspire her sent her to sleep. Darcy's diffidence added to her feeling of insecurity. Finally he rang to apologise.

"I was stupid. I forgot about the give part, as in give and take. Come down and see me and I'll cherish you."

"Maybe I broached too many boundaries," she said.

"Touché! It was me. I was thinking of you losing your job from my perspective. The other night I started looking at it from your perspective. Then I started looking at me from your perspective. Not a pretty sight. I'm sorry. Are you okay?"

"There's not one thing in my life that's certain." She felt a surge of relief at his apology.

She drove to his house and they sat on the wicker chairs, on the bumpy lawn in the too-bright sunshine.

"I'm putting things in perspective," she explained. "I was too single-minded, too immersed in my job. It was the lynchpin that held the rest together, or so I thought. I'm panicking because I don't know what to do without it."

"When I was on drugs, I used to panic that my supply wasn't coming in."

She looked at him, amazed. "But you weren't an addict or anything, were you?"

"Cass, I told you. Asia. Ten years. Stoned out of my head. Not knowing whether my family were dead or alive. Does that suggest light recreational use? Control?"

"You stopped using it. It's not as if you ended up destitute."

"I don't know what you'd call living in an old men's home in downtown Sydney. It sure ain't the Hilton."

"So you were addicted?"

"Extremely."

"A drug addict? I'm stunned." Despite their intimacy she had missed the obvious. There were other things she should have known too. She had a sudden sense that she should not be seduced back into corporate life, that there were different things in life to be explored and discovered, even unpleasant ones.

"You never . . . take them . . . now?"

He laughed at her hesitation. "Never. I still like a moderate amount of wine, but I can't touch a drug. Cass, this was fifteen years ago."

"Why were you addicted?"

"For fun."

"Why? I mean was it your upbringing, or something that happened?"

"It was fun," he said defiantly. "I got onto drugs and it was the most fun I ever had. I took hallucinogens, and I saw things I'd never seen before. It brought me right out of suburbia, all the way to a magic place. And I was hooked. I'm lucky to be alive. By the time I saw what drugs were doing to me, I didn't care."

"So why did you decide to go straight?"

"You don't decide. I did a deal for some people and they couldn't pay me. Instead, they gave me a ticket back to Sydney. Which seemed like a good idea, seeing the supplier was about to kill me. I scrounged some money here and got it to him, so I was safe. Safe, but fucked."

Cassie tried to balance her shock against the memories of her father. His had always been a tenuous connection with drugs, a side issue, quarantined, separate, as so much of his world had been. Protection and standover were part of his particular southern Italian heritage, part of how the markets had worked then. Drugs had upped the stakes. As a dying man, he was the ideal courier for a large deal. Except, he wouldn't touch it. He fled to Italy, knowing he'd die soon enough to be irrelevant. She'd pieced it together from what she'd seen, what she'd heard, what he'd told her, but she didn't really know the full story. Some day, she would tell Darcy.

"So why did you decide to go straight when you came back here?"

"No decision. My sisters put me in a drug rehab. I split. I don't know what happened. I ended up with the Salvos. I don't have many memories. Except one day, I literally woke up in the shower and I thought, I'm clean and sober, and I feel okay and maybe there's a life, maybe I can get back to that kid who drew and painted and carved and loved a beach. Maybe. And by the grace of a lot of kind people, I did."

"So that's why you don't have any ambition?"

"Jesus, Cass. Stop trying to box me up." He got up and leaned against the tree.

"It's not a criticism," she said lamely. "It's an observation."

"I've never had great ambition in a conventional sense but I'm passionate about doing my thing, not being intruded on, living my life. Even before I was in Asia, I thought the world was this wonderful, exciting, terrifying place full of demons and devils, good and evil. I want to be an observer, a creator of things important to myself and hopefully to others."

She stood next to him. "I don't think I could be like that. I need outside approval." She wondered if that was what was wrong with her now – that she had no audience.

"This is waiting time. Trust that the world is going to provide." He put his arms round her and they kissed. She felt the oneness of them together, the deep safety of it. Today, she told herself, it feels right.

Susan pulled into the driveway after picking Elin up from school, when Anthea's car swung in behind her.

"I've come for the baby clothes," called Anthea. "Is now an okay time?"

"Fine." As Anthea got out of the car, Susan noticed she was now visibly pregnant, her face flushed with pleasure. She remembered being pregnant with Elin, and how every little thing connected with the pregnancy had been suffused with meaning and happiness.

"They're all packed up inside," she said. "How is it being back at school?"

"Lots of rude jokes about me being pregnant," said Anthea. "It makes you realise what a strange view of the world adolescent boys actually have."

"Here's the big stuff," said Susan, lugging bags and baskets down the stairs. "Your bassinette. The lining, sheets, covers. And the bouncer. You use that from about two months. And this little chair. Prop them up in front of the TV and they soon get the knack of watching it." She laughed. "Just kidding. Car capsule. You have to get that fitted." She lifted up a tangle of straps. "This is a thing you suspend from doorways. They're supposed to bounce. Mine used to just hang there looking sad, but some people swear by it."

"There's so much," said Anthea.

"More," said Susan. "You need heaps, loads of jumpsuits. My kids lived in them till they started crawling. Hundreds of booties, all unused." She looked around the room. "You won't need the cot for six months or so. And books. They're like Bibles with your first. You don't need them after that."

"This is definitely an only child," said Anthea, "given my age." But she felt a sort of pleasure in this mindless maternal chat.

"I wish Cass would have a baby," said Susan. "She'll leave it too late and then she'll be sorry."

"She's made up her mind not to," Anthea said. "And when Cass makes up her mind, it's made up for good."

"It would be good for her to be wrong about something." Susan folded some of the tiny singlets that were spilling out of the bag. "You know, to want something and then not be able to get it."

"She thinks she failed at her job. She's pretty cut up about that."

"Oh," said Susan vaguely. "I thought they just fired her. Put the stuff there and we'll have a cuppa."

Anthea sat down on one of the kitchen stools. The baby gave her a backache now, and she shifted herself into the seat. She patted her stomach. Every twinge, every manifestation of the child seemed to blend them together, to increase Anthea's feeling for her. Her cynicism had shrunk to nothing.

"How's it going with Nick?"

"Awful," said Susan tragically. "Awful, awful, awful. I can't think about it."

"Did you write to him?"

"A really nice letter. Just asking him to cool things with the family, to accept some of the responsibility and to come back home."

"And what happened?"

"He's got no problem with any of it except the coming back home. I mean, he's called Nonna off, which is a bloody miracle. Christ, I'll have a time with her if we ever do get back together. It's awful to realise that your in-laws, who you thought liked you, actually hate your guts."

"But Nick won't come home?"

"He's got this theory – what's done is done. No going back. The magic has been broken." She sighed. "I sort of understand that, except the magic was broken before he went. We've got three kids. He may not love me like he did. I may not love him in the same way. But we've still got a marriage."

"So what are you doing?"

"You would not believe it," said Susan. "Leotards, tight shorts and brief top. He's not interested."

Cassie and Darcy lay in the hot February sun, their feet in the water. The sky was a deep, cloudless blue. Cassie raked the sand through her fingers. There were some large white shells, but the orange shells had disappeared from the beach.

"Lucky I got them when I did," he said.

"Mmm . . ." murmured Cassie. "Did you do anything with them?"

"I framed one for you," he said, offended. "The first time we made love."

"Very pretty. But I meant the other three thousand."

"I'm broke," he said. "I can't afford the materials to do what I want for the exhibition."

"What happened to the money for the whaling book?"

"I spent it. Then they offered me a roo assignment – carving prototypes which they get made up in Korea. All this new age capitalism – dancing round on headlands and getting kangaroos mass-produced in Korea. I suppose I have to do it."

She felt the same about getting a job. She could apply, could get one, but there was no meaning in it. She had to engender her own passion, pull herself up by her own bootstraps. At least Darcy had things he really wanted to create.

"When I've sold the unit and I'm settled in the mountains, I'll start to look round seriously. I should start now, but . . ." She shrugged. "After summer."

"When we first met, you told me you didn't like summer and you didn't like the beach."

"I've changed."

"I'm not sure I approve. You and me – we thrive on difference."

"Maybe you changed me."

"I refuse to take the credit."

"Is there any way *you've* changed? Because of me?"

"I doubt it." He drew a circle in the sand with his finger, and revealed one of the small orange shells. He blew the sand off it. "See? Unchanged."

Cassie was silent.

"But I've been thinking. That maybe I should," he said hesitantly, "use a bit of that grit you've got to get my exhibition together."

"Yes."

"And I've thought I'd like to go back to Asia, with you. For which I'd need more money than I'm making. So I'll have to really get thinking about this exhibition."

"Even make a piece or two," she said archly. But something in her was stirred at the idea of travelling with Darcy. To date, what had seemed so rich and powerful had only tested the waters. What he was suggesting now implied some sharing of their lives.

"I thought I might come and spend some time up in your mountain retreat," he said tentatively. "You know, see how we go together."

She nodded, noting his hesitation. She had seen herself as unadventurous, cursed with tunnel vision. But it was in him too.

Nick sat in the living room, a beer in hand, staring at the TV as Susan puffed uphill on the treadmill.

"You're stubborn," she panted.

"I can't put it into words," he said, "but when something has happened like this, there's literally no way back. This would hang over us for the rest of our lives."

Susan got off the treadmill and switched off the TV. She sat down opposite Nick.

"It will be there whether you come back or not. If you came back I could put it behind me . . ."

"Susan! You are a very emotional person. I'm a very emotional person. We are not like your sister, or how your mother used to be. We can't just repress things." He stood up. "I tell you. I drive past here and I feel like crying. Or I want to come in and rip the place apart. Or strangle you. Shit! Anything!"

"So I hope you've been using that punching bag I gave you for Christmas?"

"Don't bloody mock. It's serious."

"I know it's serious. Very serious. You're the one who's making a mockery of it. We've got three kids upstairs. The little ones are upset, but they don't understand. But we're breaking Elin's heart."

Nick shook his head. "I know –"

"Stay the night."

"My mother's expecting me."

"Come home for the weekend." She stood up in front of him.

He pounded the couch.

"Think of it as a new start," she said. "Not going back. I don't mean that we should suppress it – just get on with our lives." She started tidying the room. "*You* were the one who used to say that. Now I'm in a new phase. If you let me, I can see ways to make your surgery more profitable, so you're freer. We really can make it work. I even gave away the old baby gear to Cassie's friend yesterday."

"You gave away the baby stuff?" He looked at her, incredulous.

"Well, it wasn't worth selling."

"You knew I wanted . . . we talked about . . . another kid."

"But I don't want another one. You know that. And it's one decision I make."

"You make those decisions on your own? You call that marriage?"

"Yes. It's not as if you carry the kid round for nine months, then feed it and look after it and put the rest of your life on hold. Okay, I know you take the financial burden, but it's what I have to do, every minute, every day, plus every night. It's my quality of life we're talking about here. I was so sick after Jack – mentally sick. I'm not having another baby. Read my lips."

"It mightn't happen again."

"But it could! Which would be terrible for all of us. You told me about your mother having a nervous breakdown. And how awful that had been for you. As if it were her fault that she was stuck in Australia and couldn't speak the language. Probably too many bloody babies, as well."

"And I suppose I was the one baby too many."

"Oh Christ, maybe you were!" Susan threw up her hands.

"Yeah, well, I got them out of that shit shop, working twelve-hour days, and I helped the others get a start." Susan looked at Nick, knowing where it was coming from, but angry it was being dragged into their relationship. Although she knew her parents' relationship had been part of her too – the fear, the secrets, the insecurities.

"I'm fucking going," said Nick furiously. "And I know why you're prancing round in that skin-tight thing. Stuff you!"

Every time the food dribbled out of her mother's mouth, Cassie looked away. Susan collected it with the spoon and put it back in. Susan and Cassie sat on opposite sides of the bed, the slight, wasted figure of their mother between them. An embroidered red band ran down the middle of her sheet – *Sisters of Poverty, Sisters of Pov* – disappearing into the end of the bed. A curtain separated their mother's bed from the next one, and the window looked out across the main road.

"I haven't heard her speak in weeks," said Cassie.

"She's better in other ways," said Susan. "They can get her up to shower her, and she sits on the verandah in the afternoon."

"It's hardly a great leap forward." Cassie hated this mindless point-scoring across their mother. "Listen, I'm not complaining about her being here. It's a bit grim, but the nursing is great, and the staff are a lot more user-friendly than Wisteria House." She looked at her mother's drawn face. "It's her not knowing us, not being the person she was. Sometimes, I'm scared this is what I'll remember about her."

Susan turned to their mother. "You know who I am, don't you?" Their mother caught Susan's eye for a moment, a flicker of something, and then went blank again.

Cassie looked away. "What's happening with Nick?"

Susan continued spooning food, until her mother shut her mouth. "He says too much has happened. I told him there are the kids to think of."

"*You* didn't think of them before," said Cassie coldly.

"I thought of them for a long time. As long as I could bear having a dental automaton around the house. Okay, he was bright and charming when other people were around, or when he made some money. But otherwise, it was hideous. Don't lecture me, Cass. You've got no idea what marriage and kids can be like."

"Okay, but I can't believe it's all Nick's fault." She wondered why she had started this argument. She'd made up her mind to be more tolerant and understanding of Susan.

"I don't think it's all his fault. And neither does Nick – especially with all the support he's had from you."

"I've only spoken to him a couple of times," said Cassie quickly.

"Enough," said Susan. She leaned over and kissed her mother. "Bye Mum."

Cassie took her mother's hand, while her mother stared blankly at her. She couldn't bring herself to kiss her, aware of the contrast between herself and Susan. "Let's go," she said.

They walked down the long corridor to the parking lot. The floor was a grey, polished linoleum, the walls a deadly green.

"I suppose it doesn't matter," said Cassie. "She hardly notices anything."

"She knows the difference between jelly and custard, and chicken and ham," said Susan cheerily. "Between me and a nurse, maybe. Between night and day. You know, there's a special ward for people who lose any sense of their body clock. It's weird, isn't it?" Susan ran up the steps to the carpark and stood at the top, waiting for Cassie. "Great for the thighs," she said.

"How can you be so cheerful about Mum?" said Cassie. "Don't you think it matters what the quality of her life is like?"

"That's exactly why I come."

"But it's gone! Any sort of quality," said Cassie. "It's meaningless."

"So why do you come?" retorted Susan.

"Guilt. Because you do."

Susan looked at Cassie angrily. "So go back in there, say goodbye and never see her again. Go on. It makes no bloody difference to me. If that's what you think, go back and do it. She could be pretty bloody callous herself at times." She caught the stricken look on Cassie's face and was unmoved. "Go on. Do it!"

Cassie pulled away from her, upset. "Don't you ever feel like this? That you can't stand it any more? That there's no point or meaning to it?"

"No! Because somebody's got to do it! She's our mother."

Cassie shook her head. Walking to the car, she thought of the strength of her feelings for her mother, the conflict in those feelings, the awkwardness, the intimacy. She had always hated the complications of the relationship. But now she wondered if the complications she had tried so hard to resolve were perhaps the essence of it.

Chapter 18

"Nonna." Susan opened the front door to Nick's mother. Kelly held her grandmother's hand tightly, while Elin scuffed her feet on the step. "I thought Nick was picking the kids up."

"I like to see the children." She took Jack from Susan's arms. "And he's busy. Besides, I want to talk to you."

"I don't want you saying bad things about me. I don't want you interfering. Nick and I have to settle this." It came out automatically and she wondered how many times she had said this to her mother-in-law in the last six months.

"So why can't you?"

"I don't know. But it's between him and me."

"And family."

"Everybody had their say and it got worse."

"You want him back?"

"Yes I do. Elin, darling, take the little ones and go and watch TV." She shepherded Elin and

Kelly into the house and took Jack firmly from his grandmother. "Nonna's just going. Give her a kiss bye bye." As the children kissed Nonna and then raced into the house, Susan stood firmly at the front door.

"He wants more babies?" her mother-in-law persisted.

"Yes, he does. But we'll work it out."

"His father like that. I had four. Four too much. Then he want five. I have operation."

"Nonna, please."

Nonna leaned forward conspiratorially. "Tell him you have another. Then see doctor. You have operation. Take everything out." She threw up her hands. "Everything! Clean out! Tell him it is for woman's health."

"Okay, I will." She ushered the old woman out of the porch. "Thanks for getting the kids." She kissed her mechanically, then retreated into the house and shut the door. "Shit! Nuts!"

"I don't usually go to restaurants," said Darcy, "especially this expensive."

Cassie looked round the restaurant. Pictures of the Thai king and queen, brightly coloured paper serviettes, woven bamboo cover on the counter. It was standard inner-city Thai. She shook her head. "It's not expensive."

"Luxury for the boy from Kurnell. How will we ever live together?"

Cassie put down her fork. Darcy's face was impassive. "I didn't know we were going to live together."

"We discussed it. Me coming up to the mountains."

"With a line of retreat to the coast? We discussed that, but not to live together."

"Well, I'd like to. At least part of the time. More than visiting like we do now. In the long run, that's what you'd like, isn't it?"

"Yes, I would." It was strange but simple, and she felt very sure of it. "But I'm very surprised. This from the man who was scared I might spend my leisure time hanging round his house."

"Just fear. I thought you hadn't changed me, but you have. After great thought and serious agonising time, I realise I really want to live with you – at least some of the time. And you've infected me with this horrible bug. Did I tell you about that?"

Cassie reddened. "A bug?" she whispered.

"The capitalist desire to make money – to eat in high-class restaurants like this."

Cassie looked around the restaurant again.

"I'll need to get my exhibition together. I'd need more clients, more work, more materials, more tools. To get more engaged in life. More! More! More!"

"I'm not sure I want to be responsible for all this."

"I'm not sure you are. I feel more part of life. Less abstract. Remember I was an abstract artist when you met me?"

"You weren't at all," said Cassie. She squeezed his hand and felt happy.

"We can't go out," Cassie told Anthea, as they sat in the fading afternoon sun in Cassie's living room. "This agent is going to ring any minute with an offer on my flat." She looked out over the harbour, and already felt herself detached from it. It was a wonderful view, but a distant view, nothing to do with her life now except as something to be looked at. In the mountains, she saw the pine trees from her bedroom and lay under them on warm days. From the living room, she looked over the garden, which had been shaped by her father, her mother, Susan, unfortunately by Nick, and now would be re-shaped by her.

"I still think you're crazy to sell this," said Anthea, lying back on the couch, her pregnant belly prominent under her black shirt. "It's a wonderful apartment. And it was you who made it wonderful."

"I know," said Cassie. "But even apart from the cold, hard considerations of cash, it's finished. I don't need it. And it's not like your place. It never felt like home."

"Have you ever thought that Darcy has entranced you out of being yourself?" said Anthea. "I hate to say this, but maybe you're one of those people who need money and power to burn?"

"Actually, money has had very little to do with my career choices."

"Come on, Cass. A house in the mountains, overseas trips, company car, health plan, office on the top floor. Money, money, money. It must have have been a factor."

"It was the freedom of money –"

"I know it wasn't the joy of a stack of two dollar coins."

"And the chance to be powerful. To get in there and actually wield a lot of power. I read this book, just after I started the MBA. It said if you had power, you would learn how to make choices. You'd be responsible for your choices, you could do extraordinary things."

"You think that's a good idea?" Anthea looked at Cassie, her face wrinkled in distaste. "I tell kids every day that they can make choices but they're going to affect themselves and the people around them. Maybe having power feels good, but how you exercise it is the main thing."

"And that was my big mistake," said Cassie, leaning forward. "I really wanted to learn to make choices, but instead, I kept following the rules. I used the power to encapsulate my tunnel vision. I forgot what I was trying to learn."

"Run that past me again," said Anthea.

"I want to expand myself. To get in touch with things more inside me. Like what's happened with Darcy."

"Transformed by the love of a man?" Anthea asked sarcastically.

"No, it's getting out of the box. Getting free of myself. I might go back to a corporate job, but I'd be more expanded, less constrained." Her phone started ringing and she reached for it.

"Hello, Cassandra La Rosa. Yes, that's an excellent offer. He wants it immediately? Japanese buyer? When exactly is immediately? An answer tonight and settle in a month? Wait, I'll give you an answer." She put her hand over the phone and leaned across the table. "The agent has this great offer. Five hundred thousand. Ten over the asking price. But I've got to let him know tonight and move out in a month."

"Don't do it," pleaded Anthea. "Get a job straight away. You should keep this place. Or rent it. There's so much of you in it."

"Me that was. Not me now." Cassie put the phone to her ear again. "I'll take it," she said triumphantly. "Thanks, you really earned the commission."

"Are you going to live up the mountains?" asked Anthea as Cassie hung up.

"I'll live up the mountains and come into town when I like. It's close enough to drive back or I could stay with Suzie and the kids, or with you."

"You won't want to stay with me," sighed Anthea. "With Mike it's wall to wall football on weekends."

"Are you coping with this?"

"Just. I'm winging it. He's a nice man. Most women would be proud to step out with him. He's kind. We can still have a good time together. Sometimes, at least. What more can you ask?"

More! More! More! Cassie thought of what Darcy had said. She looked at the tired lines on Anthea's face, the unfamiliar sadness of her expression. "Anthea, you don't *have* to live with anyone. You shouldn't be making yourself more miserable."

Anthea patted her stomach. "Baby makes three," she said.

"I let go of all the anxiety about what I'd do and then I sold the unit at a great price," Cassie told

Darcy on the phone. "I've organised the packing and I'm going up the mountains."

"It's not supposed to happen so quickly," he said nervously. "Shit, I'm trying to buy wood. I'm sweating on getting my money from that Korean project. All the clients have dried up, and I'm broke."

"Maybe if you didn't say 'clients' with such a horrible edge to your voice, you might have more of them," she said. She was sitting on the floor in the bare flat, leaning against the wall. Devoid of its contents, the flat made her feel young and free. After her father's death, Cassie had felt a brief freedom she had never experienced before or after. She had dismissed the experience as abnormal, but now she wondered why so much of her life she had felt so constrained and contained.

"You're supposed to suffer a little," he said. "The universe is supposed to be less compliant."

"Maybe this time it's me who's totally in tune with the universe and you're the one who's out of sync."

"I doubt it." He brightened. "When do we start this new life together? You know, with the cottage in the mountains and the seaside shack next to the oil pipe."

"I'm going up now," she said. "You want to come tonight?"

"You want me to bring some fish?"

"This is the mountains. I'll make us minestrone. And damper. You'll love it."

"This family of yours . . . will they be coming up?"

"Sometimes. You'll get to meet them eventually. At the moment, there's only Susan and the kids."

"Kids panic me."

"Darcy, what's wrong?"

"Don't worry," he said grimly. "Make the soup and I'll be there."

Susan thought that Jack looked irresistible in overalls and sneakers. It would be the first time Nick would see him dressed in these little boy clothes. She had washed Kelly's hair, with difficulty, and put a bow in it, which Kelly had torn out. Kelly was cross and petulant, tormenting Jack. Bribery hadn't worked and she hoped Kelly would brighten up by the time Nick arrived. She felt nervous, as she often did about their meetings, as if each one was critical, as if each one would decide their fate. In reality, each time was a greater retreat from the marriage.

Nick got out of the car and walked across the park. He had let his hair fall across his face, instead of combing it severely back, and he looked younger and more vulnerable. She had a good feeling as Kelly ran to him and jumped into his arms. He scooped up Jack too. Suddenly, Susan felt a surge of love for him, the sort of love she used to feel; the warmth, the physical attraction, the happiness. He sat down on the picnic rug.

"How are you?" he asked.

"Good. You?"

"Okay." He reached into the picnic basket with the familiarity of ownership and helped himself to a sandwich.

"Mum's switched sides," he said. "She's backing you."

"She told me to have a hysterectomy on doctor's order," Susan said. "No more children."

His eyes narrowed. "Will you?"

"No. If I don't want any more children, I simply won't have them."

"Would you think about it?"

"I have, Nick. I really don't want to. What's more, I don't really understand why you do. I understand you'd love another child if we had one. I know I would. But we do have three. Which is a big family these days. We've got a boy, two girls. They just take us up completely. I don't understand."

He ate the sandwich quickly, and searched round for another. She handed him one of the children's peanut butter ones. "Sorry," she said. "I should have made you some more."

"That's okay," he said, eating it. "I know you don't understand my problem with going back, about putting this behind us. Maybe it's affected me more because I didn't initiate it." He held up his hands. "I know I have some responsibility, but you said yourself you'd been thinking about leaving. So it was like a bombshell to me."

"I understand that," she said reasonably.

"Even before that, I'd wanted another baby."

"Yes, I know that too."

"That's the point we could go back to. That's the high, the beginning of something new and wonderful. When that baby slides out of your body –"

"Pushed," she corrected.

"They slide at the end," he said petulantly.

"News to me."

"Whatever. I can remember all our kids being born. I remember how I felt, the magic of it, the emotional high, and that's why I truly believe if we got back to that and worked on it, it would be a new start. And all the joy of another baby."

"Yeah," she said. "I forgot all the joy."

"You are so cynical."

"I'm not. You seem to forget all this trouble started after we had Jack." She looked at him angrily. "And don't turn this on me and tell me I don't love Jack. But I had three kids, all under six. I had a mother with dementia. I had a sister who isn't crazy about me. I know she helped when she could, but Cass had that job. Okay, Nonna was great, but you know as well as I do she's not the most relaxing person to have around. I felt swamped. I felt like I'd disappeared. I felt like I didn't exist."

"These are our children."

"Oh, fuck the bleeding heart. Don't give me this Italian madonna stuff. This is *my* life. If you want a new start with an emotional high, why don't we hire a nanny and go off by ourselves for a week? We could have one of those tacky renewal-of-vows at a casino on a cheap tropical island." He looked defeated and she leaned over and touched his knee. He pulled away. "A new baby wouldn't fix things between *us*. This isn't a re-run, Nick. This is it."

He stood up. "I just hoped."

"It's non-negotiable." She looked at him, steely. "So are you coming back?"

He shrugged his shoulders.

"Kids, take Jack on the swing." She walked over to the car with Nick. "I can't live like this. We've got to sort this out. We've got to decide."

He looked down, hands in his pockets. "The accountancy thing you're doing is fine by me. I'm not a chauvinist."

Susan could see his macho pride at war with his better instincts. "So what's the rest of your agenda? I mean you want a baby, but that's not on. If you want to be practical about this, you've got to admit that a three-child family you come home to beats a four-child fantasy family hands down. I have a feeling it's something else."

"That photo you sent me. You wouldn't understand."

"Not if you don't tell me."

"You wouldn't." He got into the car.

Susan leaned in through the window. "You're torturing me because I wanted a break from this marriage. I want you to make up your mind." He drove away without looking at her.

Susan watched him go. She'd always thought of him as the strong one, the sane one. But now, it was her. She looked over to the children playing on the grass. She had to be.

Anthea walked in and dropped her bag on the kitchen table. Nearly March. Just over three months to go to baby day. Four more weeks till holidays, and she'd stop teaching for a year or two. She often wondered what life would be like with all that unstructured time. She watched mothers taking their babies to the park, in the supermarket, feeding them, sitting in cafes together. She couldn't imagine such a life, but the prospect of it seemed more exciting than anything she had ever done. She put the kettle on and looked round the room. It was okay, she thought, living with your own mess. She picked up the newspapers and dumped them into the recycling container. Mike's mess seemed worse than hers. She wondered whether the mess would be less irritating if she loved him.

She made herself a herbal tea, and sat with her feet up, savouring her solitude, the pleasant sense of her pregnant body. She loved her dark, swollen nipples, her sense of the swelling womb. Forty minutes, she thought, till he came home. Forty minutes till family time, forty minutes to the mutual meal that was a compromise between what they both liked. Maybe, she thought, it would have been the same with anyone, whether she loved them or not. Maybe this was what life as a couple was like. Maybe if you learned it young, it was less painful. Maybe she couldn't learn. Maybe it was wrong to try so hard. She didn't know.

In her twenties, she'd lived with a man in a loud, hard-drinking communal household, with meals of Chinese barbecue duck and noodles which came from the contingent of sober Chinese students living upstairs. There had been another, a sexy live-in affair, six months duration. She couldn't remember a single meal they had together.

What had been different then had been the future, which stretched out to infinity. Now, it closing in, like a drawing with exaggerated perspective. This was real. This was it. Good as it got. She could hardly contemplate anyone else now. There was him, her and the baby. No dreams or fantasies. In the night, it was painful. Crying. Thinking about being with him, without him. The baby.

"Hi." He leaned over and kissed her.

"Hi. How was your day?"

"Okay." He turned on the television, got a beer out of the fridge and sat on the couch. "Just catch the headlines." She felt guilty, assessing him all the time, while he accepted her so easily. She hated the daily ritual of it.

"Your sister called me today," Anthea said casually. "She was very sweet. About the baby. Asked me if I'd like the wedding at her place."

"Yeah, she said something about that. I think it would be a great idea. You'd love it."

"Except I've never met her. You've never met my family. We've been living together a few months."

"We're having this baby." He looked at her longingly. "That's the most important thing."

"We hardly know each other." She felt bad saying it, but it was true.

"You're saying no wedding?" His voice was flat. He was closed to her now and she couldn't tell if he was disappointed or angry.

"Not yet. We've been rushed into this, so let's leave the wedding for a while." She looked at him, not looking at her. She despaired of him, of their life together.

He didn't look away from the TV. "Okay. If that's what you want."

When Cassie arrived at the mountain house in the afternoon, a team of workmen were re-surfacing the road outside the house. Dust from the work covered the hedge, and had blown in across the front verandah.

Dispirited by the dirt, she went inside. It was only four o'clock, but already she needed to turn the light on. She remembered, leaving the flat this afternoon, how glaringly bright it had been without the blinds. She went over to start the gas fire. The pilot light was out and she had to get down on her hands and knees to ignite it. In the kitchen, someone had left the big soup pot to soak. As she tipped it out, dirty water spilled over her sweater.

Determined not to be defeated, Cassie un-packed the car. The removalists wouldn't be bringing her stuff from the flat until next week, but she began to think where she would put it all. The house was bigger than the flat and she had a sense that her delicate prints, even Darcy's sculptures, would be swallowed up in here, passing unnoticed.

She put on a tape and got to work on the soup. Darcy cooked out of pride, and out of necessity, but Cassie never had. For the first time, what she had lost, what she had given up when she sold the apartment, ran powerfully through her head. She tried not to be depressed. She cut the vegetables, sliced the ham finely, measured out the noodles and then started on the dough for the damper. A herb garden. That would be her first project. Herb damper.

She looked at her watch. Darcy had promised to be here by five, before it was dark. He had always chided her about being late, and she wondered if he was paying her back. At half past five, she rang him, suddenly panicking, but was reassured by his unanswered phone. At six, the soup ready, she sat down and watched the news. At seven, she opened the wine and poured herself a glass and lit the open fire, more for effect than for warmth. She settled in front of it, telling herself that he must have meant he was going to leave at five. The phone rang.

"It's me."

"Soup's cooked." She tried to make her voice sound light, unconcerned.

"Cass, I can't do this."

"Do what?" she asked, knowing.

"I can't move in with you, Cass. I know I love you, but I just can't do it."

Chapter 19

Cassie had spent the afternoon on the most basic of garden tasks, the compost heap. She had picked up a load of horse manure from Blackheath, added in grass clippings, vegetable peelings, shredded newspaper and compost worms. As she worked on it, she began to look at the garden as a whole. Both her mother and her father had had traditional ideas of design. Her mother had wanted flowers for show at the front of the house and sun at the back to dry the clothes. Her father had wanted a windbreak to protect the vegetable garden, his compost heap, his beloved incinerator. His only concession to aesthetics had been the pool, now an ugly concrete circle.

Cassie washed herself off under the hose and got some iced water from the house. She much preferred to be outside in the garden than confined in the house. She sat under the pine trees and surveyed her territory. She ran her hands through the pine needles. The scent rose, slightly fetid from the wet earth. She lay back, her eyes closed, her mind ranging around the garden, imagining, planning. But instead of being able to see it, full and lush, it appeared to her as dry and lifeless with cleared beds and paths, all form but no content, as if she could shape her garden, but lacked the ability to make it grow. There was emptiness, the hole left by Darcy. She finished the water and walked into the house. Picking up the phone, she dialled Anthea's number.

"When Phillip moved out, I wasn't angry, I didn't cry . . . Darcy never even moved in and I'm going crazy." Cassie looked out the window. "Anthea, what am I going to do?"

Anthea lay on her bed, rubbing her stomach, cradling the phone on her shoulder. "I've been thinking there's something different about women like us. Not to begin with. But because of the way we've lived. Maybe if you have a relationship, a real one, a serious one, when you're young, something happens. Like learning to ride a bike. They say you can't learn bike riding when you're old."

"But look at you. You're not madly in love. But you're committed. You're making it work."

Anthea groaned. "Work is the operative word. He's sweet and I can't stand it. And underneath, I don't really think he loves me either. I suspect he's got a penchant for being trapped by women. He's still on about getting married. Weird, under the circumstances."

"Aren't you going to get married?"

"No." Anthea struggled to sit up. "And of course he's sulky about that. Cass, my stuff is really technicalities. Mike and I will work something out. The baby is the main thing." She had hung on, wanting to believe that, but knowing also that the failure of the relationship would be the end of a hope quite separate from the baby.

"If it's not working," said Cassie tentatively, "maybe you'd be better moving on."

"Yeah, maybe, but I'm worried about *you*," protested Anthea. "Stuck up there. Out of a relationship, out of the city, out of a job." She paused. "Out of spirits, Cass. I've never seen you depressed. It's not like you."

Cassie blew her nose. "It is like me. I've been fighting and struggling and trying to make something of myself all my life. And it seems to take this superhuman effort. Gathering myself up every day to meet the fray. And now I'm wondering why I ever bothered. Why didn't I lie down and let life wash over me? I could have plodded on teaching –"

"Yes, well . . ." said Anthea. "We teachers aren't all plodders."

"Not like you!" said Cassie apologetically. "I was a terrible teacher. Conscientious but terrible, but there are lots of people who just do it, who stay there, and enjoy the other parts of their lives. Anthea, I keep ringing him."

"We all do that," said Anthea sympathetically, "but it's hideously humiliating when you're in the middle of it."

"And *I* decided not to have any contact with him," said Cassie in an apologetic voice. "We either argue or it's terribly cold and civilised."

"What happened to vision and integrity and being clear about things – all that stuff you used to go on about?"

"I've lost all that."

Anthea laughed. "Well, thank God for that. You know, maybe you'd be better off at work."

"I've lost all my energy, all my fight." Cassie looked round the sitting room. She'd aimed to have it clean, the old wood polished, the fireplaces and stoves properly blacked, but it had stayed like a holiday house, with corners of dust.

"How long will your money last?" asked Anthea.

"A year. Maybe more. I can live extremely cheaply. Peasant ancestry."

"Useful."

"Except if I were to go into business, I'd need the money as capital, not living expenses."

"Are you thinking of going into business?"

"I can't. I was almost ready to . . . before this business with Darcy. Now, I'm rooted."

It occurred to Anthea that she had never heard Cassie say she was rooted. Almost earthy. Maybe losing Darcy wasn't as bad as it seemed.

After she had talked to Anthea, it was too cold to work in the garden again. But the house depressed her. Ever since that first awful night, when Darcy hadn't come, it had felt alien, relegating her to the role of tenant. It felt like a camping holiday. Everywhere she looked, there was something needing repair, weeding or painting or cleaning. Now she noticed that one of the skirting boards was damaged. Looking along the board, Cassie saw that when the carpet had been laid, the skirting had been damaged along its length. When she had the floors polished, it would have to be replaced.

Without thinking, she picked up the phone and dialled Darcy's number.

"It's just me," she said. "I need to ask something about timber."

"What do you need to know?" His voice was neutral.

"My skirting board has gone. It's quite a complicated profile. I was thinking eventually of having it stained and I wondered if pine . . ."

"Pine would be okay. Oregon would be a lot better. But more expensive."

"How are you? Are you okay?" She tried to make her voice sound light and unworried.

"I'm okay."

"I'm not," she said miserably.

"We agreed not to talk."

"Okay." She put the phone down, humiliated. His two sculptures were there, behind her, where they had been unpacked. Beautiful but disturbing. She got up and lifted the one of the woman and carried it along to the spare room. She ran her hands over the female body, with shivers of memory. That, she decided, was more destructive than the pointless phone calls. She went back and looked at the carved bird. It was harsher, almost a parody of the feminine, not as painful as the tenderness of the woman. Maybe, she decided, she should torch them, sacrifice them on a big bonfire in the back garden. But she remembered how much they had cost her. In money alone, she thought melodramatically.

Eventually, she told herself as she tried to lift the bird, she would put them in the new conservatory. The building of the conservatory was so distant that she was sure she would be over Darcy by then. It felt, at times, as if he had stolen her very soul. She struggled to carry the bird up to the spare room and stopped, panting, for a rest in the hallway. It looked right, but was still too bald a reminder of Darcy. She covered it with the old embroidered cloak her father's family had given her on his death.

"You tell me what's wrong with him," she said to the bird, "why he's got no heart." She pulled herself up. She'd really go crazy if she started talking to sculptures.

She walked slowly out to the letterbox in the fading light, pulling up the summer grass which had taken root in the flowerbeds. She looked in the letterbox every day, but most of the time there was nothing, except fliers for pizza deliveries, appropriately half eaten by snails. Today, there was an envelope, untouched by the snails and addressed to her. She tore it open.

Dear Cassie,

I really love you and I was sorry to let you down the way I did. I can't seem to explain on the phone. But I will stop ringing you and I'd like you to stop ringing me. I have been searching my heart as to why it fell apart and I think it boils down to a question of values. All your life, from what you have told me, you have valued status and money and prestige. That is okay, because that is your choice.

On the other hand, all my life, I have been in search of a feeling of oneness with nature and my fellow man. I may not have been successful, but that has been my direction, and in pursuit of that I have had to largely disregard any thoughts of money and prestige. Yes, of course, I do love you.

Darcy.

She walked up and down the hall, past the bird in the cloak. "You'll keep," she told it. After that, she didn't call him. But he was still there, festering.

Anthea stood waiting as Cassie came out of the steam room. "Getting hot isn't good for the baby," she said. "And I don't know that the tub is a great idea either. I'll keep you company and then we'll eat together."

"Don't you and Mike like to eat together?"

"We've moved from 'this might work' to 'this mightn't work'." Anthea looked pained. "I think I'm on the slippery slope to no man's land again. Literally."

"Are you okay?"

"I'm okay. He's okay. We're just not okay together," said Anthea with finality. "I'm sick of talking about it."

"I'm sweating out poisonous hatreds," said Cassie as she slid into the spa. "Ever since I got the letter, I've felt so angry. Sanctimonious bastard."

"What are you doing about it?" asked Anthea.

"I've written about ten well-considered, well-written replies," said Cassie. "Like corporate reports. None with quite the edge I want."

Anthea looked at her thoughtfully. It seemed to her that now, they talked the same language. Cassie caught her glance.

"What do you think I should do?" she asked.

"Go and see him. Let it rip," said Anthea. "Get him out of your system."

It wasn't her style but Anthea's suggestion stayed with her. An exorcism was needed if she was to get on with her life. Darcy had changed her, expanded her horizons, had helped her to see painful and difficult things about herself. His letter, however, put her back in the very box from which she had emerged. She needed to demonstrate to him and to herself that she had really changed. She needed to confront him.

In Cassie's mind, the enterprise had an almost religious feel to it – somewhere between a pilgrimage and an exorcism. She picked a day and marked it on the calendar, a week ahead.

After breakfast, just before she was about to go, it seemed important that the house be left in order. Cassie wanted to claim it, to have herself sown into it like a seed. She stacked a pile of newspapers next to the wood stove in the kitchen. She picked some azaleas and put them in a Japanese raku vase on the dining table. She plumped up the cushions on her mother's window seat. There was a flowered tapestry cushion that she remembered her mother stitching, and a round, red, pleated velvet cushion. Feathers worked their way through the velvet and she pulled a couple out and then put the cushion beside the tapestry one. She was going to add one of her Kurdish cushions, but it didn't look right. The corner was her mother's. She hadn't seen her mother since her visit with Susan. It wasn't so much what Susan had said as the paralysing despair she felt at her mother's condition.

She remembered the story her mother had told her, time and again, of coming to Australia, coming to meet her father, on a bride ship, the only English woman amongst the Italian girls. Her fear, later her reality, was that she would never see England again. Cassie thought of her mother and father, adrift in Australia, a family, but also two strangers. Maybe her mother had been looking for an escape from politeness, from the restraint of the pretty little village. Maybe she had been looking for adventure and romance, but had been disappointed by her father. Maybe her mother had had more courage than she ever had.

She swept the front verandah, brushed away the spider webs and moved the big Balinese brass gong out there, to hang on the wall. Beside it, she set a large Chinese cylindrical pot. It looked right, but invited theft, so she moved them back inside, into the hall, opposite Darcy's bird. She looked into the sitting room. The sofa and chairs she had brought from the flat looked wrong there. They would never look right. The bulky, dark lounge and chairs that her parents had bought second-hand were better. In time, she could get them re-covered. She'd paint the white walls, something deeper, smoky. She couldn't get the colour, but it gave her satisfaction that, in time, she would.

Cassie lugged the surplus, unplaced furniture into the back bedroom, a small, cheap addition in fibro. She could demolish it and build her conservatory here, bringing the sky and the row of pines into the fabric of the house. Darcy's words came back to her then ... *you have valued status and money and prestige. That is okay, because that is your choice.* Stuff him. She'd get a job and build the conservatory and show him. Under her grief, she could feel the rage building. It scared her, not knowing what she would say to him, how she would feel and react.

The housekeeping had its effect. Cassie now had a sense of the house being hers, and of herself being part of the landscape here. She would find tracks through the bush, tend the roses, plant bulbs; the map no longer empty.

But still Darcy ate at her heart, and inspired her fury.

As she left the house, she could feel it imprinted on her mind. She knew that the map would become more complex. Slowly, she would rebuild her life and that would be imprinted within her.

Cassie backed the car out of the garage and decided she would not go down the expressway. Bell's Line of road was quieter, slower. A portent of her new way of life.

She drove slowly, noting the landmarks. There were several versions in her head of what she should say to Darcy. One involved the dissection and destruction of his letter, the defence of her virtues. Another concentrated on his fear of commitment. Another held forth the promises of mountain life, sweetness and light, no recriminations. In reserve, she even had a spirited defence of the market economy. At Bilpin, she remembered that he was not going to be in the new map of her life. The realisation shook her.

She stopped at a roadside stall to buy some fruit. There were cases of apples, pears, and jars of runny jam set on a rickety display shelf. A small, bent Italian woman looked at Cassie critically.

"You want a case? Lovely apples. Justa picked."

"I'll have four red delicious, thanks."

"You want jam?"

"No thanks. Is that your orchard?" She indicated the orchard behind the stall.

The woman packed the four apples as two nondescript puppies yapped in the dirt. "No. We off the road. Down the lane. Renta the stall. You know, to sell."

Cassie nodded. "Hard work, an orchard."

The old woman handed her the bag. "Too hard. We a selling. Live in Parramatta when we sell." She shrugged her shoulders. "Work, work, work. All my life. Now, stop."

"Is anyone interested in buying?"

"Not yet. Long time to sell."

"Could I have a look? At the orchard?"

The old woman looked at her sceptically. "You buy? Orchard?"

"Maybe."

"Down the lane." She pointed to a tiny dirt lane. "Stone house." She looked at Cassie with mistrust and then picked one of the pups up by the neck. "You like a pup? Very good. Foxie. Catcha rat. Ten dollar."

Cassie smiled and shook her head, and got back in the car. For a moment, she was tempted to forget the orchard and drive back down the highway. But she was in no hurry and turned down into the lane. It was narrow, dusty, with the trees planted close on both sides. It opened out a little where a great mound of wrecked wooden packing cases lay on one side of the road. Pale green lichen grew over a decaying dry stone wall. Further on, there were packing sheds, dilapidated, but obviously still in use, and a graveyard of discarded agricultural machinery. But the soft green of the trees, and the distant line of mountains made it all somehow romantic. A little further, there was a clearing on one side of the orchard. In the clearing was a tiny stone house, with a flagged area in front, covered by a trellis with grapes. In a patch of sunlight, before the soft dappled shade of the orchard took over, were rows of vegetables, silver beet, cabbages and beans. The roof of the house was a soft patchwork of faded red and pink corrugated iron, the window frames a strange, bright blue. At the back, a tilted Hills Hoist, rusting, looked like a giant spiderweb against the trees. She was stunned by the beauty of it, the sort of decrepit beauty so loved by Darcy.

It was crazy, Cassie reminded herself, to be indulging the idea of such a folly, to be thinking of Darcy, here, with her, loving this. She scribbled down the estate agent's number from the For Sale sign, telling herself it was impractical, stupid and unaffordable. She got into the car, and drove back down the lane without looking back, but stuffed the scrap of paper in her top pocket.

She drove down the highway and stopped at Parramatta, where she went into the hardware shop. The garage at the mountain house was full of her father's old tools, with peeling, red-painted handles and touches of rust. She wanted new, easy, shiny female power tools. She wandered round the shop, feeling how different it was to shop now that she had limited money, an individual rather than a corporate charge card. She liked it, and it seemed to her that she could and would get another job. Something simpler, closer to ordinary, she thought. The orchard. Perfect apples. Clear apple jelly. Export quality. She tried to calm her mind.

She still had the drive to Kurnell. She remembered Anthea's phrase of "let it rip" and felt angry with Darcy again. She got back in the car and began to drive faster, not so much with a sense of urgency, but a desire to finish this.

As she drove along the beach front, the wind was lifting the water along the shore, the waves white-tipped. Seagulls swooped and dived and a lone pelican sat on a pylon. Cassie stopped outside Darcy's house and looked up to see him sitting outside his tree house, with a mug of coffee, hopelessly trying to read the paper in the wind.

She got out of the car. "Come down," she called.

"Come up," he called back without getting up.

"No." She stood on the bottom step, feeling hopeless, wanting him again, the rage at his letter, the fear of her own powerlessness surfacing.

"What do you want?" he asked.

"That letter of yours was such crap," she told him angrily.

"From your point of view." He was colder than she ever imagined he could be.

"And yours."

"How?"

"It was because of you, not me, that you didn't come up the mountains. Not because of what's wrong with me, what's wrong with *you*. You know it."

"So is that why you're here?" He was distant, supercilious.

"Yes."

"To prove yourself right?"

"No." Why had she come? Fury, but also to get him back, make him see. "If you had come up the mountains, we could have had a life together. Stop being lonely – both of us – and start being people." She wasn't even sure if it was an invitation or an explanation.

"And reach for the stars together." His voice was laden with sarcasm. "Scale the heights. No horizons, only the infinite."

"Just an ordinary life with cups of tea and walks in the bush and holidays by the sea," she said impatiently. "Arguments and difficulties and whatever."

"Sex?"

"Yes." She said it before she realised what a put-down it was.

"How lovely."

She had become cold now. Cold and brittle. The ice maiden. Maybe that was really what he had liked. But it was too late. The whole thing had fallen apart.

He stood up. "You never get mad. You're always reasonable. You've got no bloody passion, Cass."

She felt herself contracting, categorised, in the box again. The organised, sensible, good and well-mannered box into which she fitted perfectly. Without passion, filled with a cold dislike for herself, wanting to be something else. He was standing above her, blocking the sun. She moved towards the gate, nearly tripping over the hose. She wanted to say she did have passion, that there was more in her than he could ever guess or dream of, that she was as full of despair and confusion and elation as anyone. But she was scared it might only come out as a polite protest.

She stood by the pelican carving next to the tap, and she suddenly picked up the hose, turned it on. At first, it dribbled ineffectually, but she put her finger over the nozzle and squirted it at him. The water came on hard and he winced and jumped back, trapped between the tree and the stairs. She came closer and sprayed him hard, trapping him, soaking him, punishing him.

"Fucking stop!" he yelled.

"You laugh at the whale watchers dancing on a headland. You mock me because I'm a corporate woman. You laugh at people and mock them so you never have to have a thing to do with them, so you can maintain your oneness with nature and life at a distance. You've been thinking about this stupid exhibition forever and never done a thing. You won't come and live with me because you're too scared or too mad, and I'm not sure I want you anyway, you prick!"

Cassie flung the hose onto the ground where it spun round wildly, wetting the bottom of her jeans. She walked out of the gate, got back into the car and drove away without looking back, although she had a picture of him, satisfyingly cold and wet. And sorry, she hoped.

She had planned to drive home, but she decided, on the spur of the moment, to call in on her mother. Walking through the nursing home, she felt she shouldn't have come. Weary, familiar despair settled on her. The bed next to her mother's was empty, and the curtain between the beds billowed and subsided like a sail in the afternoon breeze. Cassie sat down next to her sleeping mother. She sat back in the vinyl chair, sticky in the heat, but glad to be there. She realised it was a long time since she had been alone with her mother, without the busy presence of the nurses, Susan or other patients.

"Oh, Mama," she sighed. They had used to call her that, mimicking their father, when there had been a rare, light-hearted family moment. Her mother turned her face towards her, still asleep.

Cassie felt tears in her eyes. She laid her head on the bed and clasped her mother's limp hand across her hair. She could smell the lavender perfume their mother had always used. Susan must have put it on her, a dab behind the ears, a dab on each wrist, a ritual whenever she had gone to town, a tiny, foolish vanity. She felt grateful to Susan for remembering, for doing it. She lay, in the hot room, the occasional breeze, her mother's hand on her head, tears. There were no words, only a reverberation from a time long before words.

Eventually Cassie sat up, and held her mother's hand. Her mother was still sleeping peacefully. Wet-eyed, she leaned over and kissed her on the cheek.

She got back to the mountain house in record time, taking the expressway. She walked in, started the fire, and poured herself a drink. She sat in her mother's window seat and warmed herself in the late afternoon sun. The bottoms of her jeans were still wet and she took them off and sat, bunched in a rug, waiting for the sun to set, sipping her drink as her mother had used to do. She felt a great calm, looking out into the garden and the bush, hearing the birds. But there was also an ache in her. She had wanted Darcy, even with all his stupidity and pretensions.

Chapter 20

Susan tiptoed up the surgery stairs and unlocked the door. She turned on the light and put the two folders she was carrying in Nick's pigeonhole. She took them out, flicked through them again with pride, and then put them back.

There was a sudden noise as the light went on in the surgery behind her and she whirled round to see Nick, standing in the doorway.

"Fuck," she said, holding her hand over her heart. "You were here? In the dark?"

"We finished late," he said. "I was thinking."

"You sit here in the dark, thinking?"

He looked at her angrily. "I sit in here or in the car. I don't have any place else."

She indicated the folders. "I brought you the accounts. And I did a couple of cashflows too, if you're interested."

"Business is the last thing on my mind," he said brusquely.

"You don't have to worry about it. It's doing okay. Could be better, but the cashflow is fine."

"Shut up!" he said furiously. "Just shut up! My life's fallen apart and you're talking about the cashflow."

"You could stick your life back together again," she flashed back. "It wouldn't be easy, but you could do it. You could come back, talk about it, think about it. We could even have counselling. It's all there for you."

"I don't know if I can go back. You know, for years and years I was nothing except the smart one in my family. But I was uptight, scared. The only other thing I had going for me was that I could eventually earn money, help the family out. The only fun I ever had was that motorbike – till I met you. And I fell in love with you – with your mind, your body, the way your hair curled, the way you laughed. That photo you sent brought it all back – how I felt. And I was more and more in love when you had our babies and suckled them and raised them. Even when you were crazy."

"Spare me," she said.

"This is serious, Susan. It was true. And it's been broken. No!" He raised his hand. "I'm not saying it was your fault. I'm past that. It was an act of God, maybe. We can't just walk back in the door and play happy families."

"God save us from playing happy families," said Susan. "We're just two ordinary people, Nick. That's all we are."

"Two problems," said the doctor. "Foetal heartbeat. It's very irregular. Second problem is that the placenta seems to be detaching itself from the uterus."

"So it's serious?" said Anthea stupidly. She took her hand off her stomach, not wanting to add to the pressures on the baby. It had been very quiet the last week. She could hardly breathe for the fear, although she tried to remember to take in air for the baby.

"Serious," said the doctor. There was no smile. "I'll get Kate to ring Admissions." Anthea started to get up. "Stay there," the doctor barked. "We'll get the orderlies to take you over. No movement unless you need to."

"It's thirty weeks," said Anthea.

The doctor looked into her face, and squeezed her hand. "We'll do everything we can," she said. "It's nothing you've done. Sometimes these things happen."

"Do you want us to ring the father?" asked the nurse in Admissions.

"He's in Hong Kong this week," said Anthea. "Ring my friend. Cassie La Rosa. Ask her to come." She scribbled down Cassie's phone number for the nurse and began to cry. This morning she'd been teaching her final lesson in women's history to a class of sixteen-year-olds. Now, she had a drip in, a hospital gown, a monitor across her abdomen, a concerned nurse standing at her side. They had wheeled her across the road in the busy lunchtime traffic, into the hospital, and now she was in a ward where she had a view of street lights, tree tops and sky. The baby hadn't moved for hours. That was a bad sign.

The nurse had left her, still hooked up, but alone. Maybe that was a good sign. The drug they had given her was sending her to sleep. Maybe that's why the baby hadn't moved. Except it hadn't moved before that. A little faint kick last night, not like the big lusty kicks she was used to.

She couldn't talk to the baby. She wanted to tell it to hang on, to stay there, to get better, not to be born, but she couldn't. It was there, suspended, frightened, paralysed as she was.

Cassie stood beside her, white, frightened but comforting. She stroked Anthea's stomach with her fingertips. "Hang on, baby."

Anthea knew they had told Cassie something, but she looked at her friend, wordlessly willing her not to tell. She had to hang on, had to believe the baby was okay. Cassie clasped her hand, thinking she had never seen such fear as she now saw in Anthea's face.

"Oh God," said Anthea, suddenly white, and Cassie saw the pinkish stain spreading between her legs. She pressed the buzzer, but already there were nurses running into the room, two orderlies pushing the trolley, Anthea's face pale and scared, her blue eyes enlarged, like a child's.

"You stay there," said the nurse to Cassie, indicating the corridor, as they pushed Anthea into the theatre. "I'll call you when it's over."

Anthea remembered nothing, until she woke, a light blazing above her, the doctor holding the dead baby in her arms, Cassie beside her, sobbing, her arms around her, nurses. "I'm sorry," the doctor said. "It was baby's heart. And the placenta coming away. Didn't have a chance."

Anthea looked at the tiny blue body in the blanket, one leg curled in, the other, strangely straight, a tiny elf-like face, waxy skin.

"Was she born . . . ?"

"Survived about half a minute. She didn't have a chance," the doctor repeated.

Anthea looked at the doctor, who was red-eyed and strained. She wanted to protest. It was her baby. This was hers. This baby. It couldn't be dead. Not hers. She reached down and felt her stomach – deflated – and looked at the thing they placed in her arms with horror. She thrust the bundle at Cassie and screamed, a scream that she had never known was in her. She looked at Cassie as she screamed, Cassie with the pathetic bundle, the stiff little leg outlined against her, no chubby baby flesh, but that strange, unknown creature, a smear of pink blood on Cassie's shirt. The scream turned to a deep sobbing. She was aware of the noise she was making, of herself looking at them, and they, all strangers except Cassie, looking at her.

"Do you want . . . ?" asked the nurse, taking the bundle with the stiff foot from Cassie and proffering it to her.

Anthea shook her head. "Take it."

The sobs subsided, as if they had never belonged to her, and she lay staring at the white wall, feeling the death that had started inside her. It was still there, rapacious and black, and, she knew, would never leave her now, but would remain the most basic part of her. Anthea thought it was strange that Cassie was the one who kept sniffing and reaching for tissues. The only time Anthea felt affected was when she thought of the foot poking out of the blanket, the strange, stiff little leg. She concentrated on not thinking about it.

Later, they brought the bundle back and Cassie left. The bereavement counsellor wanted her to hold the body, but she wouldn't and the little bundle lay between them, as the counsellor talked. Anthea deliberately didn't listen, knowing how easily the black inside would expand and take her over. Later, they discharged her and she and Cassie drove up the mountains. Cassie rang Mike. He cried and said he'd ring Anthea in the morning. Cassie rang Anthea's mother in New Zealand, then rang the school and made arrangements for Anthea to have leave till the end of term.

She lay, sobbing, clinging to Cassie. Later, Cassie put Anthea to bed, and went to bed herself, but lay awake, looking out into the dark, thinking about the body of the tiny dead baby, wanting to ring Darcy. Anthea's baby was over, she and Darcy were finished. Loneliness, loss flooded her mind, and she wondered how Anthea would ever recover.

She looked up to see Anthea standing in the doorway.

"Did you call Mike?" Anthea asked.

"I rang him earlier," said Cassie. "He'll ring you in the morning. He was pretty devastated."

"He'll go back to Perth," said Anthea. "He had a job offer there, but he was going to stay here because of the baby. But we'd had the big showdown. He was doing this contract in Hong Kong for three weeks, then he was going to move out." She sat down on the bed. "Could I sleep here?"

Cassie thought of how she used to resist Susan, who had always wanted to sleep in her bed when they were children. Now, she could not refuse Anthea's ravaged grief. She surprised herself with her capacity to respond. Through the night, she turned to comfort Anthea, to hold her tightly in her arms, to pat her hair, to soothe her tossing sleep. In the morning, they both woke early and then went back to sleep. Cassie got up at midday and Anthea slept on. At night, Anthea walked in the garden. Cassie waited for her, sat with her as she slumped on the window seat, staring into the blackness, oblivious to the blankets and cushions Cassie arranged around her.

The following day Anthea slept, and over the weeks slowly edged towards more normal times. She continued, in silent withdrawal, Cassie watching her, feeding her like a small child. Sometimes she put her arms around her until Anthea moved away, back into the silent shell. Eventually, Anthea began to mention the pregnancy and the baby, lightly, in passing, as if the events had happened to someone else. Cassie continued her vigil. Anthea developed a protective veneer, thin and brittle. She lost weight. Her old brashness returned at times, but it was lifeless. She began to spend occasional nights in her apartment in Sydney, but always quickly returned to the mountains, as if the blackness inside her would overwhelm her if she was alone.

"I took your sister back her baby gear," she said one day.

"That must have been hard. You feel okay?"

"Actually, I liked seeing her children. I thought children would be hard for me, but they're not. They're just children." She shrugged her shoulders.

"How was Susan?" asked Cassie, wondering if she was a coward, if she should more actively encourage Anthea to talk about the baby.

"She's okay. Still doing the devoted daughter bit."

Cassie realised she had barely had any contact with Susan since the last time they saw their mother together.

"Odd," said Anthea. "Susan's into self-sacrifice and you're into self-realisation. They seem so different, but in the end it's all about ourselves. We're all totally self-centred creatures. No-one else matters."

"Anthea . . ."

Anthea broke up some kindling and started setting the fire. She knelt down, coaxing the flame towards the wood. "They cremate those babies, you know. The premature ones. They've got the ashes somewhere. They sent me the bill, asked me what I wanted to do with them."

Cassie put her hand on Anthea's shoulder.

Anthea stood up, as if she had not felt Cassie's hand. "They charge you for storing them. Tiny little thing she was." She looked at Cassie briefly, and Cassie felt a small flicker of the enormous chasm of grief inside her friend. She put her arm lightly round her and they watched the flickering flames. "Your sister's coming up for the holidays," said Anthea.

Susan arrived with the three children and a computer which she set up on the dining table. Cassie didn't mention it and at dinner, they fed the children around it and then sat out on the back verandah for their own meal, which they usually had with a bottle of wine. The strain of Anthea's unspoken grief and Darcy's loss was relieved by the busy presence of Susan and the children, and the gulf between Susan and Cassie was somehow bridged by Anthea's presence. Hanging together, Cassie thought, the three adults and the three children, their tensions just below the surface.

On the weekend Nick came to take the children back to Sydney with him. Susan was out when he arrived. It seemed to Cassie that Nick looked older, more worn and less effectual, as he sat with her drinking coffee in the kitchen.

"It's been over six months," he said wearily. "There's not much hope of it changing now, is there?"

"Who could change it?" she asked.

He sighed, and she could see her father's stubbornness in him. Nick knew he could get Susan back, but Cassie suspected some weary male pride, nursing the hurts of his marriage, prevented it.

"We'd have to start again," he said. "And she won't."

Cassie suddenly felt sick of him blaming Susan. "She is starting again. She's up every night studying accountancy. She's smart. She'll do well." She felt a sense of surprise at her protectiveness towards her sister.

Nick spread his hands. "Don't talk to me like I'm some klutz," he said. "I understand she doesn't want to look after kids all her life, but we've always agreed that family life was the most important thing. You know, when we got engaged, she begged me, she pleaded with me, that we don't have a life like our parents." He shrugged his shoulders. "Now this."

"I don't know, Nick. I had always thought you were happy . . ."

"We were, we were . . ."

"Maybe you were." She felt uncomfortable. Until now, she had always implicitly sided with Nick, the unmentioned subject of Susan's neurosis an undercurrent between them. "But there must have been something wrong – for Susan to feel she wanted to leave. I know she's had some problems, but marriage and family have always been important to her."

"So she says."

"They have," said Cassie sharply. "I know."

"You think it's my fault now."

Cassie poured him more coffee. "It's got to be partly your responsibility. Like me losing my job. Ultimately, for me, if I see it as my responsibility, then it's going to stand me in good stead. I won't make the same mistake again." She said it lightly, the way she used to talk to her staff, but the memory of things Jennifer had said still flashed painfully through her mind.

"The girls ready?"

"You're not taking Jack?"

"He's teething." Nick grimaced. "Won't leave his mother."

"Susan left their bags."

"I'll bring them back on Sunday. She wants an answer by the end of the holidays."

"An answer?"

"Whether I'll come back."

"I don't understand," said Susan drunkenly. "You get married and you have kids. It's like somebody hits you over the head and when you wake up the world is different. The rules change or something. I guess Nick's lost the plot." She leaned forward and wiggled her finger at Cassie. "But he's a bad boy. He won't talk about it."

"Maybe he doesn't have the tools to talk about it."

"Oh Christ!" said Susan, throwing her head back. "You were always on his side."

"No," said Cassie. "I'm not. I'm on yours." A look passed between her and Susan, a tentative acknowledgment that things had shifted. But only a little, Cassie thought. They were both being careful. Like she was about Darcy, letting the idea of him go, accepting that he had gone, bit by bit. He could still rebound on her, hit her full force, sink her. Gradually, she was building herself a new life. This, three women sitting on the verandah after dinner, wrapped in warm jackets, looking at the stars, drinking, was part of it.

"You're all primed," said Anthea, who was as drunk as Susan, "with this dream of this life you're supposed to have. And you have variations, deviations so that you forget it's not actually happening. And bits of it happen, and they unhappen. And you get stuck on them. All the while, the water's busy draining down the plughole and life's disappearing. But you're too hooked on this dream that doesn't turn out. So why has everyone got the fucking dream? This universal, hopeless dream. Unmarried, married. With children, without them. Baby!" Her voice was hoarse with pain. "None of it is ever like the dream was. It's hopeless." She looked at Susan. "No wonder I've got an overwhelming sense of futility."

"An overwhelming sense of humility?" said Susan. "Why have you got a sense of humility? I think you should feel proud, after all you've gone through."

"Futility, not humility," said Cassie, but they both ignored her.

"It doesn't make me proud," said Anthea, taking a swig of the Midori that Susan had bought. "But I've changed. I used to wonder what life was about. Now, I wonder what the fuck could it possibly be about? What possible sense or meaning or coherent idea could be embedded in this mess?" She threw up her hands theatrically and stared at the stars. "Look at those stars. They're beautiful, but they are messy. All streaky and smeary and none of the dot-to-dot pictures really work. No bears or saucepans in the sky. Just an idea that some ancient Greek dreamed up." Her voice rose. "There is no God! A mess!"

"Here's to the mess!" said Cassie, raising her glass.

"The mess!" echoed Susan.

"The baby," said Anthea slowly. "That baby of mine. Rosa." She looked at them, suddenly re-oriented to the earth. "They sent me its footprint the other day, and a photo of its little dead face." Her voice took on a cracked, harsh quality. "What am I supposed to do? Stick it in my wallet? Show it to people when they ask what happened?"

"Cry," said Susan gently.

Cassie squeezed Anthea's hand.

"I can't," replied Anthea.

Nick came up the last weekend of the holidays and worked on demolishing the green concrete circle. He worked demonically, first with a jackhammer, then with a mallet, the children watching from a respectful distance. He collected rocks from the bush, laid agricultural drainage, put in a liner for the pool, and created a small spout up the hill, so that the water flowed down into the pool and then slowly drained back into the remnants of the creek which lay beyond the back boundary. He worked late into the night, stopping for leftover sausages from the children's dinner to fuel him, digging under the lights Cassie rigged for him.

"Where's he going to sleep?" whispered Anthea and looked at Susan.

"He's having some deep cathartic experience," said Susan loftily, "which will resolve the whole question for him, including where he sleeps." She rocked Jack, trying to soothe him as he grizzled sleepily and pulled at her hair.

Eventually, they were all too tired to wait, and went to bed, leaving Nick still concreting.

Susan lay awake, the children asleep around her in the double bed, the window open, listening to the sounds of construction, willing Nick to finish, willing him to come in to her, willing the torture of it all to end, for the decision to be finally and irrevocably made. It seemed as if he was punishing her. She remembered, when she was fifteen, willing herself not to eat. Now, fighting against the tiredness that had kept her up with Jack the last few nights, she willed herself to stay awake. But finally, exhausted, she fell asleep. When she woke, the lights outside had been turned off and the cold had come through the house. She lay in bed, half asleep, thinking she should get up and close the window. In the shadowy darkness, she thought she saw Nick at the bottom of the bed. "Come in, Nick," she said. Later, she was unsure whether he had ever been there. But in the grey light of morning, when there was no sign of him, she was sure it was finished.

All the tools had been cleared away and the pool finished. Nick's car was gone. The pool was perfect, exactly how Cassie had wanted it, except for an ugly Japanese lantern standing to one side of the stream. Cassie exchanged looks with Anthea, but said nothing. It was her house, but it carried both more of her and less of her than her apartment ever had. Whereas the apartment had been wholly hers, this house carried the legacy of her parents, the flow of their lives through it, the intrusion of Susan's family, the marks of her children. It was old, jerry-built in places, disorganised and complicated. It would never, unlike the apartment, be either perfect or hers. The Japanese lantern could stay.

"I chose the lantern," Susan told Cassie. "The man said it was Japanese." She smiled. "So I knew it was perfect for you."

"Are you really sisters?" Elin asked, looking at them.

The rain poured down, making rivers of yellow clay-stained slush across the lawn. The azaleas, usually robust, drooped under the weight of the water. The late autumn annuals stood bedraggled, like weeds. Inside, there were small muddy footprints across the floor, scattered card games, the girls' dolls lined up on the sofa, Jack's baby lego a minefield across the dining room. Cassie gritted her teeth. Susan seemed blissfully unaware.

They sat out on the verandah, watching the warm autumn rain as Cassie, in shorts and gumboots, unblocked the leaves from the drains and downpipes. "It's not a wet-weather house for kids," said Susan. "We might go tomorrow." Idly, she combed Elin's hair up into a ponytail. Jack, chubby, brown and naked, worked beside Cassie, making piles of leaves. "I've got to get some school uniforms," Susan went on vaguely. "And find a babysitter for Jack for the two nights I go to that course."

"I'll babysit," said Anthea. She looked at Elin. "As long as you promise to go to bed on time."

"No way," said Elin.

"I'll still do it," said Anthea and gently tugged Elin's ponytail.

"So are you okay to go back to work?" Cassie asked Anthea. She was concerned for Anthea, but at the same time longing for solitude, aching for the house to be hers, to be free of Anthea's pain. She had not called Darcy again and he had not called her. The affair, it seemed, had ended and something in her had resigned herself, sadly, to its end. Now she needed to confront the aloneness, to be solitary.

"I rang the other day," replied Anthea. "They're desperate for me, which feels good. And I get to do a curriculum planning course one day a week all next year if I agree to take the special needs group."

"I thought you were going to teach three unit HSC history?"

Anthea shrugged. "Anyone can do that. Those kids are so smart they can practically teach themselves. Or show you up as dopey." She picked Jack up out of the mud, pulled him onto the verandah and wrapped him in a towel. "You need a bath, kiddo," she said. "You too, Cass. I hope you aren't going to get old and un-glamorous and let yourself go living up here."

"Mud's good for your skin," said Susan. She got up, suddenly energised. "We'll do Jack in the laundry tub. You have the big bath, Cass. Long and hot. I'll clean up everything. And make the dinner. And tomorrow I'll go and leave you in peace." She looked at Cassie slyly.

The morning was bright, sunny and crisp. Cassie picked the snails out of the herb garden and thought it was the right day to begin a new life. She would drive down the Bilpin road, look at the Italians' orchard again and at another more developed but more expensive property. She kept getting drawn back, impractical though it was, to the little stone house, to the idea of sending clear apple jelly to Japan. With Susan and Anthea leaving, she was already wondering what it would be like to be alone again. Alone, no Darcy, no hope of his return. There was an excitement in it, in the newness of it, but also fear. For the first time, she could understand Anthea's endless hunt for contact, for touch, even of the most transitory nature.

Susan emerged from the kitchen door. "We're going," she called. "We'll get breakfast at Macca's." She hoisted her bags into the boot of the car and walked over to Cassie. "Thanks for putting up with us," she said, almost embarrassed. "You don't need to worry. We won't come every holidays."

"I like to see the kids," said Cassie, Elin's hand tightly clasped in hers. The holiday had brought down the barriers, but there was still some uneasiness between her and Susan. "Come when you like," she said rashly. "I'll get lonely here by myself."

"I got lonely with Nick," said Susan. "You've got a lot going for you, Cass."

"You might still be able to fix it with Nick," said Cassie, as the children climbed into the car.

"It's over," said Susan, after she strapped Jack in. She closed the car door, so Elin would not hear. "I'm going to see a solicitor." She smiled. "Anyway, I've got the kids to keep me busy." Cassie felt the pain of her own broken heart. They hugged awkwardly. As Susan drove off, the children waved wildly to Cassie through the back window of the car.

"Thanks," said Anthea as she came onto the verandah with her bag. She looked at Cassie with pain in her eyes. "You can resign as my nurse, and be my friend again. You did a sterling job."

"It's not alright, is it?" said Cassie.

"No."

"Anthea."

"It's a great black thing in my soul."

"I can see it there."

"I don't even want it to go. Even though it's so painful, I want her there. I want her there in you too. Remember I called her Rosa. For you. So remember, even if you suffer. It was too big to be just a pot of ashes somewhere."

She slid down and sat on the floor of the verandah. "I'm getting some help," she said. "Back in Sydney."

She was crying, making no sound. They sat, against the noise of the currawongs.

Chapter 21

"I'm sorry to inform you, Miss La Rosa, that your mother passed away. Quite peacefully. Just a few minutes ago."

Cassie looked at her watch. "When?" she asked foolishly.

There was a moment of hesitation. "At breakfast. The aide was putting the breakfasts out. They do that, and then go back to help the ones who need it. Like your mother. And when the aide got back, your mother was . . . she had passed away."

Cassie had an image of her mother slumped on the breakfast tray, a culmination of all the small but horrible indignities that her mother had suffered and she had witnessed; the mean, embarrassing incidents that had coloured these last years. She had sometimes wondered if she would ever be able to recall her mother differently, to remember her at other times of her life. "Had she been ill in the last few days?" she asked mechanically.

"The same. Except she had been sleeping a lot. We've had to wake her for meals. But nothing . . . to indicate . . ."

"I'll come. Have you told my sister?"

"We tried to call, but she was engaged. Sister Monica knows her, of course, so she's walking up to her place now. Susan should be back from dropping the girls at school." For a moment, Cassie wondered at the degree of intimacy that allowed them such familiarity with the details of Susan's life. She, her sister, had no idea of Susan's day, or Susan of hers. Unlike her mother and herself, Susan had always been good at these casual encounters, at small personal intimacies.

Cassie pulled herself into the present. "I'll be there. By midday. Thank you for calling."

She had thought of her mother's death many times, seeing it as a release from the slow, undignified process of dying. She had envisaged it as a release for her mother, as well as for herself and Susan, an end to the tiny meaningless rituals her mother's life had become. But now, she felt a tightening across her chest. The death struck her forcefully, primally. Swamped by feeling, she couldn't think, couldn't answer the ringing phone. Eventually, she got dressed and drove to Sydney. She felt numb, disembodied, during the drive.

Susan met her at the nursing home.

"You look terrible," she whispered to Cassie. "Are you okay?"

"What do we need to do?" asked Cassie mechanically, knowing she couldn't do it.

"Come to the funeral parlour." She took Cassie's arm. She seemed remarkably calm. "We need to go up there, to make the arrangements. And you can see her if you like."

Susan made the practical arrangements for the priest, the service, the notice, the flowers, the music, the chapel and the seating while Cassie sat with her mother's body in a viewing room at the funeral parlour. The room was small and cold, imbued with religiosity and pomp. The anonymous piped music gave her a sense of unreality. She was no longer crying, but the feeling of loss reverberating through her had rendered her incapable of decision-making or even thought. Her mother lay, a sheet over her, her head revealed, her face expressionless. When Cassie's father had died, his face still had his familiar expression, stubbornly fighting life, but her mother's expression was of someone truly gone. Cassie was scared to touch her under the sterile sheet, but she wanted to put a blanket over her, to check her clothes, to keep her warm, do her hair. All the tasks she had resisted when her mother was alive now would have felt natural, but she remained as fixed and rigid as the body, staring, bound by primitive fear, until Susan drove her home.

"You don't have to feel so bad," said Susan gently. "You did a lot for her. She would have never let me get her out of the mountain house. She couldn't manage. She needed to go."

"I don't feel guilty," said Cassie. "Really, I don't. Something else."

"I know," said Susan, bursting into tears. "It's ghastly." But it seemed to Cassie that Susan had known how to prepare for death, known instinctively how to respond to death, just as she had known how to respond to her mother's sickness. Even before that, she had been tolerant of their mother's vagueness, whereas it had irritated Cassie, long before it had been diagnosed as Alzheimer's. She knew more now, but she wondered how Susan had learned these skills, why she had missed out on learning them.

Susan's house was full of people – the children, Nick, his parents and brothers, neighbours, an old neighbour of their mother's, a forgotten cousin of their father's, the doctor from the nursing home. Nick put his arm round Cassie. "Stay here," he said. "Till after the funeral."

"Are you . . . ?" she began hesitantly.

"I'll be around every day," said Nick. "I've got a locum in for the week. Help organise things and look after the kids for Suzie." He was, it seemed to Cassie, back to the solid role of husband and father. He smiled at Cassie and she was reminded again how like her father he was. "After all this, who knows?" The insecurities of her father, too.

Cassie struggled her way through the next few days and through the funeral. She had flashes of memories of her mother – her blonde hair, before it faded, pinned back with a bobby pin, the pattern of an old floral apron, the lavender perfume. The memories in themselves meant nothing, except the strength of their connection.

Late that night, Susan came into her room, with a box. "Effects," she explained. "The Sisters sent it up."

It was a sad collection. A new toothbrush Susan had bought months ago, unused. The stub of a lipstick, the colour she had worn for all their lives. Handkerchiefs, of a sort you couldn't buy any more. Underwear, nightdresses, a crocheted shawl, a dressing gown, ugly slippers, laxatives. In a smaller box, there was a collection of cards, mainly birthday cards from Cassie, Susan and Elin, two letters, an old electricity bill and two photos. Susan picked up the letters.

"It's from Dad, in Italy." She began to read it. The letter, Cassie noticed, displayed the slight awkwardness with English that he'd always had.

Dear Bess, my wife, I am back at my home in Italy. I would have stayed with you, but there were some difficulties. Cassie may explain them. I think she understands.

"I didn't explain," said Cassie bleakly. "She never asked."

"What were they?" asked Susan.

"He was under pressure to do things he didn't want. There was a marijuana ring down at the markets. Dad wouldn't get involved, but he was part of the system. When he got the cancer, he was terrified they'd get him to do something really big. Courier money or drugs. Use him because he had nothing to lose. I only picked up bits and pieces from conversations he had in Italian. And little bits he told me – only because he had to."

"Mafia?" Susan's eyes were wide.

"I suppose. He wasn't a crook, but there was a system. People he was bound to – from his father's village." She paused. "There was a whole structure, a part of his life that we never saw."

I am back in my mother's house. In great pain. I will receive the last rites. We had a

*good marriage. The two girls. Tell Susan,
my little one, how much I miss her.*

Susan looked at Cassie. "She never did. It
ends, *Love Guido*." She turned the letter over.
"You know, it's only the last few years I felt
close to Mum. I had to really work at it,
though."

There was a trace of bitterness in Susan's
voice. Cassie wondered. She, more than Susan,
had been the focus of her mother's feeling,
bound by her mother's determination that Cassie
would be the perfect child. It hadn't made for
closeness, but it had been something. But then,
when her father was dying, she had made a
stand for him. Perhaps she had been wrong, but
she had only been twenty. Her mother had never
accused her, but she had never forgiven her
either. They had drifted apart, the threads of the
past that pulled them together more and more
uncomfortable. But at the end, and now, she felt
the intimacy again, unspoken, unacknowledged,
but there.

"I think she found us both pretty hard going,"
said Cassie. "I was too much like her in some
ways. You were too unlike her." They sat on the
bed together, both thinking that what had
divided them had now diminished.

"What's the other letter?" Cassie asked.

Susan picked it up. "An English cousin. Asking her to sponsor him in 1978. *In view of their past connection*. Maybe he was an old lover."

"We didn't really know her – in lots of ways," said Cassie.

"I knew the little things," said Susan. "Like the way she liked her jam spread, or her brand of talc." She shrugged. "It gave me a feeling of knowing her. Better than nothing." She picked up one of the photos. "Here we all are at the mountain house. My God, Cass, Mum and Dad look so happy. And you. And me."

Cassie picked up the photo. It must have been a year or two after they bought the house. She was about five, long blonde plaits, Susan a pretty, curly-haired, smiling babe in arms. Her father had a large garden fork. He leaned on it, smiling broadly, holding up a large tomato. Their mother leaned against him, holding Susan, as Cassie peeped out between her father's legs.

"Nick and I have photos like that," said Susan.

"What's happening – with you and Nick?"

"He's coming home."

"That's terrific." Cassie glanced at her sister. "Are you okay about it?"

"Yes. It's best. But it's different too."

"For you?" She sensed a resignation in Susan.

"Both of us, in a way. A reversal. When we got married, I was the one who was romantic, who wanted to live the dream. I thought Nick would attend to the realities. So we had this play-act marriage. Now we have to look after ourselves and each other and the kids. He's as fragile as me. I'm as strong as him. Sometimes it seems so complicated."

"Does he see all that?" Cassie pressed her. "All the complexities?"

Susan looked at her and smiled. "Come on. He's male, he's Italian. He tries." She looked at the photo again. "They probably tried, and they couldn't. They didn't have many moments like this, did they?"

"No." Cassie took the photo. "But maybe you and Nick are more suited. More love in the first place."

"Maybe," said Susan. "It was Mum's death that brought us back. The reality. The finality." They sat, looking at the photos. The other was of Elin and Kelly at the beach. If you drew them as maps, Cassie thought, in the first photo she'd had a place, there in the centre of it. The second photo was in a direct line from the first, literally its descendant. Although Susan wasn't in the photo, she was still there, in the map, central. But Cassie had disappeared, at best a footnote, an aside. She needed a map of her own.

"I feel ripped apart," Cassie told Susan.

"Me too," said Susan. She put her arm round Cassie and Cassie rested her head on Susan's shoulder. They looked at the photo of themselves and their parents in front of the mountain house. "God, just look at us."

"I thought I'd be relieved," Cassie told Anthea when they met for dinner. "I thought my mother's death would be like the end of the nightmare. I thought I'd already lost her."

"So what did you feel?" asked Anthea.

"It was the end of all this agony and angst and degradation," said Cassie, "but it was the end of her life too. It was the end of all that happiness and unhappiness, of her marriage, and her child-rearing and her childhood and her parents and everything she'd done and felt and been. I suppose it had gone already, but death is very different."

"You okay?"

"Yes, I miss her. I can't quite understand that. I mean she wasn't really here, but I miss her. Can you understand that?"

"Only too well," said Anthea.

Grief did unexpected things. It was heavy and painful, but it became part of her, and less painful with time. Cassie felt at peace with the mountain house. She asked Susan for the family snapshot and hung it in the kitchen, next to the photo of her father's family garden in Italy. She made a vegetable garden for her father and a flower garden for her mother. She couldn't say in any concrete sense that they were memorials, but they quieted the disparate spirits in the house. She started the planting and construction of a maze for Susan's children. She bought a dog for protection. She was assured by his owners that he barked at everything. He was a large amiable yellow creature, who barked at nothing, but lay in the sun, dug holes in her garden and chased balls. She had never owned a pet before and was surprised that he greeted her in the mornings with such enthusiasm, and sat with her in the evening with such fidelity. She decided she liked him very much. She worried she'd start telling people cute stories about him. She called him Edie, after Edith Wharton, whose books she had started borrowing from the library.

She began to get to know people in the local shops with an ease that had moved beyond her former politeness. Having afternoon coffee in particular places became a habit. Her time was filled with working on plans for the house, repainting the living room and cooking impressive meals when Anthea came, or when Susan and Nick arrived. She and Susan were more careful, more respectful, then more spontaneous, and more fun. They began to ring each other regularly. They talked about their parents and their childhood, Susan's children, Cassie's life, and started to develop the secrets and understandings of sisters.

Cassie was restless, and began to explore her world. The apple orchards at Bilpin drew her back continually. She began talking to various owners, who told her of unmitigated financial disaster, until they divined she might be interested in buying a property, when their stories changed to tales of the charms of country life. She began to investigate prices, to look at production and marketing. The Italian orchard stayed in her mind and on the market. She wanted to buy it, but she would have to borrow most of the money. Nevertheless, she signed the contract and started looking for a job. She wouldn't have needed one if she had sold the mountain house and lived in the one-room stone cottage in the orchard, but the mountain house no longer felt as if it was hers to sell.

"Two mortgages and no job," she told Anthea. "How did it happen?" On the surface, Cassie's friendship with Anthea had changed very little. They saw a little less of each other because of Cassie living in the mountains, though they talked regularly on the phone and frequented their old haunts. But the friendship was somehow more equal.

Cassie took Anthea to see the orchard, achingly pretty on a misty mountain winter day. "It's run down, but it's a reasonable living."

"What's reasonable?" asked Anthea.

"Twenty-five thousand."

"How the mighty have fallen."

"I don't need much more. The land value is my super. It will almost pay itself off. The only problem is that there's not enough money to do what I really want."

"Such as?"

"Develop value-added products. Fabulous boutique cider. Perfect designer fruit for the Japanese market. Berries. Gourmet apple jellies."

"I can just imagine," said Anthea. "Apple chips, apple sauce, apple jam, apple shampoo, apple air fresheners in the shape of an apple, those funny old dolls you make out of apples. Sun-dried apples, apple gum, bonsai apple trees, apple blossom, apple seed rheumatism cures. You'll get one of those awful roadside stalls and end up selling cow-hide rugs on the side."

"You don't think it's a good idea?"

"I'm not an entrepreneur. I like a regular salary and the government super fund."

"But for me?"

"Hard work, Cass. Remember I hail originally from rural New Zealand. You'll be forever stringing up nets, chasing off fruit bats, spraying bloody codling moths, weeding, spreading fertiliser, picking, packing – all that."

"I've factored all that in." She shrugged. "In the end, I'll be working to support an orchard."

"I thought I was the silly one."

"This is very silly," said Cassie. "But it's what I want," she added passionately. They shut the gate and walked down to her car. "It's impractical. I know. But I wanted something different, to grow things. Which sounds corny, but I do." She called Edie and got him back into the car. It was a cold mountain day, and as they drove down the lane from the orchard, rain began to pour. Cassie stopped and waited for the de-mister to work.

"Have you got a job?" asked Anthea, "to support this dependent orchard?"

"I'll do consultancy work," said Cassie. "I've got some contacts in a firm that does a lot of government work, researching for various departments. They've said they'd be happy to have me whenever I'm ready. Nice people. Good money. No power play."

"There's always power play," said Anthea.

Cassie started the car. She smiled at Anthea. "I'm not interested in the power this time round. I'm going to make friends."

Anthea laughed. "Oh my God. I can see it. You'll be reading high-powered manuals on the making of friendships. The etiquette of friendship. The meaning of friendship. How many friends do you need? What is a successful friendship? Qualities to have in your friends. Count me out!"

"Ohhh," Susan sighed. "Sex has been different since you came back."

"Different?" said Nick.

She propped herself up on her elbow. "Better. I like it more. My body feels different. I'm more relaxed." She hadn't used the treadmill all week and had eaten half a packet of Tiny Teddies after dinner, but it didn't worry her. She ran her fingers down Nick's back and kissed his neck. "Sensual."

"That's great," he said, and kissed her, long and slow. But she knew that in spite of the passion of the kiss, he hadn't noticed the change, that for him sex would always be more mechanistic, less spiritual, less magical than it was for her. And therefore, she thought, less fraught. For Nick, it was a release from himself, whereas for her, it was an expression of herself.

"Do you think sex is the most important thing in a marriage?" she asked.

"What do you mean?"

She lay back, looking through the French windows, watching the gum trees swaying against the black sky.

"Sex as the centre of a relationship. A sort of barometer. I mean, if you have good sex, you're not going to get into too much trouble in other areas. But . . ." she was warming to the theme, "it's more than that. It's the most essential way you connect."

"Yeah," he conceded. "It's pretty important."

"But in a marriage," she persisted, "do you think it's the most important thing?"

"One of the most."

"What's more important?"

"Family dinners." He sounded tentative. "Maybe."

She would have laughed out loud, but she knew he was serious. "Okay, family dinners."

"A home."

"Yep."

"The kids. Kids more than family dinners and the home," he explained. "The family dinners are a result of the kids. The home too, really. Although you get that first."

"Maybe we should get a dog," she said, thinking that the conversation had sunk to a low level very quickly. "That dog Cassie has is lovely." She was prepared to let the spiritual significance of sex lapse. This afternoon, after her accountancy class, she'd started thinking about it. She felt it was important he saw it and agreed to it, but maybe it wasn't. Maybe the depth and meaning she craved, the despair and hopelessness she had so often felt, weren't the most important things in life. Maybe, she thought, Nick was right and it was family dinners. They lay, comfortable together, silent. She would have liked to think that she couldn't even imagine them apart now, but she could. Quarrels building, one of them getting overwrought. A walk-out. She could see it. Tiny Teddies and the treadmill back in the centre of her life. Maybe being able to see it and imagine it would stop it. But it made her nervous. She had never felt secure. Now she knew that feeling was the truth. No-one was ever secure.

"I booked in for a vasectomy today," said Nick. "Getting it done next week."

"You? A vasectomy?" She felt his forehead. "Are you okay? You haven't got a temperature?"

He laughed, and squeezed her breast. "It's my anniversary present to you."

Chapter 22

Cassie thought of Darcy every day. He was still with her constantly, as a reference, in physical gestures, in words and phrases, smells and colours, events and meetings, bitter and sweet.

"It's like he's put a curse on me," she told Anthea in the Korean steam baths.

"We're slow learners, Cass," said Anthea, wiping herself with a towel. "We've got to adjust to forty plus."

"What difference does age make?"

"Big difference. You know, for years I was stuck on the formula man plus woman equals life." She poured herself a glass of water from the big water jug and drank it thirstily. "Which works, as a formula, if you have a life – say like Suzie – with a husband and kids."

"Which is what you wanted for years," said Cassie.

"Until I realised I'm too old for it. Past it. Finito. Gone."

"You sound happy about it," protested Cassie.

"I am happy, because it isn't a possibility any more. So the desperation is gone. I still grieve for the baby, but not for the life. Because it doesn't mean love is gone, or sex is gone, or a body in the bed at night is gone. But the nature of relationships is different. And I accept that."

"How did it happen?"

"In a highly peculiar way. I woke up the other morning, and I'm stroking my own neck." Anthea arched her neck and pointed to a small mole. "All of a sudden I discover this long, wiry, black hair, about three feet long, growing out of that mole."

"How could you have missed a hair three feet long?" said Cassie sceptically.

"I didn't miss it. It grew overnight. It's a trick of the middle-aged female body. You just wait."

"I don't see what it's got to do with anything."

"Neither did I," said Anthea. "In fact, I was so hysterical it was the best I could do to stop myself screaming out loud, or running up to casualty at Balmain Hospital and getting it removed."

"What did you do?"

"I dropped in at the local beautician, and she plucked it out and we had a little talk about future possible nostril hair. Then we talked about adding elastin to my skin at great expense to me and great profit to her, and the general ability to pretend none of this is happening. And that spun me out so much that I went and got tested and found I am now officially menopausal. Hormone replacement therapy. HRT to the initiated. I'm getting older, no bones about it. Hello calcium supplements and low-fat milk. Age before beauty. But I have this sense of release. I'm past the age of youth and beauty, agony and ecstasy. I'm going to stop worrying about my could-have-been life and start enjoying life now."

"Is there a moral in this for me? About Darcy?"

"You're a free woman. You can do what you like. No rules, no conventions, nothing. Try again." Anthea looked at her intently. "It always seemed to me that what you and Darcy had was so big, so intense. Ring him. If two people as incompatible as you managed to get along so well, there's got to be something in it."

"Jennifer Keen, please. It's Cassie La Rosa." She was shaking, but determined to go through with this. It had been on her mind for months, to make her peace with the demons of the corporate past.

"Cassie. My God, I never expected you to ring. I was so, well, brutally honest. That would be a kind way of putting it."

"Cruel to be kind," said Cassie. "But I did take it on board. All those books I used to read about accepting criticism. How's life at DMC?"

"Poisonous. Knives in backs everywhere. Hatchets coming out of cupboards. Amazing what a restructure does for a company. But it may be the solution for an opportunist like me. I've been talking to a little consultancy group, who can offer me a reasonable salary to run their joint. So I'm engineering myself a retrenchment. If I get enough to pay off the house, me and the kid will be able to live very comfortably."

"I'm working for a consultancy group too. It's amazing how much less you can live on when you don't have a proper job. For some reason, life becomes very cheap. I think we should catch up. I'd like you to come up for the weekend some time . . . if you want to."

"Love to. What about the weekend of the twelfth?"

"Fine. Your daughter Danielle?"

"She'd love it. Listen Cass, if you don't mind me asking, what money did Julian give you as a payout?"

"Thirty grand, plus the car."

"Thirty grand. I can't believe it. That's shit-house."

"I know, but under the circumstances . . ."

"Under the circumstances? Cass, where have you been?"

"What do you mean?"

"No-one's told you? You didn't see the exposé in *BRW*?"

"I don't read *BRW* or the *Fin Rev* or even the business section in the *Herald* any more. I suppose I'll have to start again."

"You'll love this! Last month, Julian sacked Simon. All those bright and shiny graphs he'd sold to Julian about our super-dooper export potential turned out to be very flaky indeed." Cassie thought how much it had changed. She didn't care about it any more. It seemed small, insignificant.

Jennifer went on. "So Julian goes back to the drawing board and put *your* plan for setting up in Asia into action. Headlines galore! DMC multi-billion-dollar push into Asia. On the basis of market research based on cultural and financial factors and economic growth predictors. Your research. Mind you, the down side was that John Anderson took over the Research Department in its entirety. But naturally, I assumed Julian had come to some very generous arrangement with you."

Cassie was silent for a moment. "I'm sure he will," she told Jennifer. "Very generous. There's a great little orchard I've got plans for."

The invitation came in a parchment envelope. *Sculptures and collages by Darcy Diamond. First public exhibition since 1969.* Cassie looked at it, doubtful. To her, the exhibition had always been a fantasy, a dream. She had certainly never known there had been an earlier exhibition. She had never known, never considered, that he might have a past in the art world. It occurred to her painfully that there was so much she had failed to see.

There was a flier enclosed, with a glowing review of the long-gone exhibition, an excited appraisal of the possibilities of the new. On the back of the invitation was a hand-scrawled note from Darcy. *Please come, so we can talk about our future, and I can make it all up to you. If at all possible.*

She lay under the pines in the double hammock she had strung up, in the weak winter sun, bundled up from the wind. Edie snuggled next to her, his nose under her arm. She looked at the sky and tried to think. She had got her payout from DMC. She had installed a part-time manager in the orchard who supervised the day-to-day work. She was planning and experimenting with cider recipes, while the current crop of apples paid the wages. Some nights, she and Edie slept in the small stone house. It had a perfection, the sense of being hers and hers alone that the mountain house lacked. She worked in the city three or four days a week. Jennifer was now a friend, which, Cassie told Anthea, meant that she had doubled her social circle. She felt in contact with the world, a growth of possibilities, a balance in her life. Darcy, who was still constantly in her thoughts, was not as painful, as unsettling, as difficult as he had been. A future? They had had it once before and it had left her heartbroken.

Cassie pinned the invitation on her notice board, but she let opening night go by. She thought about Darcy, but she wondered if the thinking, although often painful, might be less damaging to her than the reality.

"Hi," said the voice. "I'm Andy. I'm thirty-nine and a very average Aussie knockabout guy. I run my own small and struggling business, with a two-ton truck and a bad-tempered cattle dog. I'd like to meet a woman in her thirties or forties, average looking, interested in a fun relationship. I'd like to think love lasts forever, but my experience is that anywhere between six months and five years is a pretty good bet. I like movies, eating out in good, cheap dives and sailing. You don't have to pretend you like sailing. Press one and leave a message if you're interested."

Anthea reached across from her bed and pressed one. "Hi," she said. "I'm Anthea and I'm forty-two. Next birthday. I'm a teacher and I'm scared of cattle dogs. The only pet I have is a stick insect which is attached to the potplant on my balcony. I think I'm better than average looking, but I don't want to get competitive about this. I hate sailing, but I have great legs. Reply care of Box 4131. I'm wary of leaving my phone number as I've had some real nutters."

"Have you got a stick insect?" asked Andy as he lay sprawled across her bed. They had been out to dinner a couple of times and met for coffee. Instant attraction, Anthea had decided, was in her case an extremely bad predictor of compatibility. She and Andy hadn't had it. But they did like each other. Andy had been married once and had a daughter. She was silent about her past. It was impossible to relate her feelings to anyone. It would come out wrong, cast her as a victim, or as hysterical. Too intimate, too close, too soon. But maybe, at some point, she might tell.

"No stick insect," she said. "I'd rehearsed that line as something spontaneous and funky." He raised his eyebrows. "If you get to be the hottest thing in my life and we have a stick insect issue, then I'll go out and buy one."

"My dog would eat it anyway." He was tall, dark, with a thin, angular face, and none of the bastardry she used to find so attractive.

"Well it was a pretty thin story," she said, "so to speak." She rolled over towards him. "Are you still getting replies to your ad? I mean, am I part of a long line of try-outs? A sort of casting couch for whatever you have in mind?"

"Nope. I went out with two women before I got to you, but they didn't work out." He ran his hand down her body. "You and me seem like a more promising combination."

"It's hard, isn't it? Finding someone?"

"Very."

"I don't even know what I want," said Anthea. "I used to want love, and then I wanted lust. The rose-covered cottage and the picket fence was in there somewhere. And then I was happy with anything. Now, I can't think what it is I'm after."

"I don't want to think about it too much, because if I do I'll suck it dry before I even get a taste," he said, holding her. "But I don't think sex is ever a stand-alone commodity. It comes with love, friendship, marriage, desperation, hate, disdain, money, kids."

"Or any combination of the above," said Anthea. "We could mix and match."

Andy took her hand and kissed it. "Or we could just try a mild sort of love. That blinds us enough, and doesn't bind us too much."

"Don't get clever with me," said Anthea. "I've heard all the lines."

Cassie visited Darcy's exhibition late one afternoon. "It's closing tomorrow," said the attendant. "And almost everything's sold."

"I'll just have a look," said Cassie firmly. "You're open till five, aren't you?"

At first, she felt cheated. The collages she recognised as having been cut straight out of his house, sections of the massive work that had covered one wall. Despite the framing, they still conjured up in her a sense of the house, a familiarity so strong that she could hardly bear to look. But when she came back to them, she could see that he had chosen and edited the big collage carefully, perhaps even made it that way in the first place. Each one that he'd cut was a work on its own, only to him and to her a discrete part of the greater whole. But it grieved her, that he had destroyed the whole to produce the parts. And puzzled her. The entire wall of the house would have had to be replaced. Maybe he'd finally made the wall of shells.

The sculptures were displayed with the preliminary sketches behind them, so the evolution of each piece was apparent. Darcy's close handwriting spidered across the pages. But as she moved through the forms, half abstract, suggestive of theme and form but sometimes with a detail that was almost more real than real, she saw her life with Darcy. She saw their lovemaking, their cups of tea on the lawn, their intimacy, the things they had seen in the bush, the jaggedness of her life in the city. Solidly, if not explicitly, it was all there. Strangely, since there was no reason he should know about it, there was Anthea's baby, a small figure, almost floating, its stiff little leg, its head, wrinkled like an orange, its butterfly hands abstracted, but the ultimate truth of the baby. Anthea must have seen him or spoken to him. As Cassie walked through the exhibition, her sense of him, the feeling of him was so strong that as soon as she got back into her car, she started driving to Kurnell. She remembered what Anthea had said. She remembered how she and Darcy had been. But she remembered also the deep, dark pain of his rejection.

When she arrived, it was dark. The house had a For Sale sign out the front, Sold plastered across it. She was suddenly frightened she had left it too late. She knocked. He opened the door, flustered, embarrassed and, she could see, frightened. She was hopeful again.

"I saw the exhibition," she said.

"You saw the exhibition?" he repeated stupidly.

"It was incredible. Anthea's baby?"

"She came to see me." He looked at her face. "She asked me to do something. Commissioned me. But I didn't charge her, of course."

"Does she like it?" asked Cassie tentatively. "So stark?"

Darcy poured them each a glass of wine with shaking hands. Cassie could feel herself shaking, deep inside. It was easier to keep talking about Anthea. "It was very hard for her describing the baby," he said. "I got the picture in my mind but I was scared I'd get it wrong. Wrong in the really important sense. But when she came and saw it, she sat with it, holding it and cried. But she asked me to keep it for a while. I'll cast it for her later on. To go on the grave."

"It shocked me. But I liked it. As well as the rest of the exhibition."

"In the beginning, I was going to do all the works round the theme of futility. But it got a bit circular and the whole thing seemed pointless, as well it might. So I looked for the strongest, most involving, most passionate thing in my psyche. You and me. What else?"

Cassie sat down at the kitchen bench, a sense of familiarity and of being home, but also annoyance. "I can't see how you could produce that – about us – and yet you have been so horrible to me. The letter about my values and your superiority. And then nothing else. It was painful. And before that. Not turning up at the house. Going cold on me."

"I know. Big mistake."

"So am I simply an experience that you turned into art? Is that the sum total?"

"No."

"So what was it? This on again, off again. The nastiness. You behaved like a pig."

"Pigs are sensitive creatures."

"You wrote on the invitation about discussing our future. But let's get the past straight first."

"Okay." He toyed with his glass of wine. "It embarrasses me to remember I wrote that letter to you. But at the time, I had to distance you. I'd cut myself off from that sort of emotional experience. I said I'd live with you and then the whole idea overwhelmed me. I'm not bloody fit to live with anyone."

"Are you fit to have a relationship?" asked Cassie coldly.

"I'm trying to be truthful," he said defensively.

"That's a start," she said. "And I'm trying to understand," she added more gently.

"You cope with the world, you make your way," said Darcy, "whereas I have a tendency to get blown about, not to do the things that matter to me. You do everything, whether it matters to you or not. So both of us tend to waste really important things in our lives – our time and our talent. Love, even. I'm probably just as ambitious as you. I want fame, glory. I've always had talent, but along with it, a tremendous capacity for dissipation."

"I'll say."

"So I had to cut you off. Invent an ideological defence. All that stuff about values was a throwback to the sixties, where I get stuck at the best of times. But it was because you'd got to me – heart and soul – which is why the exhibition is as it is. Because I love you. I'm not sure we can live together or even how we can be together, but you're the love of my life. And the moment I realised that, I knew how stupid I'd been. So I'm sorry. Very sorry, Cass."

They sat silently, drinking the wine. Darcy leaned over and touched her hand lightly. "I hope it isn't irreparable?"

She decided not to tell him, not just yet. No rules, no conventions, what Anthea had said. They could work it out. Later, they would go to bed, make love, discuss the future. "You cheated with the exhibition a bit, didn't you?" she said.

"Cutting up the wall for the collages?" She looked round at the bare fibro shell of the outer wall.

"I was selling the house anyway. It'll go for a development site, so there was no point in wasting the artwork. And the collages have sold very nicely."

"How come you're selling the house?"

"Thought I might buy a shack up the mountains and try to woo you again."

The map in Cassie's head became complicated again. Complicated and changing, domestic, local, metropolitan and global, some paths like a lioness' trails, others more lightly trod. In the map were paths such as Edie's favourite walks through the scrub, and the fastest route to Sydney. The road to Darcy's house at Mount Victoria she knew by heart, by night, by day, by dusk and dawn in every season. It was the centre of her map and she gave up thinking that they could or would ever live together. She had lines out to Susan's, to Anthea's, to other friends she had begun to make, to places of work, to her orchard, to the nursery suppliers, to her secret picnic places, walks down the valleys and along the ridges.

One night, she confessed all the years of mental map-making to Darcy. Inspired, he sat down in the middle of the living room, with an enormous piece of cartridge paper, and sketched it all for her, with them both getting drunker and drunker, putting in worry lines, silly lines, vital relationships, neuroses, small happinesses, major triumphs, petty victories and stupid quarrels. There were clear boundaries and undefined dark edges, clean lines and smudges. He added the deaths of her parents, the darkness of the Mafia, her Italian and English origins, his own Irishness and signed it with a flourish.

"Wonderful as a cathartic experience," Cassie told him, looking at the picture the next morning. "Appalling as a piece of art."

"Just like life," he answered.